About the Author

Frank was born in Aldridge, Staffordshire in 1936. He left school at 15 and began his working life in the coal mining industry. He joined the army in 1956 and spent three years as a Seaforth Highlander, serving in Gibraltar and Germany. After he was demobbed, he returned to the mining industry, where he spent the rest of his working life. In his spare time he took up dog training and founded the Aldridge Dog Training Club in 1970. It is still going 50 years later. After moving to Rugeley in 1974, he retired from the mining industry and then moved to Spain, where he lived for 20 years. This is where he started writing his books.

To Charlotte

Many Thanks

Frank Hutton

Frank Aulton

Beneath Pastures Green

Austin Macauley Publishers™
London • Cambridge • New York • Sharjah

A CIP catalogue record for this title is available from the British Library.

ISBN 9781788237017 (Paperback)
ISBN 9781788238632 (ePub e-book)

www.austinmacauley.com

First Published (2021)
Austin Macauley Publishers Ltd
25 Canada Square
Canary Wharf
London
E14 5LQ

Chapter 1
Another Dawn, Another Day

The alarm clock went off at 6 o'clock, awakening Billy from an erotic dream. A dull grey light peeped through the curtains, heralding another dawn and another day. "Kin hell," he murmured, easing himself up and placing a foot on the floor. He managed a fart that would have measured at least five on the Richter scale.

The pungent smell of a filled nappy brought him into the world of reality. Standing up, he glanced over at the twelve-month-old result of a passionate night, gurgling away in his cot. Little hands flailing away, he leaned over and kissed his little son, Steven.

Christine hadn't moved; she was still in the land of nod. Billy looked over at her lying on her back. Her nightdress had slipped a little, exposing a bare breast. He couldn't resist gently squeezing the exposed nipple. "The baby's crapped himself. Can't you smell it?" he asked as she pulled her nighty over her.

"It's you that stinks," she murmured. "I should think the neighbours heard that."

Grabbing his clothes off the ottoman, he made it to the bathroom. A quick piss and another fart and he started to get dressed. He splashed his face under the hot water tap and reached for his toothbrush. A quick flick with the comb and he was ready.

Downstairs, the cat and dog waited patiently by the patio door. Sliding it open, he peeked through at the grey dawn. He reached for the packet of cereal and then put the kettle on. Whilst he was waiting for the kettle to boil, he sat down at the table and put on his trainers. The cat and dog came running back in and sat looking at him. Cat food and dog meat scraped into their dishes and they were happy. Billy ate his breakfast and drank the coffee. His jacket and snap bag hung in the broom cupboard. Christine always prepared his snap last thing at night and left the plastic box on the table with an apple or orange and sometimes a KitKat tucked in with his sandwiches. He packed them into his bag with the bottle of orange juice. Picking up his car keys, he left the house and made it to his car in the drive. As he got in, a noisy moped sped by with Jegger pipping his horn. *Noisy bastard*, thought Billy as he waved.

Jegger had already reached the road junction as Billy was backing out and had disappeared by the time Billy reached the end of the road. He waited as the pit bus made its way down the road and fell in behind it as it went towards the driveway leading up to the pit. 'Armitage Colliery', the sign said as he passed through, following the stream of traffic leading to the huge car park. The bus had disappeared around to the front of the canteen. He parked his car and started walking across to the baths.

He walked in and made his way to Bay 5 where his locker was. Alf was already in there, poised with one leg on the footstep, untying his shoes. Billy bumped into him on purpose, upsetting his balance. "Bastard," called out Alf as Billy walked by.

"Sorry mate," laughed Billy. "Jesus Christ, what stinks in here?" he said, unlocking his locker.

"It's Rosebud, he's just gone down the other end," said Alf.

"What makes a man stink like that?" asked Billy.

"He reckons he sweats a lot," answered Alf.

Bodger was down the other end of the bay. "Did you see 'em on Saturday? What a team, get your colours, come on the blues," he called out. "Watch out for 'em on Saturday, they'll beat any team in their league."

Billy quickly changed into his clean pit clothes and followed Alf down into the dirty lockers. The smell of Rosebud lingered. "I'm glad he don't work with us," said

Billy, screwing up his nose. "Have you seen Norman? I've seen Jegger." Alf said that Norman had already gone through the baths. "Wait outside the lamp house; when we are all together, we'll go and see the boss," said Billy.

Jegger was the last to arrive. "I had to go and get a screw of bacca," he said.

"Right, let's go," said Billy, crossing over the crush hall and knocking on the undermanager's door. He gently opened the door and peeped in. "Can we have a quick word, boss?" he asked the man sitting at his desk. The man was already talking to the overman and looked surprised as Billy entered his office.

"Not at the moment, Billy. I'm coming down the pit today. If I get a chance, I'll pop into your rock head and see you. I'm a bit pushed at the moment. If I don't make it, come and see me when you come up that pit."

Billy nodded his head, "OK boss."

Alf shook his head. "Another promise."

Jegger turned and headed down the crush hall towards the pithead. "A waste of fucking time," he yelled at Billy as they queued up to go through the airlock.

"We'll see. If he doesn't come and see us, we will call on him when we come up the pit. That's what he said," replied Billy. The onsetter loaded them onto the cage and rang them off. The cage descended slowly at first and then got up to man-riding speed. Billy let off another fart that echoed around the cage.

"You smell worse than Rosebud," said Alf.

"On the Guinness again last night, sorry mate," replied Billy.

As the cage reached the bottom, Norman said to Jegger, "Go and get a carriage, Jeg; not a closed-in one with Billy smelling like that."

Jegger was the first off the cage and hotfooted it through the maze to where the train was waiting. "I'm here!" he shouted as his mates looked up and down the row of carriages.

"Who's got the cards?" asked Norman.

Jegger produced a well-fingered pack from his snap bag. "I meant to get a new pack but I forgot, didn't I?"

The haulage lads bundled in the section behind them, but there was one short. "Where's Ray?" asked Jegger.

"Don't know, haven't seen him this morning," replied Abbo. "It's unusual for him not to turn up. He's saving up for a car." The whistle went and the train trundled along the track.

The first stop at the Heathen, the team clambered out followed by the haulage lads. Deputy Bruce Perry clambered out of the carriage behind them. The whistle blew and the train moved slowly on to the next stop.

Billy and his team began the slow journey down the hill. The conversation was mixed. Billy asked Alf if he'd had a good weekend. "Shopping with the missus Saturday and a bit of gardening Sunday. I did manage a pint at the club though at dinner time." Jegger was talking to Norman about his moped. "I think I'm going to swap it for a Lambretta so as I can take the girlfriend for a ride. The moped struggles a bit with two of us on it." Billy turned and with a wicked smile asked, "Did you get your leg over, Jegger?" Norman butted in, "No, he serviced his moped instead."

The deputy called the haulage lads to him. "One less today, lads, unfortunately. Can you manage with the three of you until I find a replacement for Ray? I don't think we shall see him for a while."

Abbo enquired, "Why, what's happened to him?"

The deputy looked at them. "I guess you haven't heard what's happened, have you?"

A chorus of voices replied, "No, we haven't heard anything. Why, what's happened?" Bruce said he had just heard on the train that Ray's sister had been taken into Stafford hospital on Saturday night. She and her boyfriend had been on a night out at the *Disco World* nightclub when she had collapsed. She was rushed into hospital but died during the night. An investigation by the police revealed that she had taken ecstasy. Her boyfriend had been arrested for supplying her with drugs. The family were at the hospital and at her bedside when she died.

"I'll kill that bastard for doing this to her," said an angry Ray, in tears.

"It wasn't him that supplied it," said the policeman.

The boyfriend claimed it was a coloured woman they had met inside. Janet had commented on how much energy the woman had. The woman whispered, "You too can be like me if you take one of these tablets," she said, showing her a small tablet wrapped in silver paper. "They are energy boosters. I've been on them for some time now. They're harmless and will only cost you a tenner."

Janet had looked at her boyfriend. "I haven't got a tenner, have you, John?" Within minutes, she was in the ladies, taking the tablet with some cold water as instructed by their new-found friend. John had fished a tenner from his pocket and paid the woman. He had been waiting for Janet outside the ladies. Finally, she emerged, having brushed her hair and remade her face.

"Are you OK, Jan?" he asked.

She nodded. "Let's go and party."

They made for the dance floor and started dancing. Suddenly, Janet stopped and reached for John. "Let's sit down, John, I feel a bit queasy."

John looked worried as they found a seat. "It's that tablet," he whispered. "We should have known better."

Janet doubled over, clutching her stomach. "I feel sick, let's go outside; it's hot in here." They stood up and walked towards the exit. Suddenly, Janet collapsed. One of the doormen came over.

"Too much to drink, has she?"

John shook his head. "No, she's only had one coke so far. Can you help me take her outside? I think some fresh air is what she needs."

As they half-carried her outside, a St John's ambulance man came over and asked if he could help. Janet started vomiting.

"I think we need to call an ambulance," said the doorman. "If she's only had one coke, there's something else going on here." Janet had collapsed again and seemed to lose consciousness.

"Is she on anything?" asked the St Johns man. "I mean, like drugs."

John said she didn't use drugs but had just bought an energy booster from a woman they had befriended during the night. The ambulance arrived and the paramedics rushed over to where Janet lay, vomiting again. "Let's get her onto the stretcher; I don't like the look of this." John got into the ambulance with her and held her hand. "Has she taken anything?" the paramedic asked.

***

Off the train, they had a long walk to their workplace. The rock headers made their way along the long dusty road. "I bet the manager don't come down here," said Jegger. Alf said they would have to wait and see but if they had to pay him a visit when they got up the pit, he wouldn't be able to join them. "I'll miss the bus," he said.

Abbo suggested they go and call on Ray when they finished work. "We'll pay our respects and see if we can do anything to help."

The rest of the lads said it was a good idea. "You know Ray, if he says he'll do something, he means it," said Sid. "We'll have to keep an eye on him."

***

Christine changed Steven's nappy, kissed and cuddled him. She straightened the cot and pulled back the blankets on their bed. "Right, Mr Cuddlebum. Let's get you downstairs and get you fed and watered." Steven chuckled as she blew raspberries at him. She placed him in the carrycot and put him on the kitchen table whilst she prepared his feed. She glanced at the clock; it was 9 o'clock. Billy was well and truly down the pit so she had two hours to do things before Clive, the insurance man, would be knocking on the door. Her heart rate increased as she thought of what was to come. Clive was a handsome man, the same age as

Billy but more suave and gentle when he touched her. Billy was more like a bull at a gate.

***

Peter limped through the baths, leaning on his walking stick. He quickly changed into his working clothes and passed through the lamp house, registering his check number with the lamp-house man who booked him in. Peter stood at five foot eleven inches with broad shoulders, dark hair and a warm smile. He was one of the good guys and well-liked by all. "Morning," he said to Allan as he entered the oil sampling office or, to put a posh name to it, the Ferrographic Analysis Department.

"Morning Pete, yer all right, mate?" Allan was one of the main testers; John was the one in charge and usually the last to arrive.

"Yep, not bad for a Monday morning. Has John arrived yet?"

"Not yet, but you know what he's like."

The door opened. "Who we on about now?" John asked with a cheeky grin. "Has the kettle boiled yet?"

On cue, the kettle started to whistle. "You know it has to have your permission," said Allan. John took off his jacket and hung it on the back of the door, before turning on the radio.

As they sat drinking their tea, the door opened and Ken walked in and sat down next to John. "How did you do on Friday?" he asked.

John put down his paper. "Won easy," he said, referring to the snooker match at the club.

All looked at Pete. "How about you, Pete, did you score?"

Pete laughed. They always took the piss out of the two snooker players. Ken finished his tea and got up to leave. "Got a lot on today. The tractor is playing up a bit. I'll go and see if it starts all right."

Peter filled the sink with hot water ready for washing the syringes. His job was to clean them and prepare them for use again. The oil sampling kits had to be handed out to the underground fitters to take oil samples from the machinery underground every week. The oil samples had to be tested. By doing this, tracing metal in the oil gave a good indication if the machines were breaking down. Peter had himself carried out this task before his accident.

***

Joe Fiddler raised his head off the pillow. "What time's your doctor's appointment?" asked Rosie.

"Not until 10:30," answered Joe. "I'm getting up now and having a quick shower in case they want to examine me." He moaned as he got out of bed.

"You want to put some of that stinking ointment on your back so that they can smell it in the surgery," said Rosie.

Joe had a quick shower but didn't do as Rosie had suggested. He used a pleasant deodorant before getting dressed. He hurried downstairs and finished getting dressed before doing his two rounds of toast for breakfast and a coffee. Checking his wallet, he shouted, "I'm off. I might be late getting back; I promised to look in on Mum today." Slipping on his jacket, he reached for his NHS walking stick and hobbled out of the door. He felt in his pocket for his bunch of keys. It took twenty minutes for him to hobble up to the clinic, stopping occasionally to rest his back.

"Good morning, Mr Fiddler, please take a seat; you will be called shortly." The receptionist gave him a quick smile that showed no affection. She had seen Mr Fiddler many times over the last few months. Ten minutes later, Joe heard his name called out. With a look of pain on his face, he hobbled down the corridor.

"Good morning, Mr Fiddler, how are you today?" Joe gave a half smile to Dr Elaine Johnson. She hadn't been there very long and treated Joe respectfully.

***

Christine looked at the clock and checked herself in the mirror. Ten minutes more and the car would pull up outside and Clive would knock on the door. Steven was in his carrycot, sucking on his soother, almost dropping off. She opened the patio door and let the animals out. A final check in the mirror and she was ready. Her pants and tights lay on the chair. She allowed Clive to relieve her of her bra; he liked doing that as she unbuckled his belt.

A quick look through the window, checking whether the street was clear. It always was; the few inhabitants of the street were workers and had departed, leaving the coast clear. She watched as Clive's car pulled up. She waited for the gentle tap on the front door before opening it to the smiling young man. Hardly had the door closed and he was pushing her into the lounge. Their lips met and a very passionate kiss passed between then. She helped him out of his smart jacket as he fiddled with the zip on the back of her dress. No sooner had his shoes and trousers been discarded than they fell into a clinch on the settee. They were hot passionate kisses, nothing like the quick pecks that Billy planted on her as he lifted her skirt. That was the difference between love and lust. Billy was *wham-bam, thank you ma'am*, while Clive took his time exploring her body. His fingers touched her in the right places as she manoeuvred into position.

"I've missed you," he whispered as he entered her. Very soon, she was at the height of ecstasy as he gently thrust into her and sucked her nipples.

***

Dr Elaine examined Joe's back. "Still very tender, Mr Fiddler? Are the tablets helping?"

Joe eased himself off the bed. "Yes doctor, but they are making me constipated and I get very tired."

The doctor looked at Joe's notes. "Yes, these painkillers do that. I suggest you cut down on them and take them only when the pain is unbearable. I think I will put you forward for some physiotherapy; it may help."

Joe hobbled out of the surgery down the street into the estate where his mother lived. He didn't go to her house but made his way around the back to the lock-up garages. He checked that the street was clear before unlocking the door to the garage allocated to his mother. Switching on the lights, he closed the door quietly. He then opened the wardrobe at the back of the garage. It was a bit of a squeeze getting past the car covered by a sheet, but he managed it. A variety of clothes hung in the wardrobe, mainly suits. Dark suits, striped suits, white suits, ties and shoes. They were all there. Joe kept his wardrobe immaculate. He hung his walking stick up and began to strip off. First, he chose a shirt and then a tie. He hovered between suits, finally choosing a charcoal grey with a thin stripe. A businessman always looked his best to impress. Within a short time, Joe was standing in front of the full-length mirror attached to the inside of the door. A thin strip light illuminated the area. Finally, he reached for the wig inside the box. It was a dark wig with flecks of grey. The moustache completed the hairpieces. He checked that both pieces fitted correctly and felt comfortable. Next, he opened the locked drawer and took out his leather briefcase. He checked the contents: entrance passes to the N.E.C., parking permits, advertising paraphernalia, car keys and car phone—it was all there. A quick spray of deodorant and he was ready. Checking the time on his expensive wristwatch, he began to pull the sheet off the car. It was a red BMW executive class, two years old and in pristine condition. Closing and locking the wardrobe, Joe opened the garage door, first checking whether the coast was clear. The car was his prize possession and had taken every penny from his disability pension plus what his mother had loaned him, but he was gradually paying her back.

He eased the car out of the garage and quickly locked the garage, making sure the inside lights were off. Carefully, he drove off the estate onto the main road leading to Litchfield. He pulled in at a secluded lay-by and connected the car phone. Janet was the first call. "Yes, I'm ready; pick me up in the usual place."

Denise answered her phone. "Yes, I'm ready."

The third call was to Veronica. “Yes, see you in a few minutes.”

After picking up the three ladies, Joe sped down the motorway towards the NEC. “What’s on today?” asked Denise.

“It’s the Motor Show so there will be plenty of people there,” said Joe.

Chapter 2
Fiddlers Three

"It's snap time and he hasn't showed," said a disgruntled Alf.

Billy climbed down off the drill rig. "Well, he said if he didn't make it, call into his office when we go up the pit."

Jegger walked up the hill to where he had hung his snap bag. "Fucking typical," he shouted.

Norman sat down by him. "Well, I'm not going to miss the bus. You three will have to go and see him."

George waited until the men had finished their snap before he fired the head. "Maybe he won't do anything. We start levelling out shortly and everything will be OK. We might even have to change the machines; there's talk of putting a Doscoe in."

Billy looked at George, "How much farther have we got to go then at this gradient?"

George opened his notebook. "About a hundred metres, I reckon."

Alf walked a few yards up the hill to take a piss. "That's still another month where we won't be making any money."

The team returned into the head and moved the machines back so that George could fire. The men moved back and waited until the dust settled before Norman climbed up onto the Eimco bucket and started filling out onto the conveyor.

***

Peter started preparing the oil sample kits. "I need some more of the information sheets to put in. John, have we got any more?"

John looked in the cupboard. "No mate, let's go and print some off." Peter followed John back along the crush hall and then up some steps. "This is where all the offices are," said John, pointing to the different doors. "Engineers, Mechanical and Electrical, Training Office, Safety Office, Manager's Office and the one at the end, the office staff. That's where the photocopier is, that green painted door. John opened the door to the small office. The photocopier stood against one wall. Lifting the lid at the top revealed a glass panel. John placed the sheet of paper they wanted to copy and closed the lid. "Right, Pete, once you have placed your copy under there, just press this button to start it and this one to indicate the number of copies. Simple to use, mate. I'll leave you to print off however many you want." He looked at his watch. "It's nearly snap time so don't be long."

John closed the door and left Peter on his own. After a few copies had been printed, the machine shut down, leaving a red light flashing. Peter looked over the machine and pressed the buttons that started it, but nothing happened. "Oh shit," he muttered under his breath.

The door opened and a woman came in. "Oh sorry, I thought it was empty," she apologised.

Peter looked at her. "I won't be long but it's stopped for some reason and I don't know anything about it." The woman smiled. Peter couldn't help notice how beautiful she looked. She was about his age with long, shoulder-length hair. She had beautiful white teeth and her dark eyes flashed when she spoke. She reminded him of someone he had seen but he couldn't remember who.

"It's probably run out of paper," she said. "Let me look."

She leaned over and Peter stepped back out of the way. He cast a furtive glance over her body as she checked the machine. She was built just right, a firm bust, built for fondling and a pair of hips built for seduction. As she leaned over the machine, she raised a leg to balance. Pete noticed how good it looked. At the same time, he noticed the wedding ring on her left hand.

"Yes, it's out of paper," she said, straightening up. "There should be some in that cupboard." She squeezed by Peter and opened the cupboard door. Her perfume was beautiful and Peter took deep breaths. "Right, how many copies have you got to do? I only want five so I don't want to overload it."

Peter quickly counted how many he'd already got. "Another twenty," he said. She took a small wad of paper and squeezed past him again. She was almost as tall as Peter and built perfectly. "I do appreciate your help," he said.

"Don't mention it, we all have to learn." she replied with a smile. "What department do you work in?" Peter told her he worked with John in the oil sampling office, but only until his leg got better. Once again, she smiled, revealing her pearly whites.

Peter watched as she put the paper in the machine and pressed the start button. "Thank you very much. I would have had to fetch John if you hadn't come along," said Peter.

"I'm in that office over there if ever you need any help," she said, pointing to the door opposite. "My name is Susan."

Peter told her his name. "Thank you once again, Susan." He picked up his pile of papers and made for the door.

John looked up as Peter entered the office. "I see you managed it, mate."

Peter gave a huge grin. "Yes John, with the help of a beautiful woman who came to my rescue when the paper ran out."

***

Abbo, Sid and Andy sat eating their snap.

"We must go and see Ray," said Abbo. "Perhaps he needs a bit of comforting; it's the least we can do."

Sid agreed and said, "We can go up there when we knock off."

Andy agreed. "It's on our way home, we might as well."

None of them knew who Janet's boyfriend was, but they would certainly find out. "Ray will tell us," said Abbo.

"Why, what can we do?" asked Sid.

"Pay him a visit and beat the crap out of him before Ray gets to him," said Andy.

"I'm concerned about Ray," said Abbo. "When he says something, he really means it."

***

Joe Fiddler eased the car into the parking space allocated to executive visitors; Joe Irwin from East gate Oil Seals Ltd. was there to promote his company's products. He handed out samples he had brought from a catalogue, tearing off the manufacturer's label. He wasn't there to sell bloody oil seals, he dealt in sex and his three samples were experts at it. "Remember, girls, show a bit of class, flash the samples and give away nothing. Rub up against the older guys. They are the company executives with the huge expense accounts, but don't play easy to get. Remember, nothing less than a hundred quid for two hours."

Joe put on his dark-framed glasses with the plain lenses; it gave him a touch of a business-like man. He presented the passes as they went in, which he had phoned for and had been sent to his private address as he had been out of the country at another motor show at that particular time. The lapel badges had been issued to Joe and his office staff and were useable for the whole three days of the show.

The group browsed around for a while, noting various vulnerable victims behind the many stalls displaying car components and other saleable goods. Usually on the stands displaying the new cars, the company executives were in the older class, puffing on fat cigars and giving off an air of authority. Joe pointed out several vulnerable victims to the girls. "Don't forget girls, finish by 4:30, meet back at the main entrance and don't work too cheap. At least one hundred quid and that's for lunch at the hotel and room entertainment."

***

The four rock headers got off the train in the pit bottom. They had completed their yardage that shift because it had been dry in the head and the drill rig had tracked back all right this time, but it wasn't always like this. If water had seeped up through the floor, the machine wouldn't have tracked back that easy.

"Right," said Billy, "let's go and see the boss." Norman said if he went in, he would miss his bus. "That's OK, mate, we'll let you know in the morning what he says," said Billy. They hung up their lamps and walked across to the boss's office. Billy tapped on the door and peeped in. The boss sat at his desk, writing.

"Come in, Billy, I'm sorry I didn't get down into the head, but I've been talking to Ken, the deputy engineer, and he's going to come and see the situation for himself; he promised me it would be sometime this week. That's the best I could do, Billy."

The boss promised that something would be done pending the engineer's report. Billy murmured his thanks and the team filed out of the office. "Well, we will just have to wait and see," said Alf.

Abbo waited in the canteen for Sid and Andy to finish showering. He'd paid for the three mugs of tea. Abbo was always first out of the showers because he never got as dirty when he was just sitting on his arse in the motor house. Usually, Ray ran the haulage but Abbo had also been trained to drive it. Sid and Andy finally showed and joined him at the table. "We'll just call in and ask if he's all right," suggested Andy. "We don't want to be too intrusive, do we?"

They emptied the mugs and made their way out onto the road, crossing over the allotments, which was a shortcut onto the estate. Abbo knocked on the door of the mid-terraced house where Ray lived. They waited a while until someone came to the door. It was David, Ray's younger brother. "Is Ray in, Dave?" asked Abbo.

David shook his head. “No, he’s gone off somewhere on his own.”

Andy spoke quietly, “Sorry to hear about what’s happened, Dave, we just wanted to offer our condolences and see if there was anything we could do.”

Dave gave a weak smile and said thanks. He closed the door and the boys turned to leave. The door opened again immediately and Dave came out. “I know where he is but he doesn’t want anyone to know.”

Abbo looked at Dave. “We’re his mates. Dave, he needs us, that’s what mates are for.”

Dave told them to hang on. “I’ve got to go and take him something he’ll need.” The boys waited outside on the road. Dave came out carrying Ray’s fishing tent and sleeping bag plus something else in a carrier.

“Let’s help you with that,” said Andy. “It looks as if he plans to stay out a while.”

They followed Dave over the waste ground into the forest area, carefully observing that they weren’t being followed. “I bet he’s over by the pools,” muttered Sid. “I’ve been over here with him fishing sometimes.”

Finally, after quite a trek, they reached the pools. Dave led them up a bank to a clearing in the bracken. Sid looked around. “There he is, Dave, go first and tell him we’re here.”

Ray looked up from where he had been lying down. Seeing Dave, he stood up. Dave gave him what he was carrying and then pointed to where the boys were emerging through the bracken. Ray greeted them but did not look very pleased. “Ray, we’ve come to see if you are all right. We know you want to be left alone but we’re your mates. Don’t blame Dave, we persuaded him.”

Ray sat down again and invited the boys to join him. He reached in his pockets for cigarettes and offered them around. “I like to be on my own when I’ve got a lot of thinking to do. This has really cut me up. You know how I felt about our Jan. I can’t believe that bastard got her on drugs. I’m going to kill the bastard, believe me; I’m going to do it.”

The boys sat close to him. Dave asked Ray if he wanted his little tent put up. "I've brought your sleeping bag and some sandwiches and your lamp. I guess you will be staying here a while, Ray?"

His brother looked at him. "Thanks Dave, but don't tell anyone else where I am. I've got a lot of thinking to do."

Dave stood up. "I'm going back now. I'll see you tomorrow, Ray." He looked at the boys. "See you guys, you can find your way back, can't you?" He waved and disappeared into the bracken.

Ray said he appreciated the boys' concern but wanted to get away from the house as his mam and dad were crying a lot and Dave had been upset. "I need a bit of space; I'm sure you guys understand. I'll be back at work next week when the funeral arrangements have been made, but I mean it, lads, I'm going to kill the bastard."

The boys hung around for a couple of hours. "We'll come and see you tomorrow, Ray. Will you still be here?" asked Abbo.

Ray nodded. "Yes, bring a couple of beers with you and some cigs; I'm getting low."

The boys made their way back onto the estate. "See you tomorrow," said Andy and Sid as they broke away and went off in different directions.

***

Joe Fiddler checked his watch; it was getting near 4 o'clock. He had browsed around the stalls and was looking at the array of cars on show and talking with the reps. "Where is the next exhibition being held?" he asked casually.

"London in three months' time," he was told.

"I thought you usually held one in Manchester," he replied.

"Not this year, it's the Men and Women's fashion show up there next week and then the Exhibition Centre closes down for refurbishment. Making it bigger and building hotels onto it."

Joe moved on and made his way towards the exit. He enquired at the main desk what was on next week, taking the leaflets handed to him. He met up with the girls and escorted them to the car. Joe asked if they had had a good day. "Yeah," answered Denise. "You can always rely on the dirty old men, always got a wallet full of notes to spend."

Denise and Janet handed over their takings to Joe, who handed out their shares. "I gotta find some other function if I can for this week. I'll give you a call when I have." He drove the car back along the motorway, dropping off Denise and Janet at the appropriate stops.

Veronica looked at him with a smile. "Are you coming in for a coffee, Joe?" He pulled up at her flat and they took the lift to the third floor. Joe went into the bathroom and removed his hairpieces and moustache. He quickly undressed and followed Veronica into the bedroom, where she quickly undressed and joined him in her bed.

"That last guy I pulled was all talk and no play. What he promised, he couldn't deliver," said Veronica.

"As long as he coughed up, it doesn't matter, Veronica, does it?"

She smiled. "Oh no, Joe, I hope you can deliver."

Chapter 3
Hard Times

Dennis Mason, the union man, opened the door to his office. The phone was ringing like mad. "Hello, Dennis Mason." He recognised the voice on the other end right away. 'King Coal', he had been dubbed. "Dennis, something big has come up, an urgent meeting here at CMU offices Saturday morning. All union branches to attend. Very urgent, Dennis."

Dennis put the phone down. "I wonder what's up now," he said as the electrical and mechanical union official walked in. "Big meeting up Notts on Saturday morning, urgent, he said."

The other man looked serious. "I know, the Power Group have been notified as well."

***

Peter began putting the oil sample kits by the door. "I'll drop these in the charge hands office as I go. See you guys in the morning." A quick shower and he limped across to the car park. He had to pop into town for a few necessities on his way home. He decided to combine his efforts by doing the weekend shopping as well instead of on Friday. He pulled into the supermarket car park and grabbed a trolley. Nothing special was on his mind as he trawled the rows of shelves but the one thing he was looking for he couldn't find. It was a special brand of cereal he liked but it wasn't on the shelves. As he browsed, he suddenly thought, *perhaps it wasn't from here*. Occasionally, he went into Litchfield and maybe he had picked it up from there. He bagged up his supplies and went to his car. Just one more place to go—'Williams', the do-it-all shop. One more tin of emulsion for decorating the hallway of his flat. Once again, he searched the shelves without any luck. "Not until next week," he was told by the assistant. "Maybe our branch in Litchfield has some."

Peter drove home disappointed, as he had wanted to get that bit of painting finished before the weekend. As he unloaded his shopping, it suddenly came to mind that he could go straight into Litchfield on Friday and get what he wanted. That would still leave the weekend free if he got the paint.

***

Joe left the flat and Veronica was smiling. "Give me a call, Joe, when the next job is lined up, I need the money." Joe said it shouldn't be too long, as he had already got it planned out for a show in Manchester. He waved and pulled away, heading for his lock-up garage. It was clear when he arrived so he put the car away and changed back into his street clothes. Picking up his walking stick, he hobbled into the estate and headed home.

Rosie greeted him. "You're late; I bet you've been to the club."

Joe said he had met an old pal and had been persuaded to go for a pint. "It's not very often I get to see anybody, is it?"

Rosie looked at his sick note. "Another six weeks," she said and handed it back to him. "Fill it in and I'll post if off."

Joe drank the coffee she had made him. "They're going to arrange for some physiotherapy shortly," he said.

She replied, "It might help, but I doubt it."

***

Billy arrived home as Christine was changing the baby's nappy. "Shall I make you a cuppa, love, I'm ready for one."

She refused saying she had one a little while ago before she fed Steven. "Did you go and see the boss?" she asked as he sat down in the armchair with his mug of coffee. She held out the baby. "Here you are, Daddy, say hello to your little one."

Billy put his mug down and reached out for the baby. "Yeah, they're going to sort something out," he said.

"Again," Christine replied. "How many times have they said that?"

Billy drank his coffee and played with baby Steven. He loved to see him smile and try to blow raspberries. Christine took him and put him in the carrycot. "It's time for his nap."

Billy walked over to the patio door. "I think it's going to rain." He let in the dog who had been chewing at a bone on the lawn. "I'll take you out later; mate, after I've had a nap." He stretched out on the settee and was soon in the land of nod.

***

Abbo made his way through the estate towards the clubhouse. Andy had said he might pop in for a pint after he had watched *EastEnders*. Abbo ordered his beer and looked around to see who was in. His dad raised his hand. He was sitting in the corner with a beer in front of him. "I thought you were going down the allotment," said Abbo, drawing up a chair.

"Well, I was, but when I got here, there were a few spots of rain so I thought I would wait and see what it's going to do."

Abbo nodded. "Yes, it still looks a bit iffy." His dad took a swig of the Guinness and lit up a fag. "Did you hear about Ray Mullens' sister, Janet?" asked Abbo.

His dad nodded. "Yes, it was all the talk on the face this morning. They should hang the bastard of a boyfriend." Another man came and sat at the table. Abbo looked at Ken, his dad's mate and greeted him.

Ken leaned over and whispered, "I've just heard there's a big meeting with the union leaders up in Nottingham this weekend. Keep it to yourself, but I believe it's a serious one."

***

Susan waited in the hallway for her husband, Derek, to emerge through the doors leading to the planning department. He was a tall man with fair hair and wore glasses. He was one of the main planners, responsible for the pit's roadways and junctions. He greeted Susan and led the way to the car park in front of the office block. His parking space had his name on the board, Mr Derek Manning. It had started raining. "Damn this weather," said Derek.

Susan smiled. *Did this mean he wouldn't be off on one of his weekend-long trips with the boys?* "I don't think it will last long though."

"I hope not; we've got an important match at the weekend."

Susan looked at her husband. "Does this mean you're going to be away for the weekend?" she asked.

"Afraid so, luv, this one's down Northampton on the River Ouse. It will be a Saturday and Sunday morning contest, so I shall be away until Sunday afternoon." Susan heaved a deep sigh, but Derek was oblivious to her feelings. "You will be able to arrange a shopping trip with your sister. You wanted to go to Birmingham, didn't you?" He thought he was doing her a great favour.

***

Friday morning came and Billy was always glad when it came around. Not only was it pay day, but it meant a Saturday morning lie-in the next day. He kissed Christine on the cheek before he did the usual routine of getting ready for work. The dog and cat did a quiet run outside, but were soon back as the rain pelted down.

Alf, as usual, was already making his way to the dirty lockers. "Morning, Billy. Take your time, Rosebud's just in front."

The crush hall was already heaving with miners getting their lamps and grabbing the last chance for a smoke before descending down into the bowels of the earth. There was some hushed talk in the cage as it sped down the shaft towards the pit bottom. The smell of Rosebud still hung in his nostrils.

Norman was trying to listen to the hushed whispers going on between the men in front as they got off the cage. Jegger caught up with them as they looked for an empty carriage on the waiting train. "Here, take this one," said Billy, climbing in the back compartment of the one nearest the loco. The four men clambered in and Jegger fished out the pack of cards.

Abbo, Sid and Andy followed them and sat at the opposite end of the carriage. George, the deputy and fitter, sat in the middle compartment. Billy farted, which brought comments from all the other passengers. "You should smell Rosebud if you think that stinks," laughed Billy.

Norman said he had tried to listen to the conversations in the cage. "Something's brewing," he said. "There's talk of a big meeting this Saturday up Nottingham. Couldn't grasp everything but it's pretty hush-hush."

The loco rumbled along the rails, drawing nearer to the first stop at the Heathen. Billy led his team, followed by the haulage lads. Bruce said that they were still a man short, but could they manage? Abbo said they could. Harry, the fitter, followed the rock headers down the hill. "The deputy engineer is coming down today. He's probably coming down the back end into your 'head'. Look out for him, Billy!"

***

Peter limped down the crush hall into the oil sampling office. He carried oil samples left by the night shift. Allan was just putting the kettle on. John followed Peter into the office and straight away pulled out his newspaper and began scanning the racing section. "Another hot favourite?" Allan nodded his head in John's direction. "How much shall we put on Peter?" Pete laughed.

John said, "You can laugh; wait until you see my winnings."

Ken entered the office and sat down beside John. "Are you playing tonight, mate?"

John shook his head. "No, I got something on tonight."

Allan butted in, "It's Friday, Ken, you know, 'Grab a Grannie Disco' at the club. John's got his eye on some crumpet he met last week. Isn't that right, John?"

John pointed to the paper. "Here you are, Ken, put a fiver on that one."

Ken declined, "No thanks, mate, I'd sooner spend my money on booze."

***

Abbo looked at the row of tubs carrying supplies down the hill. He leaned on the first one as Sid coupled on the rope. "We going to see Ray when we knock off?"

Sid straightened up. "Of course we are and we'll take some beer and fags to him. Won't we, Andy?"

Andy looked at his two mates. "I was thinking last night how we can help Ray get that bastard boyfriend. There's too much drug-pushing in our town and it's time somebody did something about the pushers. The fucking police are useless. I know quite a few guys on drugs."

Abbo looked at his mate. "What can we do, Andy?"

Sid leaned over to listen. "We can act like vigilantes and gang up on the bastards once we find out who they are and stuff the drugs down their throats or up their arses."

Abbo nodded his head. "Yep, that's a good idea, Sid. There's four of us; we could manage something and I bet Ray will agree with the idea."

***

Deputy George came on the tannoy to the back of the head. Norman answered it. "The engineer is on his way in. Have you drilled the head yet?" Norman shouted down to his mates, "Take your time, Billy; the engineer's on his way. Leave the drill rig where it is; let him see how it is."

George said it would be half an hour before they reached the back of the head. "What's the ground like, Norman?" Norman said it was slushy and just right for the engineer to see.

***

Dennis Mason locked the union office door and made his way to the car park. He put his briefcase on the passenger seat and drove off. He would go home and change, shave, shower and pack an overnight bag for his trip to Nottingham. It must be something big for the 'King' to summon all the county's union officials to a meeting.

***

Christine pushed the pram through the estate to Billy's Mam's house. She would look after little Steven whilst Christine did the weekend shopping; it was better for her to shop alone. Billy was a pain in the arse and only wanted to watch any sport on the TV. It gave her a chance to meet up with old friends in the town all doing the same thing. It wasn't like going dancing or out for a meal, but a coffee in a café was second-best and she could catch up on local gossip from her mates. Who was pregnant and who was shagging who. Of course, the latest gossip was the girl on the estate who had died after taking ecstasy at the *Disco World* nightclub. One or two of Christine's friends said they knew of guys and gals in the town who were druggies. It was a common practice these days to want to dance all night with the help of a little pill. "They can fuck that," said Christine. "I'll do without the pills and powders."

***

Abbo, Sid and Andy made their way through the estate and over the field to where Ray was chilling out. Abbo had brought half a dozen cans of lager and Sid had brought cigarettes. Andy had filled a bag of goodies, like Mars bars, bags of crisps and a pack of sandwiches. If Ray wasn't hungry, he was. They made it over to the pools and cut their way through the ferns to where Ray was. Dave was already sitting with Ray outside the tent. "Hi, you guys. What took you so long?" he said, beaming all over his face. Ray reached for the cigarettes and opened a packet. "I've been gasping for a fag all day. Help yourself, lads." Abbo had already opened a can and passed it to Ray. "Couldn't wish for any better mates than you lot," said Ray.

Andy looked at the gang sitting drinking and smoking their heads off. "What are we going to do about that bastard of a boyfriend?" he asked.

Ray said that he had thought about it a lot. "When everything has cooled down and when we've put Janet to rest, I'm going after him."

Abbo said, "And we are going with you, Ray. We've been talking between ourselves; it's time somebody did something about those bastards who come into our town pushing drugs. We're going to nail them."

Ray interrupted Abbo, "I don't want to get you guys involved in this, thanks anyway, but this is personal."

Abbo stood up and paced up and down. "But Ray, it's our town. Who's going to be next, my sister or Andy's sister? No Ray, we're going to clean up our town and stop those bastard drug pushers from Stafford and Litchfield from coming in and selling their shit."

Chapter 4
The B.A.D Boys (Boys Against Drugs)

The gang said their farewells to Ray and made their way back into the estate. “Get your thinking caps on,” said Abbo, “and come up with some ideas and ask around about the drug-pushers. Let’s find out who they are.”

Billy and his team had waited for the engineer to arrive in the head. Billy powered up the drill rig and finished boring the bottoms. The water sprays pumped water to lay the cloud of dust, making the ground a bit slushier. “Right, I’m going to track back now so watch yourselves, stay well clear of the rig.” He raised the boom slightly and powered the tracks. All went well for about two feet and then the tracks began churning up the floor in an effort to climb back up the steep climb. Soon the rig was slipping and sliding about without tracking back as it should do. Billy stopped the machine. “See what we mean, boss? The fucking thing won’t take it.”

The engineer walked around the machine. “How many more yards before you level out?” he asked Bruce.

“We’ve got at least another hundred yards like this; maybe a bit more.”

The engineer admitted that there was a problem and it would have to be solved. He walked back up the road a few yards as Billy powered up the drill rig and attempted again to reverse it away from the back of the head. Billy struggled for at least half an hour to inch the rig back to the safe place so that George could fire the head. The engineer was looking at the belt structure and rings supporting the roadway. “OK lads, I've seen enough, let's see what we can come up with. When you eventually level out, we'll change the machines."

***

Peter took the oil sampling kits to where the area assistant engineer dished them out to the fitters. His leg was beginning to throb. A warm shower and a cup of canteen tea and he was crossing over to the car park. It was pissing down with rain so Peter drove home instead of going into Litchfield for paint. He decided to go on Saturday morning instead. For now, all he wanted to do was lie down on the settee with his leg up.

***

Christine completed her shopping and took a taxi back to her mother-in-law's place. Steven was asleep so Christine said she would take him home while he was quiet. The rain had eased off a bit as she made her way through the estate. She walked past the house where the girl who had died lived. There were flowers laid out on the lawn. The funeral was due to take place Saturday afternoon, she had been told. She arrived home just as Billy was driving up the road. He pipped his horn, which woke Steven up. "Daft bastard!" Christine shouted.

Billy got out of the car and helped carry the shopping in. Christine picked up Steven and asked Billy to bring in the buggy. "Did you hear about that girl on the estate?"

Billy said he had. "It was all the talk at the pit. Somebody ought to do something about those drug-pushers," he said.

***

Peter had fallen asleep. The tablets he had taken for the pain had made him feel dozy. It was 6 o'clock when he woke up. The cat had made herself comfortable on top of him. Peter scooped her up and put her on the floor.

Immediately, she started meowing for food. He looked in the fridge for something easy to cook and settled for the rest of the cooked chicken. It didn't take long for him to place a jacket potato in the microwave and soon he was sitting in front of the telly, watching the remains of the news. Nothing much of interest so he switched it off and picked up the daily paper. At 8 o'clock, he decided to take a bath and soak his leg in the Radox. After a good soak, he put on his jammies and settled down to watch the telly again. He wanted an early night so that he could get to Litchfield early. He forgot to set the alarm clock so it was 9:30 before he was aroused by the cat meowing to be let out. He let her out onto the balcony where her litter tray was. Peter was tempted to climb back into bed but put the kettle on instead. After a cereal breakfast and a second cup of tea, he got dressed ready for going out.

***

Susan watched as Derek packed his bag and checked his fishing gear. "I shall make an early start," he said. "I'll try not to wake you." She didn't say anything; she just gave him a fed-up look. She would be spending another weekend on her own. Nothing unusual, this was the practice for Derek to sod off with his mates, fishing. Why on earth had she married him? Five years of this and not even a baby by him. He didn't want children. Susan thought he would change his mind but he didn't, he insisted on Susan going on the pill. She often thought she had married a selfish bastard, but had also thought she could talk him around, but no, he was adamant. "No kids to tie us down."

She woke early to find Derek had gone. She looked out of the window to see what the weather was like. It was fine; a light grey morning greeted her. She showered and dressed, choosing a dark trouser suit. She had decided on a trip into Litchfield to do some shopping and browsing around the clothes shops. She always found Litchfield to be a nice place to shop.

***

Abbo waited for Sid and Andy to meet him at the corner of the road leading into the forest. They arrived, carrying beer and other goodies for Ray. He greeted them. “The funeral has been arranged for Wednesday instead of next Saturday,” he told them. “They’ve done everything they gotta do so now Mam and Dad have made all the arrangements. Will you guys be able to come? It’s not until half past two, so if you can get an early note, you won’t have to lose a shift’s work.”

Abbo said that they would be there. He said the flowers on the front lawn of Ray’s house looked good. “Yeah well, everybody thought the funeral was today, but it was postponed. Still, the flowers will keep fresh.”

The boys opened the beer and lit up the cigarettes. “We’ve been thinking up ideas on how to do something about the drug-pushers in our town,” said Andy.

“Yeah, we’re going to form a vigilante group and crush the bastards,” added Sid.

Abbo looked at Ray. “We going to do something, Ray, do you want to be part of it?”

Ray’s eyes lit up. “Yeah, you bet the fuck I do, but I don’t want you guys getting into trouble on my account.”

Sid looked at his mates. “We gotta do this right. No slip-ups and we gotta make sure we are not identified. Boys Against Drugs, eh lads?”

***

Dennis Mason pulled into the car park of the union office in Nottingham. An early start had gotten him there with plenty of time to spare. He wasn’t the first to arrive; there were other cars parked. He noticed the president’s BMW parked in his designated parking place. His bold nameplate was fixed to the wall. Inside, he was greeted by familiar faces he had met at other union meetings. The long table had been set out and name cards had been arranged around the table. The deputy president waved to him from across the room. Finding his name halfway down the table, Dennis sat down. He noticed that he was sitting nearest to the Power Group Union rep from his pit so at least they could discuss between them whatever the King had brought them together for. Soon the room was full and individuals were looking for their allocated seats.

They were all seated when the president of the CMU walked into the room, accompanied by his assistant and secretary.

"Good morning, gentlemen. I can see we have a good turnout. I'm sure that you will agree that it was necessary to call you all together when you hear what I have to say."

He cleared his throat and took a sip of water. "As you are all aware, our industry is under threat from the government. We have always been a thorn in their side and they have always sought ways and means to curb our power. Any demands that we have put to them have always been practically denied. I don't think we have been too demanding. All we ever wanted was a decent wage and good working conditions. All they ever demanded was increased production and a cutback in manpower. Now we have reached a stalemate situation and they have refused to meet us to negotiate, but that isn't the reason for today's meeting. As you are aware, I have an informer in the government who keeps me up to date with what's going on. This week, I received disturbing information from him." At this point, the president held up a sheet of paper with a long list of names on it. "Here is a list of pits earmarked for closure by the government in the not-too-distant future. There are seventy pits listed. I have copies that I will pass around for you to see. They are preparing to rape our industry like they did with the ship-building. Many of our colleagues will lose their jobs and end up on the scrap heap. Families will lose their income and be left to starve if we let them get away with it. Are we going to stand by and let this happen?" The president paused for a moment while the 'Hit List' was passed around. He took a sip of water before addressing the meeting again. "Gentlemen, there's more distressing news. My informer has also confided in me regarding a hitman who has been brought in from America to oversee these closures at a cost of 1 million pounds for his dirty work. He is a ruthless individual by the name of MacKenzie. All these pits listed are not viable according to his report and are not reaching their targets. Now we know that some pits are struggling due to various geological problems, but it has always been that way and the pits that are producing good output make up for losses elsewhere. But the Coal Board and the government won't accept this. They want full production from all pits. Gentlemen, I have brought this matter to your attention. Now we will take a coffee break and let you talk amongst yourselves."

***

Peter backed his car onto the road. He could do a quick shop around Litchfield and be back for lunch. Then he could carry on with the decorating. He followed the stream of traffic through the town and then took the road to Litchfield. He opened up the car and gave it a good run into the city centre. He parked in the supermarket car park and walked into the store. He picked up a few things and headed for the cash counter. Putting his shopping in the boot, he headed across to find the do-it-yourself store. He found the tin of paint he was after and headed back towards the car park. He checked the contents of his shopping bag and suddenly realised he had forgotten the cereal. He went back into the store and scoured the shelves. Lifting the carton, he put it in the basket. As he looked up, he was aware that someone was looking at him.

"I thought it was you," said Susan, giving him a big smile.

Peter looked at her. She was a beautiful woman. Her dark hair cascaded around her shoulders and her eyes lit up. Her smile would melt any man's heart. "Hello Susan, I was miles away. I wouldn't have noticed you if you hadn't spoken. Just picking up a few things," he said.

"Do you always shop here?" she asked.

"No, not always, now and then for things I can't get back home. How about you?"

She pointed to her trolley. "Yes, I like Litchfield. It's such a nice place to shop and I like to browse around. The clothes shops are a bit more upmarket here." Peter said he had finished his shopping and was heading home. Susan said she had finished getting her groceries. "Off to dump this lot in my car and then browse around for a while."

Peter followed her to the checkout; he could smell her perfume. She reminded him of someone he had seen on the telly, but couldn't put a name to the person. They walked together to the car park and oddly enough, her car was parked almost next to Peter's. "My little Mini," she said, pointing to the blue car.

Peter unlocked his car and put his things in the boot. He looked at her as she offloaded the trolley. His heart was in his mouth as he plucked up the courage to ask, "Would you like to go for a cup of tea or something, Susan?"

She closed the boot of her car. "Oh yes, Peter, that would be most welcome."

They walked back into the city centre. "There's a nice café just around this corner," she said. "I often use it when I'm in Litchfield. There's a nice view of the cathedral from here." Peter followed as she led the way. The streets were busy as you would expect on a Saturday. They found a table just inside by the window.

"What will it be?" Peter asked as the waitress approached.

"Oh! Coffee for me," said Susan.

"Two coffees, please." Peter looked through the window at the cathedral spires towering above the city. It was a nice place; he agreed with Susan and he felt very relaxed in her company. He didn't very often stop for a coffee on his shopping trips as he was always in a hurry to get back home. But today was different, he was in good company.

"Any more shopping to do?" Susan asked.

He shook his head. "No, not that I can think of. I did want to look for a couple of nice shirts but I can leave that until next Saturday. It's such a nice day now the sun is shining, I might just browse around."

She sipped her coffee. "Would you like to go for a walk along the river? That's what I do sometimes."

Peter's heart was fluttering. Did she want company or what? "If you will accompany me, Susan; I haven't been along there for years and I might get lost or fall in."

She gave him a lovely smile. "Why not, I've got nothing else to do and as you say, it's a lovely day."

***

Abbo, Sid and Andy always met up for a pint in the pub on the estate, mainly to watch a football match on the huge telly, but today Abbo was going to lay out his plans for actions against the drug dealers. "Listen! There'll be four of us. We will find out where the bastard comes and waylay him. I suggest we pump him full of the shit he's dealing and then let him go with a warning that if he comes back, we'll do it again. A good idea, eh?"

Sid butted in, "What if somebody sees us and recognises us?"

Abbo thought for a moment and then suggested to his friends that they should wear ski masks or something.

Sid was beaming all over his face. "I've been thinking of something as well. Why don't we buy four bomber jackets? You can get reversible ones in Stafford. Black on the outside and whatever colour you want on the inside. Along with a pair of black jeans and a ski mask, nobody will recognise us."

The boys were showing interest now and more ideas were coming up. Andy piped up, "And we could have our logo on the backside." Andy looked at Abbo. "What's it going to be?"

"B.A.D.," answered Abbo. "Boys Against Drugs."

"Everybody will think we are a pop group," chimed in Sid.

Abbo smiled. "We only wear the dark side when we're hunting the druggies and then we reverse our jackets. It sounds good to me."

***

Joe Fiddler made his way through the estate to the lock-up garage. Saturday was a good day for business and he had his mind set on the fashion show in Manchester. It was clear in the garage area as he unlocked the door and slipped in. He connected the car phone and made contact with all three girls. It didn't take him long to change into his business suit and do his makeover. He checked his briefcase for the sales leaflets and took out the four show admission passes acquired by phoning up the organisers on behalf of his company, Cottons and Fabrics Ltd.

He picked up the girls, Veronica being the last, and soon they were speeding towards Manchester. "It should be good here today," said Joe. "A mixture of men and women and plenty of clothes to look at, but business first, remember girls, we're here to make money, not spend it." He pulled into the car park and despatched sales samples for the girls to show clients. The show was well under way and the hall was heaving. "4:30 finish, girls, meet you at the main entrance."

Joe browsed around the stalls, inspecting the goods and brand names. His lapel badge enhanced by the company's name, Cottons and Fabrics Ltd., soon got him noticed. The girls also browsed around the women's fashions before venturing over to the menswear. "I wonder if there's any free samples," said Janet loudly so that the middle-aged man displaying the goods couldn't help but hear.

He moved in on her, noticing her lapel badge. "Well, maybe we could exchange samples?" he said jokingly. Janet stood, feeling the quality of the goods, whilst he did his best to further the conversation. Denise and Veronica moved on, leaving Janet to hook the fish.

“I’m going back to the women’s clothes,” said Veronica. “I noticed a dashing bit of stuff clocking me. I’ll go and dangle the bait more.”

Denise moved on, picking up the odd leaflet and trying to look interested. She hadn’t gone far before a well-dressed representative moved in on her. He noticed her lapel badge. “Hello gorgeous. What are you selling?” She could smell his strong deodorant and aftershave. He was about fortyish with broad shoulders and with the look of an athlete.

She gave him a flash of her pearly whites. “Whatever you’re looking for,” she answered.

He gave her a broad grin and a come-to-bed look. “Oh,” he said. “If you’re selling, I’m buying.” She smiled and handed him a leaflet advertising the firm, Cottons and Fabrics Ltd. “I was looking for personal offerings,” he said, handing back the leaflet. “Such as lunch and a happy hour in my hotel room?”

Denise moved away to a quieter spot. He moved in on her. “It’s not cheap,” she whispered.

He rubbed up close to her, “Whatever it costs, I’ve got to have it.”

Denise had hooked her fish. “What time and where?”

He looked at his watch. “In one hour here. My assistant can look after the business for a couple of hours.”

Chapter 5
A Time for Action

John told his wife he was going to mow the lawns and went into the garage for the mower. "Make sure you get the lines straight, not like last time."

John went back into the house. "Well, if you want to do it, you can; I'm not as fussy as you."

She gave him a look. "What time did you come in last night?" she asked accusingly.

John gave her a vague answer. "Christ knows, I was drinking with Ken till late, arranging Sunday's match." In fact, he had been over in the woods with the woman he had arranged to meet at the 'Grab a Granny Disco'. He had parked up and they had been on the backseat, steaming up the windows with their hot sex. She had been hot stuff and did it all, from a blow job to stripping off and sitting on his lap, thrusting her buttocks into his groin. John didn't give a fuck if the lines on the lawn were straight or not. His wife lived in another world.

***

The Coal Miners Union president called the meeting to order. "Well, lads, you have had a chance to mull it over between you, now let's talk about what we are going to do about it. We will take it in turns to have our say in an orderly fashion. Starting off on my right, I want you to stand up and identify yourself and the area you are representing. Placed in front of you are sheets of A4 paper. Write your name, the name of your pit, the date and your comments and hand them in at the end of the meeting. I know some of you have travelled far to attend this meeting. I hope you have arranged overnight reservations as I think this is going to be a long day. Right, let's start the discussions." He pointed to the first union representative on his right. "Let's begin."

***

Abbo and Sid downed their beers. "Are we going to see Ray?" asked Andy.

The boys looked at each other. "Yeah, why not," said Abbo. "Let's take him some beers and fags." They left the pub and called in at the supermarket. Loaded up, they made it through the estate into the woods.

A voice called out through the undergrowth. "Hey, you fuckers, wait for me." It was Dave. "I thought it was you. I could hear you a mile off."

Dave had a bag of goodies in his hand. "Ray wanted his little radio to listen to so I made up some sandwiches and stuff to keep him going. Mam has asked me to persuade him to come home, she is worried about him. She knows how volatile he gets when things upset him. I want to know if he's going to be at Jan's funeral."

They found Ray sitting on the grass outside his tent, smoking. "Hello, you guys. Heard you coming a mile away, you noisy bastards."

Abbo dumped the beer in front of him. "Hi Ray, how you bin, mate?"

Ray looked out across the pool. His eyes were watery. "I'm fucking miserable; I can't get Jan out of my mind. Sometimes at night, I walk around just calling her name."

Andy gave their mate a brief hug. "We feel for you, mate, and we'll get the bastard responsible."

Sid looked at his mates. "Shall we tell Ray what we're going to do? It might cheer him up a bit."

Abbo looked at Sid. "I doubt if anything will cheer him up."

Ray turned his gaze to his brother, Dave. "Did you bring my radio, Dave?"

Dave opened up the bag. "I got it and I've brought you some sandwiches and Mam wants to know if you are coming to Jan's funeral."

Ray looked at his mates. "Are you coming?" Abbo said they would all be there. "If that bastard of a boyfriend turns up, I'll go for him," said Ray.

Andy looked at his mates. "The police are only charging him for possessing drugs. He was only carrying weed. They're after the woman who sold them the pill. She's gone to ground. Nobody knows who she was, but she's been to the *Disco World* before, according to one of the bouncers."

Ray lit up a fag and offered them around. "I still don't want to see that bastard at Jan's funeral. Dave, make that clear to Mam and Dad."

***

Peter paid for the coffees and they left the café. "Does your leg hurt when you walk?" asked Susan.

"Not if I walk slowly but I couldn't run for a bus if I tried," replied Peter. They walked past the cathedral towards the river. There were lots of benches scattered around and Susan suggested to Peter that if his leg caused any discomfort, they could at any time sit on one of them for a while.

"How did you hurt your leg anyway? Was it down the pit?"

Peter shook his head. He told her that he had been indulging in his favourite sport, motorbike scrambling. "I used to be a part of the Hednesford team and we used to compete against other teams. We were riding against a team from Northampton on their grounds. I was leading, doing quite well when one of their riders decided to push for the lead. He cut in front of me on a downward stretch, very muddy and slippery. He came up too close and we collided. I went head over heels down a bank into a ditch. My bike flew into the air and landed on top of my leg breaking it in two places. That was six months ago. It put an end to my bike and my hobby."

Susan shook her head. "You men and your hobbies! My husband isn't that active. He likes to wade in streams up to his waist, fly-fishing. He's part of a team and goes off every weekend with his mates. He doesn't give a shit about leaving me alone at weekends."

Peter pointed to a bench along the river. "Do you mind if we sit awhile?" They gazed into the river, observing the ducks and other wildlife. "Well, at least I was divorced," said Peter. "I suppose we men are a bit selfish like that. My wife was only interested in shopping and dining out or dancing at weekends. It was all right during the early years but when I bought my scrambler, she tended to drift off on her own and eventually met someone else."

Susan nodded understandingly. "Any children?" she asked.

Peter shook his head. "No, she wasn't maternal, she liked freedom." Peter looked at his watch. "Are you all right for time, Susan?"

She checked hers. "I've got nothing to rush home for; have you?"

Peter got up. "Let's walk a little further while the sun shines." He held out his hand to help her up, to which she remarked that only a gentleman did that these days. Peter smiled; he liked being with this woman. They walked along the river making conversation. Peter asked what her husband did when the fishing season had finished.

"Oh, he'll find some excuse to visit somewhere up Scotland where there's private estates offering all year round fishing; he just doesn't want to stay at home at weekends. Sometimes, it's golf. He's a member of some club."

The thoughts rushed through his mind. *What a wanker, fancy preferring your mates to a beautiful woman like Susan.* They sat on another bench, still embroiled in light conversation. "Where do you live?" Peter asked.

"Colwich," she answered. "How about you?"

Peter smiled. "Not too far away, I have a flat in Hixon."

***

The coal miners' president listened to what the union reps were saying. How true was this information? Who was the informer in the government supplying the King with this information? "I will never divulge to anyone who my informant is. All I can tell you is that I would trust this person with my life. He is high-ranking and sympathetic to our cause."

As each representative had his say, the atmosphere in the room became electric. Some believed the information and some didn't. "Ask for a meeting with the Coal Board and demand to know what they are going to do about it."

The president pointed out that he had already done this but had received no reply. "They simply don't want any confrontation with us and are dragging their feet. What I want to know is how our members feel about this and what action are we to take. I'm asking you for your support, gentlemen and your membership. Go and talk, arrange meetings and come back and let me know how things are. By the way, there are shiploads of foreign coal already on their way from places like Bolivia and Russia. The government is secretly building up their stocks with cheap coal in case of any confrontations." It was late in the afternoon when the president held up his hands. "Gentlemen, we can stay here and talk all day and night but the problem will not be resolved. We need to know the exact feeling of our membership. I would like to close this meeting now, but I will arrange another one in a month's time to hear what you have to say and I will also try and arrange a meeting with the board if I can. Thank you for your attendance."

***

Veronica moved slowly amongst the women's fashions, aware that she was being watched. A tall smartly dressed assistant moved in on her as she inspected the stitching. "Very well made," said the assistant.

"Yes, I can see that it has quality." Veronica handed her a brochure, saying that she represented the company. The assistant, who wore a name badge with Elizabeth on it, glanced at the brochure.

"Oh yes, I've heard of your company but never done business with them." Veronica could smell her perfume as she edged closer. Her blonde hair was cut in the familiar butch fashion and her cream trouser suit fitted her neat figure. Veronica could sense the feelings being emitted. She had been in the occasional lesbian involvement in the past, but for some time since meeting Joe had refrained. But now something was stirring inside her. She gave Elizabeth a warm 'come on' smile and moved further into the rows of fashions on display. Elizabeth followed. "Would you fancy a drink or something? I take a two-hour break at 12 o'clock."

Veronica held up the bunch of brochures. "I do have to try and get some contacts for my company or else I don't get my bonus," she replied.

"Well," said Elizabeth, "you've made one and we could discuss business at lunch in my hotel and I'll cover your bonus; don't worry about that."

By now, Elizabeth was hooked and Veronica felt a tingle down her spine as Elizabeth brushed against her. "I'll be here at 11:45, is that early enough?" asked Veronica.

Joe made his way around the show, chatting to the different reps and distributing the occasional business card. He made eye contact with his three girls, making sure they were doing the business. Three thumbs up told him that all three had scored. Joe made further contacts with the reps, getting to know where other shows were being held. Nottingham was to be as good as any next week. Joe made a note and made his way to the show organisers for further information and free entrance tickets for his company.

Back in the car, speeding on their way home, the three girls were discussing the day's events. All had scored and handed over the takings to Joe, who quickly distributed their shares. Veronica said the day had been interesting and very fruitful. "What was your bloke like?" asked Janet.

Veronica giggled uncontrollably from the front passenger seat. "Oh different, only it wasn't a bloke, it was a gorgeous-looking lesbian and we had a fantastic time."

The two other girls screamed with delight. “Did she have one of those dildos or whatever they call them?”

Joe looked in the mirror. “You mean a *strapadicktome*,” he said, laughing.

Veronica looked across at him. “She had everything and gave a good service.”

Janet butted in from the back, “I still prefer to be humped by a bloke.”

Denise said she did too. “Especially if he’s good-looking and well-blessed.”

Joe reminded the girls that they were in the business for money, not to be enjoying themselves. “It’s Nottingham next. When I get more information, I will call you so keep your phones on the hook.”

He dropped off Veronica first, who gave him a strange look. Next, he dropped off Denise. Janet got into the front seat. As they sped along the road, she rubbed her hand over Joe’s crotch. “You want coffee, Joe, or what?”

Joe looked at her. “Or what,” he replied.

***

Peter looked at Susan and said, “I’ve enjoyed your company. It’s been a while since I’ve chatted to a woman.”

Susan smiled back at him. “And I’ve enjoyed being with you.”

Peter thought for a while. *Was he moving too fast?* He decided to chance it. “What about going for lunch, Susan? Let’s make a day of it.”

She looked away and Peter wished he hadn’t asked her. After all, he was being a bit presumptuous. Finally, she said, “OK Peter, why not? We’ve got nothing else to do, have we?” Peter held out his hand to help her get up. “Forever the gentleman,” she mused. They made their way back into the city, looking at different menus on the way. “Mmm…that looks nice,” said Susan, pointing to one outside the pub/restaurant.

Peter looked inside. “There’s plenty of tables and seats; yes, let’s try this one. They’ve got a good choice on the menu as well." They were shown to a table and given a menu to choose from. They found it easy talking to one another and the conversation flowed easily.

"We must do this again," she suggested. "Peter, you have made my day." Susan flashed a warm smile across the table. "And I have enjoyed being in the company of a gentleman who knows how to treat a lady."

Finishing their meal, they left the restaurant and made their way to the car park. Peter's mind was racing; he wanted to be with her longer but he didn't want to spoil things by being in too much of a rush. "I shall look forward to our next meeting, Susan. Maybe next Saturday if you are at a loose end."

She looked at him as he held open the car door. "Same time, same place," she said, leaning forward and giving him a peck on the cheek. "Thanks for a nice day, Peter."

***

It was 7 o'clock when the president called the meeting to a close. Dennis decided he would find somewhere to stay the night and drive back in the morning as the union paid his accommodation bills anyway. He stopped and chatted to some of the other union reps and noticed from their comments that there were mixed feelings amongst them. "If he's right, then it's the thin end of the wedge. They intend to get rid of the coal industry like they did with the steel industry." Another voice spoke up, "Yes and the shipping industry. All they want is to sell off to private enterprise. We'd be silly bastards to stand by and let them. Let's see if he can get a meeting set up with the management; we'll learn a bit more then."

Dennis drove to a hotel down one of the backstreets. He'd been here before and got on well with the hotel manager's husband and wife team—Gladys and Henry. "Been a long day?" said Gladys, booking him in. "Haven't seen you for a while." Dennis took the keys and moved towards the lift. "I'll come up with you, Dennis, and just check whether everything is in order."

The lift door closed and Gladys pressed the button. Her perfume filled the lift. She wasn't a bad-looking woman, somewhere in her late forties and in good shape. "How have you been keeping?" Dennis asked as the lift climbed up to the third floor.

Gladys turned and gave Dennis a pleasant smile. "Oh, I've been all right. Henry's been off it for a while. He's had to take things easy, slight heart problem. We've had to employ a couple more staff to help out; I'm not getting any younger myself."

Dennis shot her a warm smile. "You still look good to me, Gladys."

She opened the door to the room and pointed to the bed. "Here you are, Dennis, a new bed and it hasn't been used yet." She gave him a wicked smile. "And a larger TV for you to watch if you get bored."

Dennis looked around the room. The bed looked inviting. "I'd sooner try out the bed," he said, looking at her.

She gave him a wicked smile again. "Will you require a meal, Dennis? I can rustle something up for you and bring it up to your room. The restaurant is closed for the evening."

Dennis nodded his head. "Yes please, Gladys, anything will do."

She brushed past him. "And how about drinks, I can recommend a nice wine."

Dennis had a wash to freshen up; it had been a long day. A knock on the door and Gladys waltzed in with a trolley that she wheeled over to the table and began to lay the food out. "Scrambled eggs, bacon and beans, Dennis; will that do?"

Dennis sat down and began to tuck into the meal. "This is great, Gladys, thanks."

Gladys went over to the bed and picked up Dennis's jacket. "I'll put this in the wardrobe for you." She then began to fiddle about with the pillows on the bed. As she bent over, Dennis noticed the elastic line of her knickers showing that she had on the briefest of underwear. Her skirt was short and revealed a good pair of legs and she wasn't wearing tights. "Oh, I forgot the wine," she said. "I'll just go down and fetch it. I put it to cool and forgot to pick it up. I won't be a minute, Dennis."

The meal went down well and Gladys soon returned with the wine and two glasses. Dennis wiped his mouth on the napkin and placed the plate and utensils on the trolley, leaving the table clear for the wine. Dennis took it from her and removed the cork. "Are you going to join me?" he asked Gladys.

She gave him a warm smile. "Well, yes, if that's an invite?" She pulled up a chair and sat down. "You don't' like drinking alone, do you? Neither do I," she said. "Do you smoke, Dennis?"

A packet of cigarettes appeared on the table. Dennis took one out and offered Gladys the packet. "I do, on occasions." Their eyes met as she reached across the table and a lighter appeared in her hand. Dennis held her hand as he lit his cigarette. "So Gladys, what's life like for you running this hotel?" he asked.

Gladys puffed on her cigarette and blew the smoke up in the air. "It could be better. Things have got harder since Henry took ill. It has had its ups and downs like every other job. I have to manage the upper floors as Henry can't do much; he remains on duty downstairs. We hired part-time cleaners but you have to check whether they are doing the job properly."

Dennis refilled her glass and his own as the conversation continued. "Do you get out much?" Dennis asked.

She shook her head. "No, it's all work and no play for me." She got up and walked over to the window. "This room has good views and when it's dark, the city lights are pretty."

Dennis left the table and stood behind her, peering over her shoulders. She leaned against him and he put his hands on her waist to support her. Reaching up, she drew the curtains. Her perfume was strong and Dennis could feel her body heat. She turned around to face him and their eyes met. Leaning forward, their lips almost touching, Gladys whispered, "Do you want me to sleep with you?"

Chapter 6
Demons

Two fitters and an apprentice made their way down the steep hill into the rock head. Ken, the senior one, looked at the small winch that had been lowered down the hill and was still loaded on the flat truck. Brian, his mate, looked at it too. "We've got to fit this onto the belt structure and hose it up to the hydraulic pump somehow."

The apprentice looked confused. "What's it for?" he asked.

The fitters had been asked to work Saturday and Sunday to install the winch. The idea was to hook it onto the drill rig and help pull the rig back. Brian looked at the steel rope. "I have my doubts about this one, Ken."

His mate said that they could only do what they'd been told to do. The engineers upstairs had dreamed up this idea. "Better run the rope out first and see how far it reaches." By the end of the shift, the winch had been mounted and secured on the belt structure and the rope pulled out to reach the drill rig. "Just a matter of hosing it up tomorrow," said Ken, pleased with the day's work.

***

Abbo, Sid and Andy browsed around the market stalls, looking at the jackets. "This is where I saw them reversible ones," said Sid, looking through the rows of jackets on the rails.

"Can I help you?" said the guy in charge of the stall.

“Yes, you showed me some reversible bomber jackets last week.”

The man led them to another rail and pointed. The boys looked at the jackets—black on the outside but different on the inside. “It’s like having two jackets,” said the man.

Abbo took one off the rail and tried it on. “How much?” he asked.

“Ten pounds to you, my friend,” was the reply.

“Do you print logos on the back?” asked Sid.

“No, but there’s a guy on the market that does that sort of thing,” said the man.

Sid was trying one on and Andy reached one off the rail. “How much for three?” asked Sid.

Abbo had reversed his and was admiring himself in the mirror. “Four,” he said. “Don’t forget Ray.”

The man was looking at the boys. “I can knock a pound off each one,” he chimed.

“Make it one-fifty and we’ll buy,” said Sid. “We’ve still got to get the logos printed on them and that will cost.”

The man said he would settle for eight-fifty per jacket. The boys chose their sizes. “What’s Ray’s chest measurement?” asked Andy.

“Fuck knows,” said Sid.

Abbo thought for a moment, “I’m a forty but he’s bigger than me. He’s built like a brick shithouse, better take him a bigger one. I think a forty-two” he replied.

***

Monday morning soon came around and once again a stream of traffic filled the road to the pit. Billy parked and walked across to the bath entrance. Alf saw Billy coming in and stood up, making sure he was well balanced in case Billy did his usual thing. “Morning, Alf.”

His mate acknowledged Billy with a big smile. “Shall we pop in and see what the gaffer has to say?” asked Alf.

Billy said that if they were all right for time, it might be a good idea to find out if anything had been done. They hurried through the baths and drew their lamps. “I can’t see

Norman or Jegger. We'll just pop our heads around the door," said Billy, crossing over to the boss' office door. He gave a gentle knock and peered inside.

The boss looked up. "Come in, Billy. They've fitted a winch on the structure to help in getting the drill rig back. Try it out and let's see if it does the job."

In the cage, Norman asked what they had done. Billy said they had fitted a winch. "Let's hope it does the trick," piped up Jegger. "Perhaps we can earn some bonus now."

The assistant engineer called out to Harry, the fitter, as he booked in. "Harry, will you go down the back and into the rock head and see how they got on with that winch they had fitted to help pull the drill rig back?" Harry nodded and made his way to the cage waiting to send them down the pit.

The loco pulled out of the pit bottom. Harry had to remember to get off with the rock headers at the heathen and follow them down the hill into the back end.

Abbo, Sid and Andy mustered at the top of the hill. "Nothing to take down yet," said Sid, checking the empty supply cars.

The deputy joined them. "There's a journey of supplies coming in soon, lads, so do your best and get them down the hill."

Billy led the way and went straight into the back of the head. It was dry and the rig was already just a couple of metres back. "Ready to start when we've had a bite, Alf? Let's see what this winch is like." They walked back a few metres to the belt structure. The winch had been mounted on the backend and hosed up to the pump. "That rope doesn't look strong enough to me," said Billy.

Alf agreed. "We'll soon see when we try it."

Harry joined them. "When can you try it, Billy?" he asked.

Alf said that they had to bore the head first and then it had to be fired. "Probably snap time before we're ready."

Billy agreed. "Don't go away, Harry; I got a funny feeling about this."

Harry walked back a few metres to where he had dropped his tool bag and snap bag. He took out a sandwich and his newspaper. He had shared the same compartment on the train as the haulage team. The conversation had been unwelcoming as they had talked of nothing else but the funeral on Wednesday. Harry didn't know who the girl was who had died, but it reminded him of one he used to know many years ago before he worked down the pit. She had been a young girl of 16 who had worked in the same office as Harry. She was a beautiful dainty-looking girl and Harry had been very keen on her. One Monday morning, the news had been buzzing around the office that she had been killed in a car accident on Saturday night. Two girls and two boys had crashed their car, killing all four of them. Harry was devastated. He had run into the toilet block and vomited and the tears had flowed. It had haunted him for years and every now and then, he would see her face in his dreams. Now he was hearing of another young girl who had met her death. As he sat eating his sandwiches, other faces ran through his mind. When he had first started down the pit, he had made lots of friends. The haulage lads and electricians and many of the face workers. Tony had been the first, a young eighteen-year-old who had just finished his training and had been working with an experienced man ripping along the roads. A piece of rock had fallen and caught him on the wrist. Six months later, he had been diagnosed with cancer and died.

Dennis had been next, a young lad working on supplies. He had thrown himself under a train. Then there had been the electrician who had decided to ride a flat dam down the return airway instead of walking and carrying his tool bag. This all had done at some time, but this time, the electrician had hit his head on a low part of the roof, breaking his neck.

Len had worked nights, cutting the face. The machine had been like a giant chainsaw. The jib was the blades and was pulled into the face and it cut into the wall of coal. Once in, the jib was secured by a steel pin. Len had walked alongside the cutter, putting blocks of wood into the 'cut'. Suddenly, the blades had hit a piece of hard rock and the machine had jumped and bucked, shaking out the jib pin. The jib had slipped out and almost cut Len in half.

Harry used to go down Walsall, dancing at the Mayfair. On Saturday night, he asked this young girl for a dance. They started talking. She was a nurse at the hospital. She asked Harry where he worked. When he said down the pit, she asked him if he had known Len. He said he had. "I was the nurse who laid him out when he died," she said and tears had welled up in her eyes.

Harry had moved on to another pit when the old one closed. He soon made friends and enjoyed his job as a fitter's mate. He had a good relationship with all the miners and it was another sad time before the old pit closed when one of the face workers a few years older than him had been killed on his motorbike. He had been courting a girl that Harry had gone to school with.

It was to be a big shock to Harry when he went to work one day. It was a Monday morning and he was filling his water bottle. Someone behind him said, "That was nasty what happened over the weekend."

Harry thought he was referring to some football match. "Yea," he said casually. When he joined the rest of the fitters, the real thing hit him. Three men had been killed when a complete road junction had collapsed on them. As he heard the names of the dead, he felt sick. He had known all three of them. Jim…he used to walk down the road with him every morning. Patrick…the happy-go-lucky Irishman was always cracking jokes and Roman…the Polish man…all good men crushed to death in seconds. The pit that day was a bad place to be with everyone talking about the accident. As Harry finished his sandwich, he was reminded again of Brian, a young twenty-one-year-old newcomer. He used to sit by Harry at snap time and chat away. He had been married with a newborn baby. Six months later, he had been dead, killed on his motorbike.

Harry got up and shook his head, trying to forget his nightmares that haunted him all these years; they never went away. He still saw all those faces in his dreams. Why wouldn't the demons let him forget? He was going to have to get some sort of treatment.

The sound of the drill rig labouring reached Harry's ears. He made his way into the back of the head. Billy was reversing the rig. "Let's see if that winch is any good, Alf." Harry watched as the rope was played out. Jegger hooked it onto the rig. Alf powered it up as Billy reversed. It was labouring as the rig slipped and slid on the wet muddied floor. Alf kept the pressure on the winch, it helped a bit but not a lot. "Fucking useless," said Billy. He had got the rig far enough back to protect it when Bruce fired the head, but that was all. Nigel said that the winch wasn't big enough. The track of the rig was just slipping and sliding all over the place. "I'm going to get the boss on the phone and let him come and see for himself."

An hour later, two lights were seen coming down the hill. Harold, the charge hand fitter, and Mr Johnson, the deputy engineer, walked straight into the back of the head. The rig was about five metres back. Mr Johnson asked Billy to operate it. Billy tried tracking back while they watched. The winch was being operated by Alf. The rig slewed from side to side as Billy tried tracking back. The machine was labouring and the rear end kept lifting up as it struggled to track back. Mr Johnson told Billy to stop. "There are several problems here," said Mr Johnson. "The ground is too wet and the gradient is too steep for this machine and its front is heavy. We could put some ballast on the backend to try and hold it down. It's lifting up off the tracks and the ground's too wet for the tracks to grip. They've got about fifty metres before they start levelling out." He looked at Harold. "Let's try using ballast on the backend to hold it down and I'll see if we can lessen the gradient a bit. One in four is a bit steep. I don't think the next fifty metres will make much difference, we will then put a Doscoe in when it's on the level."

Harold took out his tape measure and started measuring and drawing. "I'll get a steel box made to fasten on the backend and then fill it with heavy ballast. If that helps, it will do for a while."

Harry looked on. *More bright ideas I reckon*, he thought.

***

Ray looked up as his mates made their way through the bracken, carrying their bags of goodies. "I can hear you fuckers a mile away," said Ray, trying to smile. "Looks like you're getting ready for Christmas. What the fuck have you brought me?"

Abbo sat down on the grass beside his mate. "Here you are, you big bastard. Try your new jacket on."

Ray looked on in amazement as Abbo pulled out the bomber jacket. "Jesus Christ," said Ray. "What the fuck is that? I ain't that cold." He looked at the logo on the back. "Who the fuck's the Bad Boys, some poxy pop group?"

Sid and Andy were laughing their socks off. "No, you daft prat; it's our cover for when we go after the drug-pushers. Here, try on this ski mask and hide that ugly mug of yours."

Ray stood up and tried on the jacket. It fitted him perfectly and so did the ski mask. "I feel more like a fucking bank robber," said Ray.

The lads were laughing. "That's the idea, Ray, nobody will recognise us. Now take off the jacket and reverse it." Andy began to explain the plan. Abbo and Sid helped Ray. "Poxy black on one side and green on the other, my favourite colours," yelled Ray amongst the laughter.

As they sat smoking and drinking their beers, Ray said that Dave would want in on the action but he didn't want Dave to be part of it. "He's too young to get involved."

Abbo looked at Ray. "How about you coming home now, Ray? Your mam and dad are worried about you. Come home with us and get yourself ready for the funeral on Wednesday."

Ray looked away and Abbo could see the hurt look in his eyes. "It's going to be tough, Abbo, I'm hurting all inside and I can't get my head around it."

Sid and Andy said they understood how he felt but now Ray had to face up to it. "Be strong, Ray, for the sake of the family. You are their rock and be there for young Dave; he's suffering more than you think. We will be with you at the funeral, mate, let's put Jan to rest."

Ray got up and started gathering his things. "What would I do without you lot," he said quietly.

They helped him pack everything up and led the way out of the forest. His mam and Dave greeted him and thanked his mates for their part in looking after him. The lawn at the front of the house was festooned with wreaths and bunches of flowers. Abbo and the other two said cheerio to Ray and his family and made their way back home.

Wednesday arrived and the boys were anxious to get their work done. They lowered the journeys of supplies down the hill, clearing everything brought in. They were at the top of the hill now, eating their snap. The deputy had written an 'early note' for all three and they would be able to get up the pit at 12 o'clock. They agreed to make their own way to the church and then, if they could, get a lift up to the cemetery for the burial.

Abbo was the first to arrive. He stood outside the gates and waited for the others. Soon there was a crowd waiting and as the hearse arrived, more people seemed to try and get closer. The coffin was carried into the church amidst a flow of tears. Ray followed, holding onto his mam and Dave with his father behind them. The church soon filled with friends and relatives and the service began.

Abbo, Sid and Andy stood together as the coffin was taken out after the service. They followed the crowd and managed to squeeze into cars driven by friends and family. Along the streets, people stopped and bowed their heads. It was enough to make the hardest of men weep and Abbo was the first to admit that he had shed a few tears. At the graveside, Ray held onto his mam and Dave was comforted by his dad. As the coffin was lowered, Abbo suggested to Sid and Andy that they walk back through the estate. They hadn't gone far when Ray joined them. "I need to walk a bit as well, lads, to try and clear my head. Are you coming back to our house for a drink or what?"

Abbo looked at Sid and Andy. “No, we will leave it to your family now. We are going to the pub.” Ray expressed his gratitude and said he would see them later, probably.

Chapter 7
All in a Day's Work

Joe Fiddler eased the car into the car park. The exhibition this time was at Stoke on Trent. It was 12 o'clock and the show was already under way. "OK girls, do your stuff and make the bastards pay if they want it." He handed out the leaflets advertising kitchenware. His lapel badge bore the name, Mr Lewis, Household Appliances. The exhibition was 'Modern Appliances for the Home' and the place was packed. Denise went first with her bunch of leaflets. She headed for the dishwasher and kitchen utensil section. Janet headed for the cooking equipment area and Veronica casually looked around the electrical stuff. It wasn't long before the salesman started to take interest. She handed out leaflets and got into discussion about her company. "We were too late to get our company a stall because we were exhibiting in Germany," she lied. The salesman soon began flirting with her and followed her around his section of the exhibition.

"I like exhibiting abroad," he said, winking his eye. "The continental girls are easy to get on with."

Veronica gave him a smile. "Well, we're not that bad, are we?"

She started to move away but the salesman reached out and held her arm. "Perhaps we could have lunch together?" he suggested.

"I do have to earn my bonus by advertising my company's products," replied Veronica.

"Well, if things went well, perhaps I could help you out there," he said. Veronica gave him her best smile and opened her coat to reveal what was on offer. The short skirt and tight blouse did the trick. "Two o'clock here?" he said, almost drooling over the sight of her voluptuous breasts.

Janet was bending over one of the cooking appliances when the slightly balding and overweight representative moved in on her. "Can I show you something?" he asked.

Janet straightened up and gave a naughty giggle. "Well, it depends on what you have in mind," she replied and gave him a come-on smile. He was hooked and didn't even know it as Janet moved in closer, handing out her leaflets. Her coat was hanging loose and open at the front. The representative didn't see the leaflet; all he saw was a low-cut dress and a heaving bosom. Janet pulled her coat together to hide her cleavage. The rep reached out for the leaflet, which caused Janet to let her coat open again.

"Maybe if we had lunch together, we could discuss business?" said the rep. "I'm also a buyer for the company." Janet said it was a nice gesture but her company expected her to promote their utensils and try to arrange company visits and she also had to distribute the leaflets in order to qualify for her hundred-pound bonus. "I think we can arrange a visit and, if things go well, settle your bonus," he said putting his arm around her waist and guiding her around his stall. "I have lunch at 2 o'clock and then a short rest in the hotel room. Please join me."

Denise noticed that a young rep about twenty-two years old had been following her around and showing interest. She liked them young despite her own thirty-five years and waited for him to make his approach. She pushed one of her leaflets at him. "Household appliances," she said as he took the leaflet.

"Do you have a stall here?" he asked, scrutinising the leaflet.

"No," she replied, "we got delayed on the continent and missed our chance."

He followed her around. "I would like to go abroad on one of our exhibitions but I'm only a junior manager. The senior management get all the best jobs."

She smiled at him. “And all the fun.” She looked around and said she had to get on and earn her bonus. “I’m also starving,” she added.

“Well, I’m ready for my lunch break too. Why don’t you join me? The hotel restaurant is pretty good, I’ve used it before.”

Denise could smell his aftershave and deodorant. “And the hotel rooms too?” she queried.

He looked away; she had embarrassed him. “Well, yes, if the occasion arises. I know what the reps get up to. Why should I be any different?”

She looked at the pile of leaflets in her hand. “If I had time, I might be interested but I have to earn my bonus.”

He took another leaflet. “Well, maybe we can talk business as well.”

Denise looked at her watch. “I can spare you two hours if the price is right.”

The rep nodded his head. “The company allows us generous expenses.”

Joe Fiddler was waiting at the exit doors and was checking his watch. Another fifteen minutes and the girls should be showing up. He had made enquiries from the exhibition offices where the next exhibitions were to be held. “We have some to arrange,” the lady had told him. “We have to cover Wales and the North of England, London and the South.” Joe made notes and then asked about the Midland area. “Oh yes, we have Coventry coming up shortly and there’s Wolverhampton. Derby is another one being organised. Give me your company address and I’ll send you all the details and dates.”

Denise was the first to arrive and she had a huge grin on her face. The other two soon followed. As Joe sped along the road, he asked Denise what she had been so happy about. The other two girls begged her to reveal all. “Well,” she began and then burst out laughing. “I pulled a young one, still wet behind the ears. We had lunch and then he went all shy. I had to ask him if he wanted to fuck me or not. He said he did but hadn’t had much experience with a mature woman. I took him by the arm and asked him to lead me to his hotel room. Once inside, I began to undress him. He quickly produced my bonus, nice crisp twenty-pound notes and then he was like putty in my hands. I asked him if he had ever had a blow job. He said he hadn't so I stripped off and went about it. In no time at all, he had shot his load and gone limp. I lay on the bed beside him and guided him down to the Bermuda triangle. I'm sure he hadn't been there before so I gently explained what he had to do. I played with him but he never rose to the occasion. Eventually, he confessed that he had masturbated the night before and also before breakfast."

The girls were in hysterics and even Joe had a good laugh. "You earn your money easy," said Janet.

Veronica said her fucker said he could last all night, "but I said not for a hundred quid, mate."

Joe pulled up and let Veronica out. "I'll call you," he said.

Janet was the next one to be dropped off. "See you next time," and gave Denise a wicked grin. Joe drove off and Denise settled herself down in the front passenger seat. Soon they had reached Denise's flat. Joe pulled up and switched off the engine. Denise got the message and as soon as they were inside, started stripping off. "Do you ever fuck your wife?" she asked as she stretched out on the bed.

Joe smiled. "No, not if I can help it," he replied. "She's only interested in *EastEnders*." Denise giggled as Joe explored the promised land. He was primed and ready for action.

***

Dennis Mason picked up the phone and listened as the Coal Miners Union president rattled on. "Yes, this Saturday at 10.30 am at the union office." He put down the phone and carried on with his paperwork. As an afterthought, he pulled out his diary and checked the telephone number of the Sherwood Hotel in Nottingham. A man's voice answered and Dennis recognised Henry's voice. "It's Dennis Mason,

Henry. I'd like to book a room for Friday night if I may; another meeting to attend." Henry confirmed the booking.

The month had passed quickly and Dennis hadn't been told a lot by the president but Dennis knew the 'King' liked to spring surprises and guessed the meeting would be very interesting.

***

Peter was sorting through his wardrobe. Last Saturday, he and Susan had been shopping in Litchfield. Their weekly tryst had developed into a regular thing now. She had accompanied him through the streets of Litchfield looking at the clothes shops. Peter had bought two new shirts that Susan had cast her eye over before he bought them. He chose the pale blue one to go with his smart leather jacket and grey trousers. He was getting excited now; he was to meet her in the car park in Litchfield but they wouldn't be shopping in Litchfield. Joe had suggested shopping in York, which was a very interesting place. "I've never been there," Susan had told him. He could see her car as soon as he pulled into the car park. He parked a few spaces down and waved to her.

It was a fine day with a blue sky promising a warm and sunny day. She got out of her car and walked over to him. She wore a light green two-piece suit with a matching handbag. Her smile said everything. Peter got out of the car and opened the passenger door for her. "Forever the gentleman, Peter, I like that."

They drove out of Litchfield and were soon heading northeast. "We are going to have a nice day, Susan; York is a nice city to visit, very historic and loads of shops and restaurants."

She looked at him. "Obviously you've been there before, Peter. I never have; we never went out much to places like that, quite a boring life actually."

Peter commented that his marriage had been the same. "Dancing and dining out—that's all she wanted. Thank God she's gone." Susan said that perhaps it was his passion for scrambling that had driven her away. “That was only on a Saturday afternoon and I was usually home by 6:30.”

Susan changed the subject. “How has your leg been these days?”

Peter slapped his thigh. “Coming on in leaps and bounds. The physio said it was much better and in time, I won’t notice the steel rods in my legs.” The signpost said ‘York: 30 miles’. Peter said they had made good time considering it was a Saturday. The car clock said 10:30.

***

Harry looked at the steel box on the flat truck that had been lowered down the hill. Six one-inch diameter holes had been drilled in the back plate and there were bags of steel ballast to fill it. He looked at the two apprentices who had been sent to help him. “I’ll go and hose up the hydraulic drill while you two see if you can get that box and ballast to the back of the rig.”

He uncoupled the hoses to the winch and stretched them out to see if they would reach the rig. The two apprentices had carried the bags of ballast down but were struggling with the box. “It weighs a fucking ton,” said one of them.

“Do your best, lads. I’ve got to drill six fucking one-inch holes in this bastard rig and it ain’t gonna be easy.” He hosed up the drill and looked for the chalk marks the engineer had made. After an hour, the drill hadn’t made much of an impression and he could hear the apprentices effing and blinding at the steel box. He stopped drilling and disconnected the winch and coupled them back up. He then operated the winch, telling one of the apprentices to pull the rope down and through the ‘D’ link on the back of the rig and then pull the rope through and bring it back up to where they had got the steel box to. Harry then fastened it to the box via a ‘D’ link. Operating the winch, Harry pulled the box down to the back of the rig, much to the relief of the two apprentices. “Fucking brilliant, Harry, you brainy bastard.” The apprentices echoed their appraisals.

"Right," said Harry. "Now uncouple the hoses off the winch and couple them up to the drill and then the fun starts." He looked at the drills that had been given to him. They were new but Harry still had his doubts. He quickly set the drill up and prepared to carry on drilling. It was slow going. Harry got the apprentices to put the weight behind the drill. The first hole was drilled after a while and Harry measured its depth. "OK, that's one, five more to go and then we've got to tap these holes out to take those bolts that will secure the box to the right, so carry on lads while I try tapping this bastard." It was hard going and the lads were cussing like mad. Two hours had gone by and only two holes drilled.

"We'll be here until fucking Christmas," one of the apprentices said. Harry suggested they swap over. One of the apprentices could try tapping the holes while Harry took over the drilling with the other lad. By snap time, it was three drilled and two tapped.

Harry gave words of encouragement. "We should manage this by knock off, lads, and then in the morning, we can fit the box."

The apprentices looked at each other. "That's if we get up in the morning, I don't get in until after midnight. It's disco night for us, Harry."

***

When Dennis had arrived at the Sherwood Hotel, he had been greeted by a woman he had never met before. "Hello Mr Mason, I'm Sylvia, Gladys' sister. I'm holding the fort while they take a little break."

"Oh yes, well, we all need a break now and then. Where have they gone?"

Sylvia was holding the key to Dennis' room, leaning on the counter and showing off a mouth-watering bosom. "Blackpool for a week. They both need a break, especially our Gladys. She said you had booked in and I was to look after you. It will be my pleasure, Mr Mason. Now let me show you to your room and make sure everything is to your liking." Sylvia was slightly younger than Gladys with a full figure and a pleasant smile. Dennis noticed there was no wedding ring on her left hand but was showing on her right hand.

"Are you local, Sylvia, being as you can stand in for Gladys?"

She closed the lift door. "Yes, about seven miles away from her, I have my own flat, just half an hour ride on the bus so it's quite convenient. My kids are grown up and fled the nest so I'm all on my own. I don't mind helping out at the hotel, they keep a room for me to stay in so when I'm here, there's no travelling." They had reached the third floor and the lift door opened. Sylvia led the way. "I think she's booked you in the same room as last time, Mr Mason."

He could smell her perfume as she led the way down the corridor. "Please call me Dennis; Mr Mason is a bit over the top these days, especially amongst friends."

Sylvia opened the door and entered. "I'll do that, Dennis. I like to be friendly; it's cosier, isn't it?"

Dennis looked around the room. It was the same one that he and Gladys had shared last time and it held pleasant memories. "I'll miss seeing Gladys," he said, looking over to the bed.

"Yes, I'm sure you will. She's such a friendly person but aren't we all under the circumstances. Now Dennis, what can I get for you, something to eat or drink? I can bring it up to your room." Dennis turned around and faced Sylvia. She was nice-looking and her eyes flashed as she spoke, "Not many interesting guests here at the moment, Dennis, the restaurant is quite boring." Dennis walked over to the window, it was getting dark. "I'll draw these curtains for you, Dennis; it makes it nice and private." She squeezed past him and he could feel the warmth of her body next to his.

"Yes Sylvia, whatever is going and I'll have a bottle of wine to go with it and you can join me if you like. I don't like drinking on my own." Sylvia said nothing as she handed him the room key but the look in her eyes said it all. "Is it all right if I smoke?" asked Dennis.

Sylvia fished out a lighter from her pocket. "Yes Dennis, just open the window slightly to let the smoke out. We don't allow it normally but you're special, Gladys said."

She disappeared from the room and Dennis unpacked his overnight bag. Half an hour later, she reappeared with the food trolley. Dennis noticed there were two glasses. "I just have to pop down and see to two late arrivals. It won't take me long. Enjoy your meal, Dennis."

He tucked in, his mind drifting to tomorrow's meeting with the Coal Miners' Union. It would be noisy and hectic and likely to last a long time. Dennis checked he had brought his paracetamol with him. The packet was in his shirt pocket, they needed to be handy.

Dennis lit a cigarette and went over to the window. He drew the curtains back a little and opened the window to let the smoke out. Sylvia entered the room. She had a packet of cigarettes in her hand and an ashtray. "I'll join you," she said, lighting one up.

Dennis moved over to allow her to stand by the window. He noticed she had applied a stronger perfume and had also changed her clothes. Her hair had been brushed too. They stood side by side, puffing away. Dennis put his free hand around her waist and pulled her closer. He was sure now that quite soon, they would be humping like two rabbits.

The president was already at the meeting and the conference room was filling up rapidly. Dennis sat next to the Yorkshire Miners Union rep whom he had become friendly with. "I bet the sparks are going to fly today," he said casually.

"Right, gentlemen, let's get seated and get this meeting under way," shouted the president's assistant, Pat O'Leary, a heavyweight Irishman who followed the president around like a puppy dog.

The room settled down and the president addressed the union reps. "Gentlemen, welcome to this meeting. Last time we met, I told you that I had hoped to arrange a meeting with the company's management in the hope to settle certain rumours regarding our industry. Despite two applications, they have not had the decency to reply. I have also this week sent a final request for a meeting, informing them that unless negotiations take place, there will be serious repercussions. I have been informed by my informer that the government has told the management that under no circumstances should they agree to meet us. Therefore, gentlemen, at this meeting today, I wish to discuss what action we should take. We will now do as we did before and ask each of you what you think we should do. As before, I want you also to write down whatever you have decided, your name and what pit you represent."

They started off round the table clockwise. The first was a Welsh Union rep. He stood up and addressed the meeting, "Mr President, I have addressed my members with the information that was given at the last meeting and my opinion is we must stand fast and fight for our industry. The fact that a hitman from America has been brought in to sort us out is an insult to the members of the Coal Miners Union and my members feel that if it's going to come to a confrontation then let it be. We will take whatever action necessary to save our industry." There was loud support from around the room and shouts of 'hear, hear' supported the speaker.

***

Abbo and the lads had met up at the pub. They were surprised when Ray walked in and joined them. "I'm coming back to work on Monday, I've got to try and focus. The doctor's given me some tablets to calm me down a bit." The lads quickly made him welcome and a pint was thrust in front of him. "I want to thank you guys for your support. What I would have done without you, I don't know, but thanks, guys."

Andy piped up, "Well, for a fucking start, my glass is empty; your round, Ray." They discussed the following sporting fixture that was on TV and followed the ongoing game.

Abbo spoke up, "You know what we discussed, Ray, about sorting out the druggies. Are you still with us on that?"

Ray looked surprised. "I thought you had forgotten all about it. Yea, I want to wear my fancy jacket. When do we start?"

Andy said that careful planning had to be done. Sid said that they had to locate the meeting place where the dealers met their customers. "We need informers who can be trusted but someone not in the gang, someone who can move amongst the younger generation without being too obvious, like schools and youth clubs."

Ray looked at the lads. "I know where Jan's boyfriend met his contact. Our Dave has seen him many a time buying weed and Dave said he wants to help."

The lads looked at each other. "He's a bit young to get involved," said Sid. "I know it was his sister too but he's still at school, for fuck's sake. What if we get caught?"

Ray nodded. "He will only be an informer, not a member of the B.A.D. boys. I think he will be ideal; he certainly moves around."

The boys agreed to Dave playing a small part in the operation but not to take part in any action. "Right, when do we start?" asked Sid.

Abbo suggested getting the information first. "Ask Dave to do some scouting around, Ray. We want positive information and not rumours. And Ray, not too fast on the boyfriend; it will be too suspicious if we do him so soon. We can wait a bit; he ain't going nowhere."

Ray agreed to put his feelings on hold. "We will need a vehicle," said Sid. "What if we have to get away quick and without a vehicle, we can't go far, can we?"

Abbo looked at the lads sitting around the table. "How many of us can drive anyway?"

Ray said he could, Andy said he could and Sid hadn't passed his test yet but hadn't driven anything since then. "We must first get a vehicle. Let's look around for an old banger that's going cheap. As long as it's a good runner, that's all we need," said Andy. "But not buy local as we don’t want to be recognised before we start. Something dark, nothing that stands out. Let’s start looking around now.”

Chapter 8
Romance

Peter held Susan's hand as they walked around York. They had visited a few shops and now were heading for the history museum and York Oldtown, which was full of interesting shops. "I love this place, Peter; it's so full of interesting things and places."

Peter agreed and then said, "You need to spend more than one day here to see and explore things."

Susan said, "A weekend here would be nice."

Peter looked at her. "Would you like that, Susan? I would." The conversation went quiet and Peter thought he had said something out of place.

Susan squeezed his hand. "Yes, Peter, a weekend here with you would be lovely." They found the museum very interesting and took in the reproductive scenes of York in the past. "They certainly went through hard times in those days," said Susan. Peter suggested they find a restaurant and trailed the streets for one that took their fancy. "That looks an interesting menu," pointed out Susan. "Shall we try it?"

Peter opened the door and made for a table near the window. The waitress came over and handed them the menu. "What would you like to drink?" she asked. Susan asked for a Britvic orange and lemonade whilst Peter settled for half a lager shandy.

Peter looked at Susan, she had a beautiful smile. He reached out across the table to touch her hand. "Did you really mean what you said about a weekend here?" he asked.

The waitress returned with the drinks. "Yes, Peter, it would be lovely," Susan replied.

Peter's heart was pounding so loudly it was a wonder Susan couldn't hear it. "Shall we arrange something then, Susan, that's if it will be all right with you?"

The waitress came back with the starter. "There are plenty of opportunities when my husband buggers off with his mates fishing, if that's what he does."

Peter looked at the sadness that had appeared across her face. "Do you think he's up to anything else, Susan? I know what you're going through; I've been there myself."

She shook her head. "I'm not sure what he gets up to. He claims it's just sitting on a riverbank, fishing and chatting to his mates and then off to the pub for a drink and lunch, but when he goes away for a whole weekend, who knows?" Her smile suddenly returned. "Let's forget about him and enjoy our meal. Anyway, two can play at that game."

***

Christine heard Billy close the front door. Monday morning came around fast and Christine was looking forward to this one. She got out of bed and looked at the little bundle in the cot. "Come on, my pretty one, let's change your bum and get ready for another day." She quickly washed and dressed Steven and fed him. She drew the curtains and looked out at the rising sun. It looked promising. Placing Steven in his pram, she quickly tidied up the kitchen and lounge. The dog and cat were up the garden, out of the way. A quick peep at Steven who was nodding off and she ran upstairs and tidied the bedroom, tearing the curtains closed. She washed and selected clothes from her wardrobe. She reached for a fragrance spray and sprayed around the room, killing the smell of fart arse Billy.

Downstairs, Steven was still awake and gurgling away, flaying his hands. Christine looked at the clock. It was 9:30. Two rounds of toast and a mug of tea later, Steven was asleep. She pushed his pram though into the kitchen and glanced through the curtains. The street was empty. She looked at the clock again. Ten past ten, where was Clive? Usually, he was on time but not today. As she looked through the window, a blue car pulled up. It wasn't Clive; he had a black one. As she looked, a young woman in her twenties got out. Christine frowned. The woman was smartly dressed and wore her hair in a bun. She was wearing a dark trouser suit that enhanced her well-proportioned figure. As she approached the house, Christine noticed she was carrying a briefcase like Clive's. "Oh bollocks," she murmured, going to the front door. The young woman smiled and introduced herself as Marianne, the insurance representative. Christine half-smiled back. "Come in, please. Where's the usual rep?"

Marianne followed Christine into the lounge. "Oh, Clive has been relocated to another area. The company does that from time to time." Christine invited the rep to take a seat and offered a drink. "Coffee please," said Marianne. "It helps keep me awake whilst I'm driving."

Christine couldn't help smell the rep's perfume. "You smell nice, what is it?" she asked.

"Chanel No. 5," came the reply. "I do like Chanel and they do nice variations." Christine said she liked the Opium range but did like to vary her choices. She noticed that the rep wore no ring on her left hand.

"Still single, I see," said Christine, pointing to her own wedding ring. "Not met the right bloke yet, eh!" queried Christine.

"I'm not into the male gender," said Marianne. "They're too rough and ready for me. I prefer the more genteel approach of a woman. I'm a lesbian, I prefer it that way."

Christine couldn't believe what she was hearing. Men would have given their right arm to screw this bird. She passed over the insurance documents to Marianne. "Is it any different lying in bed with another woman?" she asked quietly.

Marianne signed the documents and put the cheque into her briefcase. "Yes, it is, I've tried men but find them rough and ready. A woman is more delicate and not in any rush to mount you. They also understand a woman's desire and can please you more so than a man. You should try it sometime and form your own opinion, of course."

She was looking closely at Christine and the tingling sensation crept up Christine's spine. She couldn't believe what was happening but as she looked into Marianne's blue eyes, she had a sudden desire to kiss her. Marianne read these feelings and moved closer to Christine. As their lips met, Christine gave a cry of delight. Her arms embraced Marianne as her sexual desire increased to a crescendo. Marianne's hands slid inside her blouse and fondled her breast. Christine reciprocated by sliding her hand up the inside of Marianne's leg. By now, her sexual desires were at a high as Marianne felt her way between Christine's legs. Christine had left her pants and bra off because she had been expecting Clive. Her legs parted as Marianne's expert hands fondled and probed her innermost parts. Soon she was at her peak as she responded to Marianne.

"Oh my God, that was amazing," she gasped.

Marianne adjusted her clothes and reached for her handbag. "Yes, it was and it does get even more exciting if you are in the right place, relaxed and comfortable with the right person. I think you and I would be great together, but not here, not like this. I live in Stafford in my own apartment and it would be nice if you could visit me sometime, Christine. I guarantee multiple orgasms."

***

Billy led the team down the steep road to the back of the rock head. "I wonder what monstrosity they've come up with now," he called out. Harry was following a few yards behind. "You'll see, we worked our bollocks off over the weekend doing this but we never had time to try it out." The team sat down and had a quick bite. Billy was the first to get up. "I'm dying to see this," he said, walking down to the rig.

Alf, Norman and Jegger followed. "Power it up, Billy, let's see how the bastard performs." Alf made sure the cable was free. "OK Billy."

The power went in and Billy inched the rig forward. "Seems steady enough but we won't know until we've bored the head and we power back. Let's give it a try."

Alf and Norman watched as Billy raised the boom and started drilling. The water sprays used to lay the dust soon started wetting the floor. Billy said the back of the rig was now more stable with the ballast box fitted.

Harry stood watching. “Took us two days to drill all them holes and then three of us to fit that box. The fucking thing weighs a bastard ton, but it looks good. We’ll see if it’s any fucking good when he tracks back.”

They waited and watched as Billy swung the boom backwards and forwards. Jegger was clearing up behind the rig, ready for Billy to track back. “Do we need to winch back as well?” he asked Harry.

“Better get it ready, in case,” he told Jegger.

***

The Coal Miners’ Union meeting became noisy as each rep gave his report. Dennis took a couple of paracetamol. The meeting went on until 7 o’clock Saturday night and then resumed on Sunday morning until 2 o’clock. The president and his staff made notes and gave their opinions where possible.

“Gentlemen, I can safely say that unanimously, we have decided to take action against the Coal Board in an effort to save our industry. I therefore propose to inform them that if no meeting takes place by the end of the month, we will do whatever is necessary. Do I have your support on that?” The room echoed with ‘yea, yea, yea’ and hands raised in the air. The meeting ended on that note and the union reps started to leave.

Dennis made his way back to the Sherwood Hotel and up to his room to pack. Shortly, a knock on the door and Sylvia came in. “I bet you’re tired, eh, Dennis?”

He nodded his head. “Absolutely knackered and a splitting headache as well. I thought that bloody meeting would never end.”

Sylvia put her arms around his. “You should stay another night, Dennis, and rest yourself. You are in no condition to drive home.”

Dennis gave her a weak smile. "Or for anything else, Sylvia. Thanks all the same but I've got to get back; I've got a lot to do."

Sylvia sat on the bed and watched as Dennis went about packing his bag. "I hope you come again, Dennis, we have had a good time, haven't we?"

Dennis leaned over and kissed her. "You can say that again, Sylvia. It was fantastic."

He drove home, feeling very tired. His wife looked at him as he entered the house by the front door. "You look terribly exhausted, Dennis, why don't you go to bed and rest? It looks like that meeting has drained you." Dennis took her advice. Monday morning would soon come around.

***

After they had bored the head, Billy started to reverse the rig. The tracks bit into the floor and eased back. "Looks good," said Harry as the machine eased its way back.

"That's fucking better, Harry," called Billy as he parked the rig. "Perhaps now we can earn some bonus on our yardage." The rest of the team cheered and Harry said he would ring his boss and tell him all was well in the rock head.

***

Abbo and the boys were pleased to see that Ray had turned up for work. "I've been looking through the papers at second-hand cars," he said excitedly. "There are a few about for four hundred quid."

Abbo agreed it was the right sort of price and mentioned that if they all chipped in, it would be affordable. "We will have to decide who's going to be the registered keeper and where it is going to be kept," chipped in Andy. Abbo agreed that it would all have to be sorted out. They decided to meet in the pub that evening and look through the papers with Ray.

Andy arrived first with a couple of freebie papers and then Abbo with a motoring magazine. They thumbed through the 'cars for sale' ads, scrutinising those that were in their price range. "A bit pricy, some of these," said Andy.

"Yea but keep looking; we'll find something," replied Abbo.

Ray drew their attention to one. "Here, look at this. A dark blue Vauxhall Astra carefully looked after by a woman owner from new. Eight years old but in very good condition. Sixty thousand miles registered."

The boys looked at the ad. "Owned by a woman—it'll smell like a freaking flower shop," remarked Sid.

"Yea but it will be clean and tidy," said Ray.

"How much?" asked Abbo.

"Five hundred or nearest," replied Ray. "I think it would be worth a look, let's make a phone call." Ray placed the phone to his ear. The pub phone was handy and in a quiet corner. The phone rang out and a woman answered and Ray started asking questions. He seemed satisfied and asked for the woman's address. He gave his name and asked if they could call the next day to view. It was agreed and an appointment was made. A tingle of excitement erupted around the table as the lads discussed the future of B.A.D. Boys. "Get your cash by tomorrow and let's decide who's going to be the registered owner and where the car will be kept. It's a Cannock address so we need a car to get over there. Also, we need to get it insured to drive. I'll see if Dad will let me borrow his car."

Andy looked at his mates sitting around the table. "I'll be the registered owner and the car can be kept at my house. There's room at the side of our garage and Mam knows I've been looking for a car of my own." The boys all gave Andy a 'cheers mate' response. "And I'll get a quote on the insurance," he added.

***

Christine asked Billy if he would run her into Stafford when he came home tomorrow to get some curtains for the back room that was now going to be Steven's room, when Billy got around to decorating it. "Oh pet, you know how tired I am when I get home. Can't you take the car and go yourself? I'll look after Steven."

Christine accused him of not taking any interest in the home. "Just make sure there's enough petrol in it then, not like last time."

When Billy came home the next day, he jangled the keys in front of Christine. "Here you are, pet, the tank's half full."

Christine drove to Stafford and parked in the large car park in front of the shops. She knew which shop she wanted to look in, the one that specialised in home furnishings. She took her time looking around for the right material. It had to be special for Steven; it would be his first bedroom. She browsed among the materials, taking her time. She had the measurements written down but she was also looking amongst the made-to-measure ones. Finally, she chose a pair already made and carefully rechecked the measurements. A whiff of perfume reached her nostrils as she made her way to the counter. "Hello Christine, fancy meeting you here. I've been thinking of you." Marianne's voice sent a tingle up Christine's spine.

She turned to see Marianne standing close behind her. "Hello Marianne, nice to see you. I hadn't expected to bump into you. How are you keeping?"

They inched their way to the cash desk. "Oh, I'm just browsing at the moment; getting ideas for my flat. What are you doing?" Christine replied that it was curtains for Steven's bedroom that had brought her into Stafford. Her heart was beating fast as Marianne's body came closer. She was still looking very beautiful and desirable. "Where have you got to go next?" Marianne asked Christine.

"Nowhere, this is it for today."

Marianne suggested Christine come for a coffee at her flat, which wasn't far away. The tingling sensation shot up her spine as Marianne steered her across the car park. "Leave your car here and I'll run you back later." Again, she steered her along a line of cars. "This is mine." Christine recognised it immediately. She half-smiled as Marianne opened the door for her. She hadn't expected this and was a bit surprised how Marianne had persuaded her so easily, but the Chanel perfume filled her lungs and Marianne's beautiful smile sent a shiver through her whole body. Now she began to feel sexually excited.

It was a short journey and soon Marianne was turning the key in the door of her flat. It was a two up and two down block. Marianne had one of the upstairs flats. "This is nice," said Christine as she was guided inside.

"Yes, nice and comfortable," said Marianne as she moved in closer to Christine. "Make yourself comfy; I'll do the drinks. Is it coffee for you or something more relaxing?" Christine settled for a white coffee with sugar. Marianne had slipped off her jacket and hung it up. "Shall I take your coat, Christine? It gets quite warm up here."

Christine obliged and as she handed it to Marianne, she drew closer and leaned forward. Marianne recognised the signs and leaned forward. Their lips met and they embraced. "It's good to see you again, Christine. I was looking forward to the end of the month when I did my collections."

They sat together on the settee as they drank their coffees. The eyes said it all and the touching. Christine was feeling very horny. Marianne got up and took Christine by the hand. "Come on, Christine, I want you passionately." They were soon wrapped in a passionate embrace, each exploring the other's innermost parts. After some time, Marianne reached for a small vanity case. "I keep my toys in here." She opened the case to reveal a selection of vibrators and other things. "Do you have any toys, Christine?"

The first thing Marianne chose was a six-inch vibrator with which she gently stimulated Christine's nipples before going lower down. "No, I've never used anything like that." Soon Marianne was getting her aroused as she massaged her with the vibrator.

"They come in a variety of shapes and sizes. They are nice to use if you're on your own or with someone else who knows what to do."

Christine found her heart beating madly. "Let's go into the bedroom, Christine. I'm getting excited and I've got other toys to play with." Marianne was soon removing Christine's clothing. They lay naked on the bed, both exploring each other's body. Marianne inserted the vibrator into Christine and switched it on. Soon the tingling effect was doing its work as Christine writhed and moaned. Marianne knew how to get her going. Christine felt like a puppet in Marianne's hands as she fondled and caressed her. She stopped using the vibrator and sat on the edge of the bed. "Now I'll introduce you to another of my toys," said Marianne as she searched in her bag.

Christine looked on as Marianne pulled out a black thing that looked like a man's penis with a sort of harness attached. She strapped it around her waist and adjusted the straps. "Now let's have some more fun," she said, rolling Christine over.

Again Marianne massaged and fondled Christine and then she began to introduce the black thing. "What is that?" Christine asked as it was slowly inserted.

"They're called dildos," whispered Marianne as she gently played with Christine.

The phone rang and Marianne cussed but took no notice of it as she roamed all over Christine, who by now had reached her peak. The phone rang again as Marianne withdrew the dildo. She kissed Christine and left the bed. When she returned, the dildo was in her hand. "Do you want to try it on me, Christine? I like a bit of variation too."

Christine managed a glance at her watch. "Another time, Marianne, I have to go now. My husband is waiting for me to get back so he can go watch a football game."

"You see what I mean about men," said Marianne. "They dominate our lives and they don't know how to fuck either. Wham bam thank you ma'am, and it's over. Did I satisfy you, Christine? Why don't you take a quick shower and then I'll drive you to the car park. There's a shower cap hanging up."

Christine turned on the shower and pulled on the shower cap; she began a quick application of the shower gel. Marianne entered the shower and began washing Christine's body. Soon they were in a passionate embrace and Marianne's fingers were once again probing down below.

As Christine drove home, she kept shaking her head and wondering if it had been a dream or a nightmare. She couldn't believe she had just been seduced by a lesbian, but what an exciting time it had been.

***

Peter had arrived early in the car park, smartly dressed and very happy. He had managed to book a hotel in York for the weekend. His overnight bag lay on the backseat. He was hoping that Susan hadn't changed her mind. The hairs on the back of his neck tingled with excitement. He walked around the car park, looking for Susan's car. There weren't any long-term parking facilities there so they would have to find somewhere for Susan's car for overnight parking. He wandered around the council car park and eventually found a place where overnight parking was allowed at five pounds per night. When he got back to his own car, Susan had just arrived. She parked near his car and got out. He noticed she was carrying an overnight bag. "Let's put your bag in my car and then you must follow me in your car to the overnight parking area." They parked Susan's car and Peter put in the five-pound note and tapped in the details. Placing the ticket on the dashboard where it could be seen, they climbed into Peter's car. He leaned over and planted a kiss on her cheek. She seemed relaxed and in a good mood. She leaned over and planted a kiss on Peter's cheek too. The journey to York was filled with conversation about various things. Peter never mentioned her husband; it was Susan who mentioned him first.

"Gone for a weekend's fishing again, or so he says. Northampton this time. I often wonder what he gets up to on these trips. He never talks about it when he returns; he says it would be boring for me."

Peter nodded understandingly. "Well, let's try and forget him for this weekend, Susan, let's enjoy being together."

They pulled into the car park of the hotel in York. "This looks nice, Peter," said Susan. They booked in and were shown to a room on the first floor with a view of the river. As they stood looking through the window, Peter couldn't resist putting his arm around Susan's waist. She moved in closer to him and turned her head, offering her lips to him.

"I can hear your heart beating," she whispered.

Peter responded and held the kiss for a long time. "Yes Susan, it's beating for you."

It was a nice Saturday afternoon and they decided to go out for a walk and find somewhere to eat lunch. The hotel's restaurant was available but they chose to look around the city for a while.

***

Ray, Abbo and Andy looked at the car. The woman said she had looked after it and had it serviced regularly. Ray said it was in good nick as he sat in the driver's seat and tried the engine. They offered four-fifty but the woman refused. She reckoned five hundred was a good asking price and had received more enquiries. "OK," said Andy, "we'll take it," and pulled out his wallet. He peeled the notes out onto the table and let the woman count them. He confirmed that the documentation was correct and they said goodbye. Andy climbed into the driver's seat with Abbo in the passenger seat. The engine purred as they drove off, following Ray back home. They pulled into the club car park and got out to admire their new purchase.

"Well, what do you think, my friends, are we in business or what?" Andy was smiling. "It drives well and is comfortable to ride in."

Abbo looked at Ray. "We will do a test drive tonight, eh Ray?"

Ray nodded. "I'll get Dave to show us where the 'pusher' meets his customers. Let's meet up in the club car park at 8 o'clock tonight, but remember, this is just a dummy run, no action yet."

***

Joe Fiddler stood by the exit gate waiting for the girls. Veronica arrived first and gave him a warm smile. "Waiting for me?" she teased.

"And the other two," said Joe.

"They're just behind," she replied. "It's my turn in the front seat, Joe, remember my turn." The girls chatted away as Joe eased out of the car park. They had all managed to score and had handed Joe their takings. Joe split the cash and handed the girls their share. Janet said she would need to take a week off for personal reasons. Joe replied that nothing had been arranged yet for the next exhibition and would contact them if anything came up. He pulled up to let Janet out first and then drove on to where Denise lived.

"Have a nice time," she quipped as she got out of the car.

"I think she's a bit jealous," said Veronica, smiling at Joe. The car came to a halt outside the block of flats. Veronica got out and looked at Joe. "Coffee or what?" she asked, giving him a wicked smile.

Joe watched as her short skirt rode up her thighs. "Or what," he replied. Veronica walked up the path and Joe looked as he walked behind her. Veronica had the loveliest arse he had ever seen, like two bunnies in a sack. He was going to have her doggy style this time. He closed the door and walked into the lounge. Already Veronica was stripping off and walking towards the bedroom. Joe watched the two bunnies disappear through the door. He stripped off and followed.

"You've got the loveliest arse I've ever seen, Veronica," he whispered.

Veronica gave him a stern look. "I don't do arse, Joe, that's for queers."

Joe eased himself onto the bed. "How about doggy style then? On your knees, Veronica."

She rolled over and took up the position. Joe was standing proud and eased himself into her. "OK Joe, come on, fuck me American Express, if you like." Joe obliged and in no time at all had satisfied himself. “My God, Joe, you were ready for that,” she said as Joe uncoupled.

“Yeah! I sure was,” he replied, “and now for the coffee.” He watched as the two bunnies in the sack climbed into fresh underwear and made for the kitchen. Joe grabbed a quick shower and got dressed.

***

The sun was shining on the cobbled streets of York as Peter and Susan browsed around the streets. They stopped at a couple of shops just to look inside and then moved further along the river walk. There was a nice café with chairs outside overlooking the river. “This is nice, Susan, let’s see what they’ve got to eat.” They chose a salad each with a glass of wine to accompany it. “Shall we visit the museum?” Peter asked.

Susan looked at him in a funny way and squeezed his hand. “No, Peter, let’s go back to the hotel and make love. That’s what I want at this moment.”

Susan walked towards the bedroom and started removing her clothes. She was hungry for love and wanted Peter desperately. They slid into bed and started kissing straight away. Peter was also hungry for love and soon rose to the occasion. Susan received him eagerly and soon they were satisfying their eagerness. Peter explored her body gently. She was in good shape and soon she was moaning ecstatically as Peter’s slow rhythmic motion brought them both to their peak.

“That was lovely, Peter, you are such a good lover.”

Peter kissed her. “And you too, Susan. That was great.” Peter rolled over onto his back and closed his eyes. His stomach was full and his sexual urge satisfied. The sun had almost disappeared when he woke up. Susan was lying on her back with a contented look on her face. Looking at his watch, he realised they must have been asleep for almost two hours. He gently raised himself off the bed and disappeared into the bathroom. As the warm water cascaded over his body, the door opened and in stepped Susan. “Big enough for two?” she asked, slipping on the shower cap.

Chapter 9
Revenge

Harry caught the bus to the hospital. It was unusual to get an appointment for a Saturday morning but still it came up. His doctor had listened to his complaint about his recurring visions and had recommended that Harry needed to see a specialist. He handed his appointment card to the receptionist and took a seat. Half an hour later, his name was called out and he followed the nurse into another office where a smartly dressed man was sitting. "Mr Williams, good morning. I'm Mr Jennings; please take a seat. Your doctor has referred you to me to see if I can help you with your problem."

Harry nodded his head, "Yes. If you can, I would appreciate your help."

"It's these so-called demons that are bothering you, Mr Williams, so please tell me about them."

Harry started talking, telling him about the people who kept coming into his memory. About his cousin Pat who died of an epileptic fit when he was ten. How he and his sisters went to see her body laid out in her coffin. How Aunt Amy told him to touch her forehead, she was stone cold. How a couple of years later, his best friend Johnny was killed on the road at the bottom of the school green. He had run into the road to pick up a wounded bird and was killed instantly by a twenty-ton brick lorry. How the whole school attended the funeral and how they had sung '*Silent night*' as Johnny's funeral song. How two years later, Ronnie, another friend in his class, had hung himself at home playing with some rope. Ronnie was brilliant at drawing; he used to draw motorbikes racing around a track. He was buried near Johnny and even today, when Harry visited the family graves, he walked past the place where his school friends were buried. Harry went on to tell him about his friend in the army who had hung himself in the showers in Gibraltar and about the others: Tony, Dennis, Archie, Teddy, Patrick, Roman, Brian and Joan—the girl he had been keen on. All those faces came before him.

Mr Jennings listened to Harry and made notes. "You have a lot of memories, Mr Williams, and these memories are all about people who were close to you and that's all they are, Mr Williams—bad memories that are locked in your subconscious mind. A lot of soldiers came home from the war with bad memories of friends they had lost and every now and then, these memories would come to the surface, just like you are experiencing, Mr Williams. These memories…do they cause you any harm or distress you in any way?"

Harry shook his head. "No, but I can never forget them; they're always there and sometimes if I hear of someone being killed in our area, especially if they are known to me, these memories come flooding back. I can never get rid of them. I can never forget them. They're always there and they come back to haunt me."

Mr Jennings wrote something down. "Mr Williams, I'm just going to ask you to participate in a little experiment. Do you like football or any sport or any other thing that could occupy your mind?"

Harry thought for a moment. "Yes, I support Villa and I watch the local lads play if they are at home. I also like oil paintings, which I dabble with, and there's my garden. I like growing chrysanthemums."

Mr Jennings stopped him there. "OK Harry—do you mind if I call you Harry? Now can you bring back in your memory one of your friends who got killed?"

Harry closed his eyes. His cousin Pat came into his mind, she was lying there in her coffin. Mr Jennings called out, "Harry, who has just scored that last goal for Villa?"

Harry's memory was interrupted and Pat disappeared as he struggled to think of the last Villa match he had attended. He called out a name as his memory recalled the action.

"Thank you, Harry. I have just interrupted a bad memory by recalling a happy one. Did your bad memory go away?"

Harry nodded his head. "Yes, it was interrupted when I heard you ask about Villa."

Mr Jennings seemed pleased. "Right, Harry, we are on the right track. These memories are deeply implanted in your brain which controls other things such as memories. They have impacted themselves because they were very important happenings; they were friends and colleagues who had a great influence on you. Do you really want these memories of your friends deleted forever from your memory box or do you just want to control them?" Harry said he didn't want to forget his friends but wanted to be able to switch off when he wanted to. Mr Jennings wrote something down. "Right, Harry, I'll see you again in a month's time. Now remember that little experiment we have just tried. If, during the next month, your memories crop up, simply switch over to the Villa or your chrysanthemums to change your memory. You can do that." Mr Jennings stood up and shook Harry's hand. "See you in a month's time and remember your memories won't harm you, they are just part of your past experience. Just dismiss them at will."

***

Andy pulled up in the pub car park. Ray and Dave stood waiting in the shadows. They climbed into the car. Dave sat in the passenger seat. Abbo suddenly appeared and climbed into the backseat with Ray. Dave gave Andy directions to follow. They drove through the town and followed the road leading to the woods. Dave pointed to the pub half-hidden by the trees and told Andy to pull into the car park. There were half a dozen cars occupying various places. Dave looked at them. "He's not here yet. Park over there by that van. I'll just have a look around." They had been waiting for about twenty minutes before a red Ford Fiesta pulled into the car park. “I think that’s him,” said Dave. They watched as the driver sat and waited. It wasn’t long before a man came out of the pub and approached the car. The driver lowered his window and conversation took place. In the dim light of the car park, the boys watched as money was exchanged for a small package. Dave pointed to another figure walking into the car park from the road. “That’s him,” said Dave. They watched as he approached the red car. Conversation took place and once again money was exchanged for a small package. “That’s cannabis,” said Dave. “That’s all he uses.”

Ray unfastened his seatbelt. Abbo put his hand on his arm. “Not yet, Ray, it’s too soon. Remember, this is only a test drive; we will follow that bastard in the car and find out where else he goes.” The red car reversed and pulled away. Andy followed but not too closely. The car headed along the road until he came to a large car park amongst the trees, which was a well-known place for courting couples or illicit sexual encounters between married couples. The red car pulled into a quiet corner and the driver wound down his window but kept his engine ticking over. Soon he was being approached by the occupants of a car that had been parked there, obviously waiting. A young couple stood talking to the driver of the red car. He opened a small briefcase and showed them various packages. The couple picked out what they wanted and money was handed over.

Abbo was making notes in a diary. “I’ve got his number plate and the date and time. What’s the name of this place, Dave?”

Dave thought for a moment. “It’s Takeroo, I think. There’s a campsite just over the road and I noticed a sign on the gate.”

The red car reversed and pulled back onto the road. Andy followed at a distance. They approached a junction and the red car indicated left. “He’s going out of our area now,” said Andy. “Let’s let him go now.” The boys agreed and made their way back to the pub car park.

“Who’s for a pint?” asked Abbo.

***

Peter drove into the car park where Susan's car was parked. He reached for her overnight bag and put it on the backseat of her car. She got into the driver's seat and put the keys in the ignition. "Thank you for a wonderful weekend, Peter." She leaned her head towards him and he bent down and kissed her. He watched as she pulled out of the car park, wishing in his mind that it could be something more permanent. Susan, on the other hand, was thinking what if Derek was seeing someone else and these weekend fishing trips were just an excuse for something else. She mulled it over in her mind as she drove home. Derek hadn't arrived home yet, the driveway was empty. There was no sign of his car. She put her overnight bag away and started preparing the evening meal. Derek always made it home for his tea. He arrived an hour later and followed his usual routine of unloading his fishing gear and putting it away in the garage. Then his overnight bag would be put in the spare room where it would be unloaded later.

"Hi there, Susan, are you OK?" was the usual greeting. He sat down and began looking through his fishing magazine whilst Susan placed the evening meal on the table.

"Good weekend?" she would always ask.

"Oh no, not very, a bit boring actually," would be his reply. "Not much on telly, I'll go and sort my stuff out." Susan was left to watch TV as usual.

Derek entered the lounge. "Did you do anything special, Susan?" he asked, picking up the daily paper.

Susan changed channels. "No, not really. A look around Litchfield on Saturday afternoon; what else am I supposed to do when you're not here?" She looked over at him as he flicked through thc papers.

"Oh, I thought you might have met up with some of your friends and gone out for a meal or something."

Again Susan changed channels. "My friends go out with their husbands to a restaurant and such, that's the normal practice when you're married."

He looked over the newspaper at her. “But you know that’s not my scene, love. I’m more for using my skills at golf or fishing. I’m an outsider really. I’m more active.”

Susan forced a smile. “So I’ve found out since we got married, Derek. You like being with your mates.”

***

Christine heard the door close as Billy left for work. She quickly picked up Steven who was happily gurgling away in his cot. Nappy changed, a quick wash and he was ready for his bottle. She put him in his carrycot on the settee whilst she attended to her own needs. A cereal breakfast followed by a visit to the bathroom. Steven had dropped off to sleep, enabling her to spend time choosing some provocative clothing and a strong perfume. A quick tidy-up of the living room and a glance at the clock. Another half an hour before Marianne’s arrival but already Christine was feeling horny. When the doorbell rang, Christine took a quick look in the mirror before opening the door. She was confronted by an elderly gentleman carrying a briefcase.

“Good morning, ma’am, insurance. I’m Mr Foster, your new agent.”

Christine’s face fell. “Where’s Marianne?” she asked.

“Oh, another turnaround from head office. They do this thing often these days. Marianne has been moved to another area for a while and I’ve replaced her. I hope you don’t mind a more mature member of the company taking care of your investments?”

Christine was in a bad mood for the rest of the day. It had not been a good start; in fact, it had been very disappointing.

***

Rosie nudged Joe. “Time to get up. We’ve got a doctor’s appointment at 11:30.”

Joe moaned as he eased himself off the mattress. “Why are you coming with me today? Have you got a problem?”

Rosie looked at Joe. "Yes, it's a personal one and we might as well go together."

Joe hobbled downstairs. Rosie had already set the table for breakfast. "We'll go early as it's quite a walk up to the surgery," said Joe, finishing off his cornflakes.

Rosie cleared the table. "I'm ready when you are. I don't want to rush." They made their way through the estate and made it to the surgery in good time. Rosie chatted away to people she knew whilst they waited to be called.

Dr Elaine Johnson greeted them with a smile. "Good morning, Mr and Mrs Fiddler, and how are you both today?"

Joe sat down and half-smiled at the doctor. "My sick note has run out, doctor, and I need a prescription."

The doctor looked at Joe. "I can see your back is still bothering you, Joe. Has the physio not helped any?"

He shook his head. "Not a lot, doctor. The tablets are helping with the pain but are causing constipation."

She nodded her head. "Yes, some tablets do cause that but I'll give you some medicine to help you with that." She wrote a prescription and Joe mentioned his sick note. "There you are, Joe. Keep on with the physio! Now what can I do for you, Mrs Fiddler?"

"Well, doctor, it's not really for me, but can you give Joe some of those Viagra tablets? He won't ask for them himself but our sex life is non-existent. He keeps saying it's his back but he won't even try. I think he wants a kickstart to get things moving."

Joe went red in the face. "Rosie, I've got a bad back. It's painful to try."

Doctor Elaine rose from her chair and reached into a wall cabinet. "Joe, here's a booklet showing various positions you can try; have a go, Joe, for Rosie's sake."

Joe took the booklet and the prescriptions, handing them to Rosie as they left the surgery. "Here, you can go and get these. I didn't know that's what you were going to ask for."

Rosie gave him a quick smile. "Early to bed tonight, Joe."

Chapter 10
Action

The week passed quickly since the B.A.D. Boys had carried out their recce. They were now ready for some real action and agreed to meet. Dave had agreed to spy on their victim. He ran into the pub and signalled to the boys. “He’s on his way to the meeting place now.”

The boys left the pub and got into their car. “Are you sure that’s where he’s heading?” asked Abbo.

“Yes, I’m sure,” answered Dave.

The car pulled away and they drove to the rendezvous. “Nobody there yet,” said Sid. “Pull over there in the shadows! I’ve just seen somebody walking down the road.”

It wasn’t long before the red car pulled into the car park. A few minutes passed before a figure emerged and approached the vehicle. “That’s him,” said Dave. They waited as the deal was completed. Another car pulled up alongside the pusher’s car.

“That’s the pair we saw last week,” said Ray. “They must be regulars.” They waited as another deal was sealed. “Right, get ready! As soon as they’ve gone, we go and get him. Masks on and no names mentioned.”

Abbo was the first out of the car, followed by Sid. “I’ll get in the front passenger seat, the rest of you in the back. I’ll do the talking.” Quickly, they made their move. The surprised driver was just putting money in his wallet.

“What the fuck’s this?” he called out.

Abbo put his finger to his lips. “Shush, we’ll do the talking.”

"What is it you want?" asked the frightened man. "Drugs or cash?"

Abbo looked at the small attaché case Sid had passed over. "Here's his supply." Abbo opened it, revealing small packages of powder and bottles of pills. "What's this shit?" he asked.

"Medical supplies," said the man.

Ray leaned over and took a look. "Medical supplies, my arse. That's coke, they're ecstasy, they're packets of weed and there's more, probably crack or heroin."

Abbo opened a bottle of pills. "You are going to tell us these are aspirins, I suppose? Well, here, take a few cos you've probably got a headache or soon will have." Ray leaned forward and grabbed the man's hair, pulling him back in his seat. Abbo shoved a handful of pills into the man's open mouth. "Don't worry, mate, you'll soon feel better."

A packet of white powder was opened and its contents tipped over his mouth and nose. "Please leave me alone, take the money and go, please."

Abbo reached for the bottle of water lying on the dashboard. "Here, mate, wash it down with this." He gave a nod to Ray as a signal to disappear. He reached for the ignition keys and threw them across the car park. The boys made it to their car where Dave was waiting. Ray drove the car to a small lay-by.

"Right, change your jacket and hide the masks! We don't want to get pulled over wearing these." Abbo pointed to a telephone box further up the road. "Pull up here, Ray; I've got a phone call to make." Five minutes later, he got back in the car with a broad grin on his face.

"What was that all about?" asked Sid. Abbo said that he had phoned the local police saying a man high on drugs was causing a problem in the Takeroo car park. A chorus of laughter burst out as they drove away.

"I'm going to the club for a pint," said Ray.

***

It was a nice sunny morning as Joe put on his jacket and made for the front door. Rosie was in a good mood. "When shall I see you later, Joe? That physiotherapy seems to be doing you a bit of good these days."

Joe thought for a moment. "I'll be going into town to see a couple of mates. They keep me up to date on benefits and such like and then I might call in on Mam, I haven't seen her for a while. It will probably be tea-time before I get back." He closed the front door and hobbled down the road, making his way through the estate. The road into the garages was deserted. Making sure no one was around, he unlocked the garage door and slipped inside quickly, closing the door behind him. Putting on the light, he stripped off the sheet covering the car. He unlocked the cupboard and started to change into his smart gear. Half an hour later, he was ready, checking his toupee was in position and his false moustache firmly in place. Picking up his briefcase, he switched on the ignition. Another quick look to see if the street was clear and he opened the doors wide and backed out the BMW. He didn't waste much time locking up the garage and quickly manoeuvred the car through the estate onto the main road. A quick stop at a telephone box to inform his girls that he was on his way.

"It's the NEC today, ladies. The Homes and Gardens Exhibition. We should do all right there."

Janet said she had always wanted to visit the exhibition. Veronica said she did too. Denise said she hadn't got any money to spend so she would be looking for a quick pick-up. "Someone nice and tasty," she added.

Joe browsed around the show, chatting to the reps and picking up a few samples, also making enquiries about other exhibitions. One rep gave him a newsletter with information on forthcoming events. "If you phone this number, you get free updates and invitations. They also provide you with lapel badges and free car parking tickets in the executive car parks." Joe thanked the rep and said he would look for him at other exhibitions. At 3:30, he made his way to the exit and waited for the girls. Janet was already there, waiting anxiously and looked very frustrated. She saw Joe and ran up to him. “Joe, let’s get out of here fast. Please Joe, get me out of here now.”

Joe was taken aback. He looked at his watch. “We gotta wait for the other two, Janet. What’s happened?”

Janet puffed nervously on a cigarette. “I gotta get away from here, Joe, something’s happened.”

Joe said he would take her to the car and she could wait there whilst he rounded up Denise and Veronica. Janet said she would tell them what happened when they were all together. Joe hurried back to the exit where the two women were waiting. “We’ve got an emergency on our hands. Janet has had a problem she’s going to tell us when we’re all together.”

Denise sat in the front passenger seat and Veronica comforted a distressed Janet. “Well, what’s happened?” asked Joe as he purred up the engine.

Janet looked worried. “I picked up this rep and soon I could see he was up for action. I met him at 1 o’clock by the main entrance and he led me to the hotel. He was in his mid-fifties, slightly overweight but he was eager to get his leg over. We had a quick cup of tea and a ham roll before he led me to the lift and up to the second floor. He was very keen to get going and was lying naked on the bed before I had time to take a piss. There was no foreplay; he was straight up it, shafting away. One thing I noticed was five twenty pound notes on the bedside table. I tried to slow things down a bit, telling him we had plenty of time but he just kept hammering away like a steam train. It was all over before I had a chance to scratch my arse. I rolled off him and lay there, listening to this rasping noise he was making. I asked him if he was OK and he sort of grunted. I got up and fetched him a glass of water. He was sweating like a big pig. I got dressed and again asked him if he was OK. He didn’t answer and he was breathing very erratically. I quickly left the room and made my way out of the hotel, making sure nobody noticed me. Outside the hotel was a pay phone. I dialled 999 and said there was a guy in room 87 at the hotel having a heart attack. I didn’t give any more details. I just made my way back here. I don’t know if the bastard’s alive or dead. I heard the ambulance arrive so that's it, that's my day over. Get me home, Joe! I need to crash out for a while."

Joe said she had done the right thing. "Did you pick up the cash?" he asked.

"Oh yes, Joe, I'm not that far gone yet but no more overweight buggers for me again. I'm sticking to the athletic type."

Denise looked at Joe as they entered her flat. "Coffee first, Joe?"

***

Susan watched as Derek parked his car next to hers. She couldn't help notice how smart he looked, not the usual Derek in jeans and scruffy jumper with an anorak. He made the usual, "Hello Susan, are you OK?" before putting his bags in the spare room. Susan greeted him and asked if he had had a good weekend. She couldn't help notice a different look on his face as he sat down with the newspaper. It was as if something was on his mind. "Yes, quite fruitful actually; I caught the most fish this time." Susan had been doing the ironing. She finished the garment and started to put the remainder away for another day. "What about you, Sue? Anything exciting?" he asked.

"No, just the usual girlie shopping in Stafford, nothing to get excited about." She had prepared the evening meal and retired to the kitchen to warm it up. They sat down at the table and engaged in small talk about the weather and such. She still had a feeling that something was on his mind. Finally, after settling himself on the settee in front of the telly, he looked at her. "Susan, we must talk. This marriage of ours isn't going anywhere, is it? We don't appear to have anything in common anymore, do we? You don't share my interests and I don't share yours. I'm an outdoor person and I love what I'm doing—fishing and golfing with the lads. I don't think that is fair on you so I think we must talk seriously about an alternative."

Susan looked at Derek. Her intuition had been right; Derek had something on his mind. "Is it a divorce you're suggesting?" she asked.

Derek looked away, completely taken aback by her frankness. "Well, I hadn't quite decided on what we should do but if you want to go down that road…yes, that would be a good idea, Susan. I'm sure we could make a more interesting life for ourselves. I can't change my ways, Susan, and it's not fair on you, is it?"

Susan got up and left the room. In the kitchen, her heart was pounding away. A huge smile appeared on her face. She made two cups of tea and returned to sit beside Derek on the settee. "I didn't mean to make you so unhappy, Sue. I just thought we could make better lives for ourselves."

"Who said I'm unhappy?" replied Susan. "I've had those same thoughts for a long time."

Derek seemed surprised at her reply. "Then we can discuss it without any aggro like two sensible adults."

Susan picked up a magazine and started reading. "We must go and see a solicitor and get things moving right away," she said. "I don't want this thing to linger on. Let's get it over with. We must put the house up for sale and that alone can take time. By the way, Derek, have you met someone else?" He looked away and she could see the look of guilt on his face. "I thought so."

Derek got up and switched off the telly. "I intended to come clean about everything, Susan. I just didn't know how you would react. Yes, I have met a woman who shares my interests. She is a wildlife artist who spends a lot of time along the riverbanks. She came up to me and asked if she could draw the fish I had just caught. We just struck up an immediate friendship and we began meeting at various locations. She also plays golf."

A silence lapsed between them and Susan continued reading her magazine. "I didn't mean to hurt you, Susan, in any way. I just wanted to wait for the right moment to tell you all this."

Susan looked up from the magazine. "Who's hurt, Derek? Certainly not me. I'm glad it's all out in the open now. We can part amicably and make a fresh start. I have also been making plans for a new future."

Derek sat down beside her. "There's one more thing I want you to know. I'm putting in my notice at work. I've been offered a job by one of the anglers who I have made acquaintance with. He's a director of a company designing prefabricated buildings such as supermarkets and warehouses. I have accepted a position as draughtsman."

Susan closed the magazine and picked up the empty cups. "Right, tomorrow when we finish work, let's go into town and get the ball rolling. First a solicitor and then the estate agent."

***

The phone rang in the union office and Dennis answered it. "So that's final," he said as the union president rambled on.

"Yes, Dennis, that's it, there's a meeting this weekend if you can attend. It's time for decisive action. Let's take the bastards on. We will do our utmost to save our industry."

Dennis told his wife he would be going to Nottingham on Friday night. "It sounds as if it's the final push. I don't know how long I'll be at this meeting. I'll let you know if it's going to be a long meeting."

He pulled up in the Sherwood Hotel car park. It was just getting dark and a light shower of rain engulfed him as he got out of his car. Henry looked up as Dennis entered the reception. They exchanged greetings and Dennis asked Henry if he was keeping well. "Tomorrow I go into hospital to have a check-up and they're talking about fitting me with a pacemaker. I might be a bit better when that's all done. Our Gladys has just nipped into town to get me a new pair of pyjamas. She should be back soon. She will be glad to see you, Dennis." Henry gave him the key. "Same room as last time, Dennis."

Dennis took the lift. Placing his bag and briefcase on the bed, he walked over to the window and looked out. Gladys had just pulled into the car park and was locking her car door. Dennis lay on the bed and took two paracetamol. He always ended up with a severe headache before and after these meetings. He felt himself dozing off. A light tap on the door brought him around. "Come in," he called out.

Pushing a trolley, Gladys came into the room. Her eyes lit up as she crossed over to where Dennis was lying on the bed. "You poor darling, another of those terrible meetings?" She sat on the bed and leaned over and planted a full-on kiss. "It's nice to see you again, Dennis. I think of you often."

He responded, "I think of you too, Gladys."

She began to lay out the meal. "Henry hasn't been too well just lately. He's going into hospital for a few days to see if a pacemaker would help him."

Dennis nodded his head. "Yes, he told me. It must be hard on both of you having to run this place as well."

Gladys looked at Dennis. "Eat your meal and have a rest. I will have to go and see to Henry. I shall be looking after reception until the night staff comes on. I'll see you later if you want a bit of company?"

***

Susan couldn't contain her excitement as she parked her car in the usual place in Litchfield. The week had passed quickly and she and Derek had done what they had planned. The solicitor had taken notes and asked on what grounds was the reason for their divorce. "Incompatibility," Susan told him and Derek had agreed. The next thing was for the house to be sold. They hadn't spoken much during the week but Susan had told Derek he was confined to the spare bedroom. He didn't argue and had begun sorting out his private possessions. They had agreed that the house should be sold and the proceeds divided.

Peter had parked his car and had just been waiting for Susan to arrive. As soon as he saw her arrive, he pulled forward and opened the door. She gave him a warm smile and a peck on the cheek. She appeared to be in high spirits and chatted away excitedly as they drove to York. She had not told Peter yet; she wanted it to be her big surprise of the day and wanted to choose her moment. Derek had packed a lot of his belongings and loaded up his car. Susan guessed he wasn't going fishing. He merely said he would be back Sunday afternoon. That didn't bother Susan now, she and Peter would have a good weekend of their own and no more guilty thoughts would pass through her mind. They had booked the same hotel and were greeted pleasantly by the hotel staff. Susan threw herself onto the bed and waited for Peter to join her. They kissed passionately and were soon in the throes of their love for each other. Susan lay quietly for a moment and then, with a burst of excitement, revealed the good news to Peter. "We are going to celebrate tonight," he said. "I never thought this would ever happen, Susan, its wonderful news. Now we can make plans for a future together."

During their weekend, all sorts of ideas were talked about. "As soon as Derek moves out, I shall be looking for a flat to rent," said Susan excitedly.

"Won't you be coming to live with me?" Peter asked, surprised by Susan's decision.

"No, when everything is settled, I shall rent a small flat just for a short time whilst we look for a suitable property to share."

Peter thought for a while. "And then I'll sell my place and we will have a good deposit for our new home. Oh Susan, I promise you a happy life."

Susan put her arms around Peter. "And then I want a child, Peter."

***

The C.M.U. meeting started at 10 o'clock. The room was packed and noisy. Dennis took two paracetamols as the president called the meeting to order.

"Gentlemen, today is decision time. I must tell you that I have tried to arrange a meeting with the government and British Coal but they are adamant that no further talks are likely. So now is the time for us to decide on what action we are to take. I propose that we call for strike action. That's the only thing that will bring these people to the negotiating table. I have heard from my source at Westminster that the authorities are going to call our bluff. The American hatchet man has advised the prime minister not to take us on unless she's prepared to see it through to the end."

The room erupted with various calls for action. The Nottingham area rep stood up and asked for a chance to be heard. The C.M.U. president asked that he should be given a chance and the room fell silent.

"Mr President, our area has been on full production for a long time now and we reach our targets and earn good bonuses. Are you going to suggest that I ask my members to give all that up and go on strike for who knows how long just to save a few pits that have been losing money and are having to be carried by pits that are successful? It doesn't make sense to me and my members."

The room burst into an uproar again as other area representatives argued against one another. The president asked for order. When finally the room was quiet, he stood up and addressed the area representatives. "Gentlemen, I know that for some it's going to be a hard decision, but let's look at our industry as a whole. As a trade union for one of the country's largest employers, we have always supported each other. I have been informed that the government has produced a list of seventy coalmines it wants to close. How many men are going to lose their jobs? How many mining villages will be decimated? How many people is this going to affect? Perhaps not in your area but let's think about other areas such as South Wales, Yorkshire, Durham and Scotland. Let's not think of only ourselves; let's think of our fellow miners and their families. I say let's fight to save our industry and the jobs of those who have spent their lives breathing in the dust and losing relatives to provide this country with coal." The room once again erupted into uncontrollable anger. The president raised his hands and gradually the noise abated. "Gentlemen, I suggest we put this to a vote. A piece of paper will be given to each one of you. Write Yes or No for strike action. These will be collected and counted now and we will accept the majority vote.

Dennis took a piece of paper and voted 'yes' and signed it. When all the votes had been cast, they were collected and handed to the president, who tipped them onto the table in front of him. Members of his staff counted them in full view of the area representatives. They were counted and recounted. Finally, the result was handed to the president. "Gentlemen, we have a majority and I declare that as of Friday of next week, we shall withdraw our labour. I shall notify the government and British Coal of our decision. I now ask you to notify your membership of our decision."

***

Dave ran home from school as fast as he could. His mam called out to him to be quiet as his dad was having a nap and Ray had already crashed out on the settee, as was his usual routine having spent all day down the pit. "Take the dog for a run over the fields, they'll be up by the time you get back," she said.

Dave couldn't contain his excitement. On his way home from school with a couple of mates, they have been joined by another guy who Dave only knew vaguely as Kev, who was a bit older and in a higher class but he knew Dave's other mates and chatted away freely. "Went to a super disco at the weekend," he began, "in Newcastle called *Musicana Disco*. My brothers took me and got me in; they lied about my age; it was fantastic. There was some dishy talent there all for the picking."

"Did you score?" asked one of Dave's mates.

"No, not this time but I was chatting to this Columbian girl. My, what a figure and could she move her arse. We got really friendly but she had to leave early. She said she'd got to go up to Manchester to meet her brother and do some business. I took it she meant drugs. I asked but she just laughed and disappeared."

Dave had taken it all in and when Kev had mentioned the Columbian girl, Dave had felt a cold shiver down his spine. Was this the girl who had sold the 'happy tablet' to Jan?

Ray was awake and drinking a coffee when Dave returned. "Hi kiddo, what are you all excited about?"

Dave told Ray about what Kev had told them. "It must be the same woman who sold our Jan that tablet, Ray. Let's go and get her."

Ray told Dave to calm down. "There must be dozens of coloureds knocking around, Dave. How do we know she's the one? How can we prove anything?"

Dave was upset and the tears began to erupt. "She was my sister too, Ray."

Comforting his brother, he led him outside and up the garden away from the house. A light drizzle forced them to take shelter in the garden shed. "Listen Dave, we need hard evidence. How can we get that?"

Dave wiped away the tears. "Jan's boyfriend should be able to identify her, Ray, let's ask him."

Ray's face changed to anger. "I just want to kill that bastard, Dave. I don't think I could control myself if I got near him."

The following morning, as the boys clambered into the waiting train in the pit bottom, Ray revealed what Dave had told him. Abbo said, "Well, let's check it out, I've heard about *Musicana Disco* being a hot spot."

Ray replied that only Janet's ex-boyfriend could identify her definitely.

"Well, I know him and I'll have a quiet word with him," Sid suggested. Ray said he wouldn't want to meet up with the boyfriend as he himself was still seething with anger. Abbo suggested Ray could stay at home whilst the other three asked the boyfriend to accompany them to *Musicana Disco*.

"I'll leave it up to you," said Ray. "But make sure the bastard identifies the right one, we don't want to make any mistakes."

Harry listened to the conversation until Billy seconded him into the next compartment to make up the four for a game of cards. "Where's the old man this morning, Abbo?" Billy shouted as he dealt the cards.

"He's not been well over the weekend. Bad stomach, he's off to the doctor's this morning to see what's up with him. Mam thinks he may have an ulcer or something."

***

Dennis opened up his office. He was tired this morning, what with the meeting and then Gladys had come to his room wearing a see-through nighty. A night of passion had finished him off and he had fallen into a deep slumber, waking up late Sunday morning with a splitting headache. Today, he had to make plans to notify the workforce of the president's decision to call an all-out strike for Friday. With the help of the mechanical and electrical union leaders, they had planned to make up some large notices to be put up around the pithead, around the corridors and outside the canteen. They also had to make themselves available at knock-off to answer all the questions that would be thrown at them. Dennis had decided to hold a meeting outside in the car park where one of the notices had been hung. The afternoon shift coming on would be the first lot to start the barrage of questions. They also had to notify the pit management of the union's decision. Lots of things had to be done. Arrangements to keep the pit safe were a priority and teams of officials had to be prepared for safety reasons. The management wouldn't be pleased. Indeed, when Dennis and the electrical union's rep entered his office, the manager was furious at the outcome. "Do you realise what a lot of problems can arise from this action? The pit has to be put on safety, which means officials on duty twenty-four hours a day. We have to have standby crews of fitters and electricians to deal with emergencies. The pumps have to be kept running to deal with the water. I hope this bloody fiasco is over soon or this pit could be closed permanently."

The notices were put up and soon the union offices were being bombarded by men wanting to know what had happened. Dennis and Phil, the electricians union rep, decided that a table and two chairs should be placed in the corridor outside the canteen to greet the afternoon shift. As the men arrived and read the notices, the union reps were soon inundated with questions being thrown at them. Some of the miners accepted the decision but there were some who were not in favour of strike action and wanted to work. The union men told them that the president of the Coal Miners' Union had held a meeting of all area union reps and a vote had been taken. Throughout the week, angry miners all over the country had voiced their protest against the president's action. Taking note of the situation, the coal industry bosses gave instructions to all pit managers that the pits would remain open for any men to come to work if they wanted to. This caused uproar throughout the coal fields as the newspapers took up the fight, some for the miners and some for the coal industry. Notification that the miners could turn up for work if they wanted to, caused a storm of protests. Coaches were laid on to ferry willing workers past the picket lines. A lot of abuse was hurled at them as the coaches drove through the picket lines.

Chapter 11
The Price of Coal

Billy explained to Christine that the action by the union was necessary to protect jobs and the industry as a whole. "This bloody government is hell-bent on closing down the mining industry and this was just the thin end of the wedge." Christine said she hoped the strike didn't last long as she couldn't stand Billy under her feet all day. "I shall be doing my bit on the picket lines," he retorted. "So don't worry your pretty arse about that."

***

Joe Fiddler backed the car out of the lock-up and drove towards Litchfield. Janet had remained hesitant after the last episode but Joe had reassured her that he would look after her and would always be close by. "Manchester is always a good place for exhibitions—loads of northerners and they're not a bad lot, Janet, just pick a younger one this time. No pot-bellied buggers or bald-headed old farts, treat yourself to a bit of class."

When they arrived at the Exhibition Centre, Joe stayed close to Janet as Denise and Veronica sauntered off and started looking for their prey. "I'll be your company boss and you can be my secretary for today, Janet, until we find you a suitable client."

***

Derek had more or less cleared all of his stuff from the house and a 'For Sale' sign was put up on the front lawn. His notice had been put in at work and he started his new job next Monday. Susan watched as he put his fishing gear in his car. He closed the boot and came back into the house. "I won't be coming back, Susan, but I'll keep in touch. I'm glad our parting has been quite amicable and I do respect you for that. I'm sorry it didn't work out for us, Susan, and I really do hope you find someone who will give you all that you want. You are a good-looking woman. Thanks for everything." He left the house and Susan waved as he drove off. Now she could relax and sort out what she was going to wear for her meeting with Peter on Saturday.

The following morning began with warm sunshine. Susan had chosen a pink two-piece suit and a sparkling necklace with a matching handbag and shoes. She glanced in the mirror and with her shoulder-length hair and sparkling white teeth, she looked beautiful. Peter was waiting at the usual place; he waved to her as she parked her car. A wide grin greeted her and a "You look beautiful, Susan". They kissed briefly and Susan held onto his arm.

"Let's not go to York today, Peter, let's stay in Litchfield. I would just like to browse around here and then go for a walk around the cathedral and along the river; it's going to be a lovely day." She told Peter that Derek had left and was not coming back.

Peter squeezed her hand. "I'm glad it's happened like this, Susan. At least it was amicable with no arguing or fighting. I did worry about you. Now let's get the divorce over and then we can be together permanently." They walked leisurely through the streets of Litchfield, stopping for a coffee at a backstreet café. Peter talked about the forthcoming strike. "I hope it soon gets resolved. I don't like confrontation and according to some, this could get nasty."

Susan agreed. "I don't think it will last long; with no wages coming in, the families will suffer and everyone needs food on the table."

***

Sid took to walking around the estate, hopeful that the boyfriend would show himself. It was three days before Sid spotted him leaving the supermarket with a pack of six cans tucked under his arm. "Been looking for you," said Sid. "How's it going?"

The boyfriend acknowledged Sid. "I'm OK. Why you looking for me?"

Sid came straight to the point. "We think we've found that coloured girl who sold you that tablet, but we need someone to positively identify her. Could you do that?"

The boyfriend looked away. "I'll never forget her. I wish I could get my hands on her."

Sid lit up a cigarette and offered him one. "It would be too obvious for you to do anything. Just leave it to someone else but we need you to help us identify her. Will you do that?"

He nodded. "Just tell me when and who else is involved?"

Sid said he couldn't reveal any other information at this point. "We will want you to come with us on Saturday night to a disco. Are you willing to do that?"

The boyfriend said he would, but not if Ray was involved. "He's put it about that he's after me." Sid assured him that Ray was not party to anything and would not be involved. He arranged to pick up the boyfriend at 7 o'clock outside the supermarket, telling him that it was important that he showed up. If he failed, someone would be looking for him.

***

Joe led Janet around the various stands at the exhibition, talking to the reps and introducing himself and his secretary as company managers of some obscure firm. They browsed around for a while until they struck up a conversation with a rep who looked promising—a nice-looking guy in his thirties who showed an interest in Janet's full figure. Whilst Joe kept the other rep engaged in conversation, this eager young man chatted her up and revealed what he was thinking. Janet said her boss would be going for lunch in a short while, which left her free to do what she liked.

"Please have lunch with me?" the rep asked enthusiastically. "Meet me by the exit in half an hour." Janet agreed to be there. Joe told her that he would be watching from a close distance and would keep an eye on things. The rep arrived and introduced himself as Geoffrey. He was a junior manager of the company. He took Janet's arm and led her across the car park to the hotel entrance. They found a table and ordered a light salad.

"Do you stay in this hotel whilst you are here?" Janet asked casually.

The rep's eyes lit up. "Yes, we book a suite for three days where we can entertain prospective customers. Would you like to see it?" He led her to the lift and pressed the button. The room was large with other doors leading from it. The rep showed her each room, leaving the master bedroom until last. "This is my room, isn't it nice?" he said, leading her into it.

By now, he was getting closer and touching her. Janet responded, "I wish I had more time to spend here," she said. "But I have to go and earn my bonus." She sat on the bed. "Oh! This is comfortable," she said, falling back into the pillows. "Oh dear, I'm going to have to leave now. My boss pays me a hundred pound bonus if I can get some orders from the reps. Sorry, Geoffrey. Work comes before pleasure."

The rep whipped out his wallet and placed five twenties on the pillow. "There's your bonus, Janet, let's relax for a while, shall we?"

Joe checked his watch and if Janet didn't return soon, he would have to go and search for her. Another five minutes passed before a smiling Janet paraded herself in front of him. "I was getting worried," he told her.

"No need, Joe, everything is hunky dory this time and a good time had by all."

Veronica sat in the front seat as Joe purred up the engine. He gave her a smile as he noticed her short skirt had risen further, revealing her ample thighs. Joe felt in his pocket and popped a blue tablet in his mouth. "Indigestion," he murmured. Veronica made a quick visit to the bathroom where a quick shower prepared her for what Joe had in mind. She entered the bedroom, completely naked. "What's it to be, Joe?" she asked. "American express, doggy fashion or what?"

Joe peeled off his underpants revealing that he was ready to go for whatever, eyeing up the naked Veronica. "No, this time it's the slow boat through the Bermuda Triangle."

***

Billy joined the crowd of angry miners as the coaches slowly drove through the lines of pickets. Men were banging on the sides of the coaches shouting 'scabs'. The police had formed a cordon stopping the miners from blocking the road altogether. A lot of pushing was going on and policemen's helmets were being kicked around in the road. It started to get into an angry situation and the pushing intensified. Police chiefs were using megaphones to address the crowd. Miners' wives had started to join their menfolk, calling out to the police that they were just paid thugs and bullying bastards.

As the weeks passed by, several scuffles took place between the miners and the police and men were getting arrested. The women pelted them with eggs as their menfolk were dragged away. "They are just trying to save the coal mining industry," one woman told a reporter. "What would you do if you were being thrown on the scrap heap? We have children to feed. Think of that and put that in your paper." Television cameras visited pits up and down the country, filming the action, but the government refused to comment. 'The rebel miners are just out to cause trouble' was the only comment. Support for the miners came from various sources. Other unions gave their support and cash donations were made. Food stores also donated food supplies. The country as a whole seemed to support the miners at first but as the strike went on, eventually people's attitudes changed. Soon reports in the papers accused the miners of holding the country to ransom as fuel supplies began to peter out. In the towns and villages, anger began to show and in the mining communities, fights broke out, even families turned on each other. Billy walked into a pub in the town after a spell on the picket line. Several working miners were gathered. They looked down their noses at him and turned their backs to him. The pub landlord took his time serving Billy and commented, "You're not welcome here. This is for working men only."

Billy picked up his pint and threw it over the barman. "What the fucking hell do you know about work, arsehole? Stick your beer up your arse."

Two men rushed over to grab Billy but his six-foot-two frame sidestepped and slammed them both into the bar. A voice from behind him called out, "Billy lad, don't let them get to you, fuck off home."

Billy turned towards the door and made a quick retreat. "You're banned from this pub," shouted an angry barman.

Billy turned to see who had called to him in the pub. Alf's tired-looking body caught up with him. "Best thing to do is stay away from them if you can, mate. Ignore the fuckers."

Billy gave Alf a smile. "Hello mate, what are you doing down here?" Billy noticed how ill Alf looked; he was a shadow of his former self.

"Oh, just been to put in a prescription and I needed to get out for a change of scenery. This here strike is going on a bit, mate. What's going to happen?"

Billy shrugged his shoulders as he helped Alf across the car park. "Come on, mate, I'll give you a lift home. I don't know, Alf, things aren't going smoothly, the unions are split and there's talk of a new union being formed to represent the miners who want to work. I think they're calling it the Democratic Union and there's more men crossing the picket line; they've had enough, Alf. It's been going on now for nine months and you can only last for so long with no money coming in. To be quite honest, Alf, I'm thinking of going back to work. Our Christine is doing a bit of part-time work to help out but it's not enough."

Alf nodded. "Yep, it's been a tough one and I think we've lost the battle this time, mate."

Billy pulled up at Alf's house. "You take care, mate. I'll see you again soon."

***

Dennis packed his bag. Another meeting at Nottingham had been called. He had booked in at the Sherwood and was just about to leave. "Don't know how long," he called to his wife. "I'll phone as soon as I know anything." It was raining heavily as he drove towards Nottingham. As the wipers did their best to give him a clear view, Dennis thought about the oncoming meeting. No details had been given but deep down in his heart, Dennis hoped an end was in sight. With members of the C.M.U. going over to the Democratic Union, Dennis could sense disaster. He was greeted at the hotel by Sylvia. "Hello stranger," she said. "Nice to see you again, it's been a long time." Dennis shook hands but Sylvia leaned over the desk. "How about a kiss instead?"

Dennis gave her a peck on each cheek. "Where's Gladys and Henry?" he asked.

"Blackpool for two weeks. Henry had his pacemaker fitted and so they've taken a two-week holiday to see how things work out. I think it's possible they may take early retirement if everything goes well with Henry."

Dennis signed in and took the key offered. "Same room?" he enquired.

"Oh yes, Dennis, kept especially for you. Do you need me to show you the way? Only I can't whilst I'm on duty at reception, but I'll check on you later to see if you need anything." She gave Dennis a wicked smile, which Dennis reciprocated.

"I don't think my meeting will last for two weeks but then you never know."

Sylvia was the first to wake up at 6 o'clock. She shook Dennis and asked what time his meeting was. "10 o'clock," he yawned.

"OK, I'll give you time to take a shower and then it will be time for breakfast. I'll bring it up. You don't want it in the diner, do you, Dennis?"

The president called the meeting to order. All the areas were represented and the room was full and noisy. "OK gentlemen, it's decision time again. You are all aware of what's been going on and what's been happening within the union. As far as I can make out, our union has been split down the middle. Half of our members have decided to join the newly formed Democratic Union. I am bitterly disappointed but the situation that has brought on this action had been escalating beyond control since this strike was implemented. Our adversaries, the government and British Coal, have exceeded expectations beyond any comprehension visualised by us. We expected a fight and we've got one but now we have lost public support thanks to the media and their false representations. Now the union has been weakened by this split. It is with much regret that I have to say this, gentlemen, but we can no longer carry on with this fight." Opinions were voiced and suggestions put forward. The president listened to all but in the end he suggested a hands up vote to call off the strike. The vote was in favour of the president's suggestion and a motion was carried for the president to notify the government and the coal industry bosses that they were going to call off their industrial action strike and return to work, but would still want to negotiate about the pits earmarked for closure.

Dennis decided that he would stay another night at the hotel, much to the delight of Sylvia. As they lay side by side that night, Sylvia said that her sister had talked about early retirement and had asked her if she would want to take over the hotel as manager. Gladys said they would pay her a good salary and as the owners of the hotel, Sylvia could call on her anytime for help. She could give up her flat and live at the hotel. Dennis said it would be a good move but he would miss seeing Gladys and Henry. "I'll be looking after you, Dennis," she giggled.

***

The boys met at the pub with Abbo driving. "Where do we pick him up?" he asked.

Sid told him to pull up in the supermarket car park. As they did, a figure stepped out of the shadows. "It's him," said Sid. "His name is Greg Sanders. I know him vaguely from school days." Sid opened the door and beckoned to Greg to get in. Abbo pulled away without saying a word.

Andy broke the silence. "We only want you to identify this woman but make sure it's the one who sold you the happy tablet. We don't want any fuck ups, do you understand, mate? No fuck ups." Greg agreed and said he could never forget her face and although he had given a good description to the police, they hadn't traced her.

"Probably been lying low for a while," said Abbo.

They arrived at *Musicana Disco* and pulled into the shaded area near the exit. "Stay close and don't make any moves until we're sure, then we decide how to handle it." Abbo was the leader in this operation and had agreed with Ray that it must be a positive identification. The place was full and the music loud. The boys moved around the crowded floor, searching for a face, any coloured face.

Greg scoured the crowd but came up with nothing. "It's early yet, most of them get tanked up first and then show up late, already half-pissed. She might not even come here tonight; they do move around, these pushers."

Soon the boys were feeling thirsty. "Nothing strong," warned Abbo. "We need clear heads." They circulated around the dance area again, scrutinising every coloured face they came across. Some got a bit hostile at their staring and would make suggestions like, "What the fuck do you want, weirdo?" It was half past ten when another noisy bunch entered the dance area, immediately making themselves known. The boys edged their way towards the entrance.

Greg suddenly hid behind Abbo. “Look, that one! It looks like her but her hair is Rasta now, not all frizzy.” The boys moved in to get a closer look, shielding Greg between them. They moved in close just as the music ended and the lights went up. An announcement from the stage was being made about glasses and bottles being carried onto the dance area. Also, some idiot had parked his car behind another one, blocking in someone who wanted to leave. Greg took advantage of the moment and moved in to get a good look at the coloured woman. It was her; he recognised her handbag and also a slight scar above her right eye. He tugged at Abbo’s arm. “It’s her. I know it is definitely her.”

Abbo moved in closer and so did Sid and Andy. The girl observed them and moved out of their way. Sid gave her a lovely smile. “Hi,” he said, moving slowly past her. The next minute she was amongst the dancers moving to the music and joining in the fun.

“Greg, you go and wait by the entrance so we know where you are.” Abbo looked at Sid. “You, my smiling friend, get on the dance floor and give chase. Chat her up, ask her a few innocent questions like, do you come here often? It’s my first time here. I come from Stoke; where do you come from? I drive a Mini but I’m looking for something else. What do you drive? What, a Mini Cooper? That’s what I’m looking for. Sid, get the chat on with her, ask her to show you her car. Does she want to sell it?”

Andy and Abbo moved around the floor, watching Sid chase their prey. He appeared to have made contact with her and was chatting away freely. Sid had always been a ladies man and could always talk the hind leg off a donkey. Abbo caught his eye and gave him a nod. The girl said something to Sid and moved away. “She’s just going for a piss,” said Sid. “I’m getting on well with her but she’s got to be going at 12 o’clock. I’ve asked her about her car and she does want to sell it. She’s got her eye on another. I’ll be going outside when she goes as I’m going to have a look at her car. Keep your eyes open for when we go out.”

The girl came back and resumed conversation with Sid. It was 11:45, Abbo and Andy moved towards the exit where

Greg was waiting. They told him to go and wait by their car. Andy also went outside. At 12 o'clock, Sid and the Columbian made their way to the exit. Abbo followed. He watched them move across the car park to where she had parked her car. Sid looked around it, showing great interest. As she opened the door to get in, Sid asked her to pop the bonnet up so that he could look at the engine. She did this and asked Sid if she could start the engine for him. Sid looked under the bonnet. He noticed the two shadowy figures getting out of the car that had just pulled in close by. Masked and in their bomber jackets, they moved in on the cow. Abbo got in behind the girl and grabbed hold of her. Andy got in the passenger seat. The girl screamed but the noise from the engine drowned out her screams. Abbo held his hand over her mouth as she struggled to bite him. He spoke to her and told her to be quiet or he would hurt her. Andy was searching around for the drugs cache and found a small case under the seat. Abbo talked to the girl who was still struggling. Sid had disappeared, which had been arranged. As Andy opened the case, Abbo eased his hand away so that the girl could breathe. Andy opened a bottle of tablets and poured some into his hand. He guessed these were the happy pills and began stuffing them into her mouth while Abbo held her firmly. Next, Andy opened some small packets that contained white powder. He poured three down her throat and washed it down with mineral water. The Columbian was like a wildcat, she clawed at Abbo trying to reach his face with her long nails. More water washed the powder down her throat and Andy popped a few more pills into her mouth. Abbo reached over and turned off the engine. Removing the keys, he told the girl that if she ever showed her face in Newcastle again, worse things would happen. He got out of the car and threw the keys into the darkness. Andy had emptied the contents of the case all over the interior of the car before getting out. Sid was sitting in their car with the engine running.

"Right, let's fuck off," said Abbo as they changed out of their bomber jackets. "Let's pick up Greg."

Sid pulled in at the first telephone box. "I'm just going to leave a message for the police."

***

Christine asked Billy if he wanted to go shopping in Stafford but he declined, saying he would look after the baby and he wanted to cut the lawns. "There's half a tank of petrol in the car, luv. You go on your own." Christine picked up the keys. She needed to go to *Matalans* for curtain material for Steven's room. They had moved his cot into the second bedroom now that he was a bit older and sleeping through the night. Billy had decorated the room with birds and animal pictures and made it nice for Steven.

She pulled into the half-empty car park and checked whether she had the list of things she needed. With her tape measure in her hand, she browsed around the store looking at different fabrics. As she wandered around the store, she caught sight of a familiar figure. It was Marianne. Christine's heart began pounding as she made her way through the shoppers to where Marianne was standing. Christine put her hand out to touch Marianne but suddenly noticed that Marianne was not on her own. Their eyes met and a huge smile greeted Christine. "Hello stranger, how are you?" Marianne's companion looked on. "This is Elizabeth, a friend from way back. She's been staying with me for a couple of weeks before she goes back to university."

Elizabeth reached out to shake hands with Christine. "Any friend of Marianne is a friend of mine," she said, holding onto Christine's hand. Christine couldn't help notice the marks on Elizabeth's neck. The tell-tale marks of Marianne in the throes of passion. She had sunk her teeth into Christine's breast, leaving a mark that Billy had queried. "It's the cat; she clawed me" had been her reply. So Marianne had found another playmate. *Well, that's how it goes in the lesbian world.* Christine made her excuses to depart quickly. Marianne gave her a hug. "We must meet up again," she whispered. "Here's my phone number, Christine, call me anytime, I've missed you." Christine left hurriedly, she wanted to get out of the store as quickly as possible; she didn't like being used.

***

Ray couldn't wait to hear how things had gone. He was waiting for the boys to get back. It was 1 o'clock when Abbo drove into the pub car park, having dropped off the boyfriend first. Ray jumped into the car. "How'd it go, mate?" he enquired.

"It went down well," said Sid. "We gave her the same treatment as that other bastard and by now, she should be in the hospital being pumped out or in a police cell banged up and being charged. It's been a good night, Ray, and the boyfriend did the job. You can forget him now, Ray; he's paid for his mistake."

Ray still had an angry look on his face, "But it doesn't bring our Jan back, Sid, does it?"

***

Peter met Susan early Saturday morning in Litchfield. "Where would you like to go today, Susan? How about a quick run up to Blackpool? I haven't been there for years."

Susan's eyes lit up. "Oh yes, Peter, that would be a nice change—if you don't mind the long drive?"

Switching on the ignition, he leaned over and planted a full-on kiss. "I'd drive to the ends of the earth for you, Susan."

She held onto him. "Would you, Peter? Do you mean that?" It was a two-hour drive and various issues were discussed. Peter told her an old friend from his motorbike scrambling days had telephoned him, enquiring how he was coping with the strike. Peter admitted that it had gone on for longer than anyone had expected and that he would be glad to get back to work. Martin, his friend, was a senior figure in a factory making earthmoving equipment. He said that if Peter was interested, maybe he could find Peter another job. He knew Peter had experience with hydraulics and one of

Martin's team of fitters was talking about moving to Australia. He would keep Peter informed and if it happened, he would contact Peter.

"That would be nice, Peter. There's no way they're going to let you have your old job back underground with your bad leg, are they?" Susan reached out for his hand and squeezed it.

Peter looked at her. "I had thought about looking elsewhere but now I've met you, I just wanted to remain close." Blackpool loomed up and Peter followed the directions. It hadn't taken that long and soon they were pulling up in a car park near the front. It was a nice morning and already the music from the fairground was reaching their ears. "Looks like they're getting ready for the illuminations. We must come for a long weekend when they're ready."

Susan said she had never seen them and it would be a nice treat. She tugged Peter's sleeve. "Buy me a candy floss, darling, I haven't had any of that since I was a little girl." Peter still limped slightly and Susan wondered just how painful it was for him to be walking around all day.

"No problem," he assured her. "The plates, nuts and bolts have settled down. I do still get days when I have to limit myself but the hospital keeps a check on me. I do find it awkward to dance though."

Susan acknowledged that her dancing days were over. "I have two left feet and no rhythm, so don't worry about that, darling."

***

The C.M.U. offices were buzzing with newspaper reporters as the president and his assistants entered the conference room. They took their places at the row of tables at the far end of the room, facing the rows of seats accommodating the media. The president called the meeting to order. In his hand, he held a piece of A4 paper. He stood up and held up the piece of paper. "Gentlemen, I have here a list of coalmines that have been nominated for closure by the government and the coal industry bosses. There are a total of seventy pits highlighted to be shut down. That means a lot of men being dumped on the scrap heap, thanks to the prime minister's American hatchet man. He's a millionaire and well-known in the States for his ruthlessness. At a cost of one million pounds, he was brought in by our government to oversee which pits were vulnerable for closure. Don't ask me where I got this information from as it's top secret and I dare the government to deny its existence. That's what this strike has been all about, the future of our industry and jobs of our miners. I do confess that some of these pits have been struggling with production due mainly to geological conditions, but the pits that have been successful in meeting their targets have been able to make up for the loss of production and on the whole, the industry is holding its own. If we can see these pits through their bad times, more than likely they will hold their own given time. We are a nationalised industry but unlike other countries, we are not subsidised by our government, we hold our own. I have informed the government and British Coal that we have called off the strike and are ready to return to work. Now let's see what they are going to do. But I will tell you this, within twenty years, there will be no coal industry in this country. We will be buying our coal from places like Russia and Bolivia where their miners work for a pittance. Our mines are deep coalmines and it is an arduous task, but for many years, our brave miners have kept this country on its feet, but now you will see changes. The coal industry will see the power stations change over to gas turbines. Now let's see what happens when our North Sea gas runs out. Your electricity bills will go up and everything else will follow, mark my words, gentlemen. This country has lost everything it once had: shipbuilding, steel works, car manufacturing and the motorcycle industry. The only thing we are good at is making war, even amongst ourselves. Thank you, gentlemen."

The room erupted in loud applause as the president left the meeting. "Well, I didn't expect that," he said, entering his office. "Now let's see what's going to happen."

***

The pit was a hive of activity as the miners returned to work but there was an air of despondency as the miners clashed. Some made angry remarks but everybody was glad it was all over and that over a period of time, everything would return to normal.

Peter walked into the office and was greeted by John and Allan. "Let's have a cuppa before we start," suggested John.

"I got some milk from the canteen," said Allan.

"Has anybody brought any tea?" asked Peter. Blank looks and then John produced a jar of coffee and a packet of PG Tips.

"You have to get your priorities right," he beamed.

"I bet you've spent every Friday at the *Grab a Grannie* disco," mused Allan, winking at Peter.

"Well, you have to keep in touch with people," said John, "and find out what's happening in life."

Allan started laughing. "And are you still shagging that blonde from Litchfield?"

The train driver blew his whistle as the last of the men got into the train. Abbo started dealing the cards. Ray sat next to him with Sid and Andy sitting opposite. Billy shouted, "How's your dad, Abbo?" There was silence as the train pulled around a bend. The noise made it impossible to hear anything, but once back on the straight; Abbo shouted back, "Not so good, they are having him back in hospital for more treatment. It's a concern."

Harry dealt the cards, listening to the conversation. Norman said they would have to find a replacement for Alf. "It doesn't look good for him," added Billy. "I've known Alf since I first started down the pit. We've been good mates, they don't come any better."

Chapter 12
A New Beginning

Christine heaved a sigh of relief as she heard Billy leave for work. "At last," she murmured to herself. "Now I can do what I want without him creeping around feeling my arse." She had appreciated the fact that when Billy had been at home, she had free use of the car, which was handy, but now she felt bogged down with only a buggy to push around the town. She needed to go into Stafford again to *Matalans*. She only had one option and that was to go by bus. The problems were the buggy and Steven; it was hard work coping with both. She decided to phone Mam and ask if she would have Steven for a couple of hours. Mam was delighted so Christine made her way through the estate to big smiles and open arms. Quickly, she made her way back into town just as the Stafford bus was coming in. She had been thinking what would happen if she bumped into Marianne; she tingled a bit with excitement at the very thought. Maybe it wouldn't hurt just to see her for a quick chat. She searched her handbag for the piece of paper with Marianne's telephone number on it. When the bus dropped her off in Stafford, Christine started looking around for a payphone but she couldn't find one. Sadly, she made her way to the shopping centre and to *Matalans*. She quickly found what she wanted. At the pay counter, she asked the assistant where the nearest payphone was. The assistant said there was one in store for customers to use and it was just past the toilet area. She made sure she had some change and went to look for the phone. She dialled the number and waited. Her heart was beating fast as she held the phone. It seemed a

long time ringing and she was about to hang up when Marianne's voice came on. "It's Christine, Marianne; I'm just doing a bit of shopping at *Matalans*. Do you fancy a coffee?"
"My God, Christine, my prayers have been answered." Christine said she would have to wait for Marianne outside the shop, as she did not have the car today. "I've just got out of the shower, Christine, give me ten minutes and I'll come and pick you up." Christine started to feel excited seeing Marianne again but she only meant to have a coffee at the nearby café.

Marianne's car pulled up in the car park and a warm greeting called from an open door. "Come on, Christine." She bundled her shopping into the car and sat looking at Marianne. She couldn't help noticing how beautiful she looked and her perfume was intoxicating. Christine leaned over as Marianne reached out for her. She planted a kiss on Christine's lips. She turned on the ignition and reversed out. Christine felt the tingling sensation again.

"I just thought we could have a coffee," said Christine in a sort of unconvincing tone.

Marianne looked at her and giggled. "Yes, I'll make you a coffee if that's what you want." She drove to her apartment and led the way to the door. Christine followed her inside. Marianne took her coat off and then helped Christine with hers. She reached out for Christine and put her arms around her waist, drawing her to her. Christine didn't resist and put her arms around Marianne. "I've missed you, Christine, please say you have missed me."

Their lips met and Christine felt the urge to fondle Marianne. Soon they were lying on the bed naked as each gave way to their desires. Marianne had reached under her pillow and pulled out one of her toys. She inserted the dildo into Christine and gently manoeuvred it. They kissed passionately and fondled each other. Christine was almost at her peak when Marianne rolled over on her back and gave Christine her toy. "I've never used one of these, Marianne, what do I do?"

Marianne guided her hands. “Just fuck me with it, Christine, like I did to you.” They played with each other amidst their moans of ecstasy. Christine had never felt like this with Billy, he was like a bull at a gate when he mounted her and rolled off when he satisfied himself. Marianne took her time and explored her body in different ways and both would reach their peak together. Marianne eased off Christine. “Let’s have a short break, I’ll make the coffee.” They sat on the bed talking girlie talk and drinking their coffee. Marianne said she hadn’t seen anyone for a while. The insurance company had extended her area and it was usually late evening by the time she got home.

“Don’t you see Elizabeth at all?” Christine asked.

“No, she only comes occasionally on holidays. She has her own pad at the uni and she has her own friends. No, I’ve been going without the physical stuff for quite a while; that’s why I’m so hungry for you, Christine.” She took the empty cups into the kitchen. When she returned, she was carrying her small case with her. She looked at Christine. “I need to exercise my stallion,” she said, removing the black rubber harness and large rubber penis. “I want you to fuck me first, fast and furious, Christine. Give it to me, girl, I need it.” She helped Christine put it on and then lay back, waiting anxiously. “It is self-lubricating, Christine, go straight in hard and fast. That’s how I want it.”

Marianne moaned in ecstasy as Christine rode her. “Don’t bite me this time,” she whispered, “my husband noticed the marks on my boobs. I blamed the cat.”

Marianne relaxed after a hectic session. “Now your turn, Christine, and I know just how you like it.”

Marianne put her toys away after making sure Christine had orgasmed and finally wore a smile on her face. “Come on; a quick shower and I’ll drop you off at the bus station. Remember, Christine, anytime, just give me a call.”

***

Abbo and the boys met up in the pub. Sid was carrying the Staffordshire newsletter. “Have a read of this,” he said, smiling. Ray reached over and opened the paper, laying it on the table. "There," said Sid, "I've marked it."

The boys gathered around Ray, straining their necks. '*A breakthrough on the drug pushers*' was the headline. "A Columbian drug pusher was arrested last week when an anonymous tip-off informed the police that she was crawling around on her hands and knees in the car park of a well-known disco haunt. She was completely knocked out on drugs and had to be hospitalised overnight so that the contents of her stomach could be emptied. A further investigation revealed that her car was full of drugs, albeit tipped out all over the inside of the vehicle. She claimed she had been attacked by guys trying to rob and rape her, but no evidence of this was found. It was also revealed that she travelled around various discos supplying drugs and had, in fact, been at the one in Stafford on the night that the girl had died and that probably it was her who had been selling the happy pills. Police have her in custody and will be charging her with drug dealing and selling the happy pills that killed the girl. A police spokesman said she would be facing a long spell in jail."

Ray congratulated his mates on a job well done. "I'll buy the beer," he said.

"There's nothing about the other one we did at Tackeroo," said Andy. "No, not yet, but they will be getting their heads together. It's obvious that it's a similar attack, especially the anonymous calls to the cops," said Ray. "Which means we've gotta be very careful in future. Let's lie low for a while."

***

Peter showed the people around his flat. It was the second enquiry, this time an elderly couple downsizing from a three-bedroom house. They seemed interested. Peter rang Susan. "I've just had a second couple viewing and they did seem interested. Have you had anybody yet?"

She said she hadn't but the neighbours told her that someone had been looking and had driven past twice.

"Probably over the weekend whilst we were in Blackpool." Peter suggested looking for a place for Susan to move into and mentioned he had seen an advert for apartments in a new complex not far away. Perhaps this weekend would be ideal. The weather promised a wet weekend. "Yes darling, we had a lovely time at Blackpool; perhaps it's time to start looking around." They agreed that's what they would do and Susan would drive over to Peter's flat.

***

Harry pushed himself through the waiting fitters to where the assistant engineer was booking them in and deploying them. "Ah Harry, we're short of a face fitter to cover the face. Jack has hurt his back and will be off for a spell. Can you fill in for him?" Harry said he didn't mind but his tools were in the Rock Head. "I've got the key to Jack's box; he sent it in this morning. Thanks Harry."

The train was waiting in the pit bottom. Billy moved over to make room. "Alf passed away yesterday evening," he announced solemnly. "It was a sad old time watching him die. We have been mates for years. He took me under his wing when I had finished my training."

The mood was disturbing and no card games were played. "That's why Abbo isn't at work today," said Andy.

Harry announced that he had been deployed to the coalface for a while and if they wanted a fitter, they would have to call someone. He watched as the men got out at their destinations. He knew most of the face team, having done the occasional cover when Jack had been off. He didn't mind the face; it was a retreat face, which meant they only lasted so long and then everything was dismantled and moved on to a new one.

Jack's box held everything, even a couple of sex magazines. He picked up the tool bag and moved down to where the men were stripping off their shirts before going onto the face. He knew Jack was a good fitter and kept on top of the maintenance work. The power went in and the machines started cutting. Harry sat down and checked the tool bag.

***

It was Wednesday evening when Peter's phone rang. Expecting it to be Susan, he lifted the receiver and said, "Hello darling."

The man on the other end said, "Don't get personal, Peter, its Martin."

Peter burst out laughing. "Sorry Martin, I didn't expect it to be you." Martin asked Peter if he was still interested in a job. "Oh yes, mate, why, has anything come up?"

Martin said that the man who had been going to Australia had definitely made up his mind and announced that in six months' time, he would be leaving. "So how about if I pick you up on Saturday afternoon and show you around the factory and talk job prospects?"

Peter was over the moon and he couldn't wait to phone Susan. She too was excited. The estate agents wanted to show an interested couple over the house. Susan had agreed that Saturday afternoon would be fine. "So darling, we're both going to be busy on Saturday. Well, we will have a lot to talk about. I think you must come over to my place. I'll cook you a meal and we will have a night in. How about that, Susan?"

She giggled happily. "Yes darling, that sounds good."

Peter waited anxiously for Martin to arrive on Saturday afternoon. He had kept quiet about Martin's offer. His workmates would be told if anything developed. Nothing had been decided yet. Martin arrived at 2 o'clock and pulled up next to Peter's car. "OK mate, hop in. It's good to see you again. Just like the old days, eh?" Martin had given up the scrambling. "I've got two young children now to look after and they keep me on the go," he said. They talked about the good old days as they made their way to Uttoxeter. Martin was saying that he had been there quite a while and found it a good company to work for. He eased the car into the car park and climbed out. "Here we are, Peter, look at that lot all destined for the eastern countries. They are one of our best customers." Peter looked at rows of heavy-duty machinery at the rear of the factory, all kinds of earthmoving equipment and mobile cranes. "We have some very rich customers, Peter, and they like what we make." They walked around the factory. Martin unlocked a door and showed Peter inside. "This is the assembly line and this is where the hydraulics are fitted. You would be a part of the hydraulics team and I would be your supervisor. I'm sure you would be happy here, Peter, as we have a good team second to none."

"Has a job come up yet, Martin, for definite?" Peter asked.

"Yes, it has and you are my choice to fill the vacancy, that's if you are interested."

Peter admired the cleanliness of the place and said how different it was to what he had been used to. "What are the wages like?" he asked. Martin explained that Peter would start on a six-month course under supervision on basic pay, which he said would be comparable to what Peter was earning now. After six months, he would be reassessed and then regraded accordingly if everything worked out. Peter could be on the full rate within six to twelve months. Peter said it sounded acceptable. Martin said he would arrange an interview with his bosses with a recommendation by him. They walked around a bit more and then Martin suggested a beer to celebrate and talk about old times.

***

Joe backed the car out of the lock-up. It was an exhibition of caravans this time, Static Holiday Vans and Tourers. He had been before but not for a long time and he was looking forward to it. He rang Janet first but when she answered, he noticed a disappointing tone. "Sorry Joe, I've just started my monthlies, but I've got a friend who will make up the number. Her name's Val and she's a blonde bombshell. I'm sure you will be pleased; she knows what's what, I mean. She's here with me now. Are you OK with that?"

Joe was disappointed as he liked to organise things. "Yeah OK, as long as she knows the score. Be there in five minutes." Joe pulled up outside her flat and Janet appeared with her friend. He couldn't help notice how attractive she was. Janet introduced Val and opened the front passenger door for Val to get in.

"She will be OK, Joe, she knows the score."

Val smiled at Joe. "Janet says she's been with you for quite a while, Joe."

He smiled back at her. "Yes, we've been a team for at least three years. It works quite well and provides us all with an income." Denise and Veronica made acquaintance with Val and they all chatted away freely as Joe headed for the Welsh border.

The exhibition was in a large field and the caravans were in long rows across the field. The parking lots were marked out with ribbons and a special place for the exhibitors. Joe dealt out the brochures and samples he had sent off for and gave them the sales patter. "Carpets and curtains we sell this time, girls, do your best and hook 'em in." Val looked at Joe. "You will come with me," he said. "My secretary on this occasion." As she got out of the car, Joe noticed a good pair of legs and a good arse. "You'll have no problem, Val."

Veronica asked Joe where the hotels were. "There aren't any; each rep has their own private caravan over there." He pointed to a row of flags. "Just beyond those flags."

Denise and Veronica led the way to where the rows of caravans were sited. 'Sales Area' marked the beginning. "Don't forget your bonuses," remarked Joe. He led Val into the huge marquee where the reps were gathered. He introduced himself and Val to a couple of reps at the entrance. Obviously, they were ready to pounce on anyone looking interested. One rep immediately looked Val up and down. "Can I show you anything?" he asked. Joe said they would like to look around the caravans. The rep immediately took Val's arm. "Allow me to guide you around our displays."

Joe followed for a while and then said he would go and chat to a few more reps while his secretary was being shown around. “My name is Rodney,” said her guide. “I’m the sales manager’s assistant.”

Val smiled sheepishly. “Am I going to be safe with you, Rodney, now that my boss has gone?”

Rodney beamed a broad smile. “As safe as you want to be,” he said with a twinkle in his eye. “It’s early yet, hardly anybody around, it will get busier later on.”

“Which is your caravan?” Val asked, as she manoeuvred past him, brushing her body against him.

“It’s over there. Would you like to see it?” he asked.

“Just a quick visit,” said Val. “I have to circulate and get orders or I don’t get my hundred pound bonus.” Rodney took her arm and with a quick look around, escorted her along the row of caravans to where the reps’ caravans were sited. Once inside, he put his arm around her waist and guided her through the door into the bedroom. “Oh Rodney, this is cosy and look at that bed. I could just flop on there.”

Rodney sat her on the bed and sat beside her. “Val, I’ve got to be honest; I fancy you like mad.”

He pushed her back into a lying position. “Rodney, I can’t, I have to get back to work. I’ve got to earn my bonus. My cooker has packed up and I need to earn my bonus to get a new one. Oh Rodney, if only…”

With that, Rodney stood up and took out his wallet. “There!” he said, placing five crisp twenties on the bed. ”There’s your bonus, Val.”

Quickly, Val picked up the money. “All right, Rodney, thank you.” She started stripping off; Rodney was already down to his briefs and standing proud.

***

Harry worked his way along the coal face. It was safe at the moment as the machine was in the ‘main gate’. The chocks had already been pushed over for the machine to cut into the ‘tailgate’. Harry noticed the big expanse in the waste. The roof hadn’t dropped yet, leaving a void that you could get two coaches parked side by side. The machine had started on its return to the tailgate. Harry moved back down the face, watching the big drums rip into the coal face. Occasionally, the tailgate drum would shudder violently as it bit into the coal face. Harry wondered why it did that as the coal didn't show any signs of rock where the drum was cutting. He followed the machine into the tailgate. He asked the machine man if he had noticed it. "Yes, it's been doing that all morning." Harry asked if he could examine the machine when it was in the tailgate before the machine was pushed over.

"Leave the drum clear so I can just take a look." The machine man obliged and Harry looked at the ranging end. He asked the machine man to lift the drum up and down a bit. As he did, Harry noticed that a huge plate that secured the ranging end to the body of the machine was moving. It was obvious it had loosened. "I'll have to look at that at snap time," he told the machine man. "Can you arrange to bring the machine back into the tailgate at snap time and leave the drum raised? I'll tell the deputy what I want to do."

Harry went to the toolbox and sorted out the large sockets and ratchet and also the intensifier.

Chapter 13
Trapped

The machine man brought the machine down the face to within twenty yards of the tailgate before the panzer chain stopped. "That's fine, I can get to it there but lift the drum up and I want to put two pack blocks under it just in case it drops when the power's out." Harry crawled under the drum with his tools and began to block the drum up. He hadn't noticed but the machine was opposite the waste that hadn't dropped. George, the deputy, came down to the face and asked Harry if he was all right. "Yes, I'm fine. It won't take me long just to tighten up these bolts." Harry began going around the ring of bolts with the socket set. They were all loose. No wonder the drum had been vibrating. He began going around again with the intensifier. Suddenly, the place began to shake and an almighty crack shook the whole place. There was a huge bang as the waste dropped. The chocks were pushed forward and the machine began to tilt in towards the face. Dust filled the air as more rock came down. Another crack and the face line began to move. A huge slab came away from the face and leaned over towards the machine that was leaning into the face. Harry covered his face as the dust cloud covered him. He tried to move but he was trapped face downward with the machine leaning over him and a huge slab of coal poised precariously above him. Through the dust, he could just make out lights as the face team and George rushed to see what had happened. Amidst the choking dust, he could hear someone calling his name. Harry tried to shout but the dust had smothered his whole face. He was choking and couldn't speak. He cleared the dust from his eyes and spat out the dust. Again he heard someone calling out to him. The blocks were still under the drum and Harry tried to clear away the debris so that he could see the lights from the cap lamps. They were just in the tailgate and trying to assess what had happened. Harry waved his light to them but could not speak. He coughed and spluttered, trying to clear his throat. George ventured a couple of yards further, calling out to Harry. It was unsafe to come any further. Harry tried to check whether he was all right. He was lying face down between the panzer conveyor and the face. He found he could just about wriggle his body but any movement seemed to bring more debris down on him. Slowly, he began to clear away what he could in front of him. The wooden chocks had moved but still seemed to be supporting the huge drum. Bit by bit, he cleared away the small stuff, throwing it behind him. His legs had been free but now he was covering them with debris, but at least he could move them slightly and nothing seemed broken. In front of him, between the machine and the tailgate, pieces were still dropping from the roof. Finally, he managed to call out, "George, I'm all right, not hurt, but I'm trapped behind the machine; I can't get out. George, I could do with some water, the dust is choking me."

George flashed his light to let Harry know he had heard him. Turning to the face charge hand, he said, "See if you can find anything we can use to get him some water. I'm going up into the main gate to phone the manager and get a rescue team down here. Get some safety lamps on the face and keep checking for gas. Those wastes are full of it and I'm going to get the fan extended so we can get more air down the face. We have got an emergency situation here and we need supplies. Chock blocks, wooden trees and split bars. We've got to shore up this face line and try to get to Harry."

***

The C.M.U. president addressed the meeting. "There have been no promises made by the government. They have just rejoiced in the media and on TV that they were adamant they would defeat the miners and would not tolerate being held to ransom. They ignored questions on pit closures and said it was their intention to make the industry profitable. I have been invited by a television company to appear on TV and answer questions. I intend to do that and I promise to wipe the smile off the PM's face."

Dennis took two paracetamol and got into his car. Gladys and Sylvia were on reception when he arrived at the Sherwood. "Well, when did you get back?" he asked a smiling Gladys.

"Only an hour ago. Henry was tired so we had a few extra days. I'm back on duty now and Sylvia is about to go home, aren't you, dear?"

Sylvia shook hands with Dennis. "It's been nice seeing you, Dennis. See you next time."

Gladys gave Dennis the key. "I'll just see Sylvia to her car and then I'll pop up and come see you, Dennis." A few minutes later, she arrived with a tray. "I bet you're ready for this after that long meeting?" The steaming hot coffee was just what he needed but he anticipated Gladys was ready for something else as she moved in closer and put her arms around his neck.

"Later Gladys, I've got a splitting headache and I'm so tired."

She said she understood and would see him later. "Have a good rest, Dennis. I'll close the curtains; it will make it easier to go to sleep. I'll see you later."

***

Abbo carried the drinks from the bar and placed them on the table. "How's things, Ray? What a morning we've had. I don't know how many loads of timber and blocks we've sent into the backend. I've heard there's a problem on the face with someone trapped."

Ray took a sip of beer. "I've heard it's Harry, the fitter. It must be serious as the rescue team and the manager have been there quite a while and the loco driver is on standby." They looked up as Sid and Andy joined them. "There's a bit of a panic at the pit; something's going on. I've never seen so much timber going into the backend." Ray changed the subject. "Our Dave reckons somebody's pushing drugs at school. He's seen kids in the school playground darting into the bushes, not with girls but with small packages. He thinks it's drugs and someone on the outside dealing through the fence at lunchtime. He's going to find out if he can what the score is."

Andy shook his head. "We've got to stop that, these kids don't know what they're getting into. Ask Dave to hide in the bushes and find out who the pusher is, Ray. We'll take the bastard out."

***

The manager watched as another supply of pack blocks were passed along the face where once the hydraulic chocks had been. It looked like a wall of wooden blocks from floor to roof. There had been a space left for the digger to get in and dig a trench close to the face. Timber had been placed to support the slab of coal that had come away and was threatening to topple over. "How far are they in now?" someone asked.

George said, "About ten metres, it's slow going as it's such a delicate operation."

The manager enquired about Harry. "Is he getting food and water and is he still conscious?"

George said he had just been talking to him. "He said he stinks of urine because he has to piss where he is lying and he dreads the thought of what he would do if he needs to crap." The manager asked about ventilation. "It's OK; we've got good airflow and we are constantly checking for gas."

"How long has it been now?" a voice asked.

George looked at his watch. "It happened at 10 o'clock and it's 4 o'clock now so he's been there for six hours," replied George. "And we're only halfway to getting him out."

The manager shook his head. "It's that slab of coal that broke away. We've got to be very careful; if that moves any further, it will bury him." Another load of blocks was brought in.

"At least he's got a sense of humour," said George. "He asked if he was being paid overtime and could we get him home before 9 o'clock or he will miss the boxing on TV."

The manager said he would go up the pit and see Harry's wife who had been brought to the pit top. "I'll be back later."

The rescuers changed over. "That floor is rock hard," said one of the diggers. "It's hard going."

George sat down on a pile of blocks and ate his snap. "Poor old Harry. He's not a young man but he's a tough old bloke."

The face charge hand sat down beside George and took a drink of water. "He's a big bloke; we shall have to open up the trench when we get a bit closer. It's those blocks he put under the drum; they will have to come out for him to crawl under the drum. I'm worried in case the drum comes down when we remove them."

George agreed the situation was precarious. "And he keeps dropping off to sleep. We must keep him awake or we won't know if he's lost consciousness or not. Try to keep someone up front to keep him talking."

***

Susan came home from work to find Peter's car in her drive. She hadn't seen him all day so she was quite pleased. He was sitting in his car, reading a letter. "Hi Susan. I've come to show you this letter from Martin. I've got a job interview next week and he says I'm the only one to be granted an interview. Things are looking promising."

Susan read the letter. "Oh, I do hope you get the job, Peter, it will be another new start for our future together." As she opened the front door, she bent down to pick up the mail. She tore open the one from the estate agent. "An offer has been made on the house, Peter, that's ticked another box in our favour. Now we must find something for me to rent temporarily until yours is sold."

Peter stayed and helped Susan prepare the evening meal. There were lots of things to talk about. "You could just move in with me," suggested Peter. "It will save you rent money."

Susan looked hurt. "I know, Peter, but you know we haven't known each other for that long. I want to be sure before I commit myself to another marriage so soon after getting divorced. I hope you don't feel badly about this, darling. I do love you, I want to marry you, and I will marry you but just let me have a little more time to myself. A year and I'll know for sure that everything will be fine."

***

Val met up with Joe and the two other girls. "Everything all right?" he asked her.

She smiled. "Yes Joe, all went well and if I wanted to stay the night, he would make it worth my while, but I told him I had to get home to my sick mother."

Veronica asked if Joe wanted Val in the front seat. "Of course he does," said Denise, smiling. They all agreed that these exhibitions were easy pickings and better than standing on street corners and trawling the pubs. Joe pushed the BMW and soon they were back in Litchfield. Denise was first and then Veronica. "Have fun," she said, leaving the car.

Joe looked at Val. "Of course we will."

Val guided Joe to where her flat was and he pulled up in her parking space. "Is it coffee or tea, Joe?" she asked, opening the door that led to her second-story flat. Joe said he liked his coffee. Val smiled. "Yes, Janet said you had a thirst that needed to be quenched." Joe entered the living room and looked around the modestly furnished room. "I'll just put the kettle on, Joe, everything is ready in the kitchen. I won't be long." Joe watched as she disappeared into the bedroom. He popped a blue tablet in his mouth and waited for the kettle to boil. Val appeared in the bedroom doorway with just a bath towel covering her naked form. "Won't be long, Joe, enjoy your coffee."

Joe walked around the flat, sipping the steaming hot coffee. He wandered into the bedroom and noticed that the curtains had been drawn and the bedclothes peeled back. He returned the empty cup to the kitchen and made his way into the bedroom where he stripped off and lay on the bed. Val entered the bedroom completely naked. Joe noticed that she was a genuine blonde. Val joined him on the bed. "I can see you are anxious to fuck, Joe. What will it be—normal or doggy or do you want oral?" Joe said the choice could be hers. She laid him on his back and played with him before straddling him. "I'll give you a Sharon Stone if you like." Joe moaned with ecstasy as she manoeuvred her body. Before he left the flat, he asked Val if she wanted to be a part of the team. Reluctantly, she declined, saying that she really did have a sick mother in a flat down below and that she was her mother's carer, but would be willing to step in if any of the other girls were indisposed.

***

Dave crept into the bushes surrounding the school playground. He found several couples groping each other frantically as he made his way along the fence. He recognised the one they called Kev, talking to two eager youngsters no more than thirteen years old. Soon a fiver was being exchanged for a small package. Dave retreated; he'd seen enough. Kev was the one who had disclosed the information on the Columbian so Dave figured someone was supplying him.

***

Billy announced to his workmates that he would be leaving early on Friday morning to attend Alf's funeral and asked if anybody else wanted to join him. The other three men said they would and would arrange it with the deputy for 'early notes'. They would finish and be up the pit by 1 o'clock. If the funeral was arranged for 2:30, they could make it easily. Billy was pleased and said he would take them in his car and bring them back for their cars after. Abbo hadn't been at work all week. He said there was a lot of running about to be done and his mother was too upset to do anything so he and his sister were arranging things and a gathering in the clubhouse had been laid on for after and all were welcome.

***

Harry tried to move his legs. He was getting painful cramps, which were excruciating. He could see the man digging away no more than six feet away. What was taking the time was that all the dirt from the trench had to be passed back to another digger and so on; battening was time consuming and warm work. "Hi Harry," said Chris, one of the face workers. Harry could just make out his sweaty face through the void where his two pack blocks he had placed had taken the weight of the drum. "Won't be long now, mate. How's things?"

Harry said he would be glad when he was out. The cramps were terrible and so was the smell of urine. "I need a shower and a shit, whichever comes first will be a relief."

The digging continued. A new lamp and more water were passed through to Harry via a shot-firers cable that had been poked through on a long pole. Harry struggled to change his lamp but decided just to hold it in from of him. "Hi Harry, it's Rob, captain of the rescue team. How are you feeling, mate? We're going to pass you a small bottle of oxygen and a mask. If you are feeling groggy, just put on the mask and take a whiff. We're going to get you out soon, Harry. The worst is over. We've just got to get you through this narrow space between the blocks. We might have to knock them out, Harry. Can you tell if the beam is resting on them or on the block of coal that's come down?"

Harry shone his lamp and looked at the blocks. "The one is right under the drum on the coal side but the one on the panzer side could be taken out so that the machine is leaning into the coal but is being supported by the drum leaning into the coals. I'll try and poke around it and see how it is."

Harry took a whiff of oxygen, which helped make him a bit more conscious. He then started to poke around the block on the panzer side. The cramps in his legs started again, causing him a lot of pain. He was also getting pain from his arse from fighting the need to crap.

Another hour passed before two men appeared within reaching distance of Harry. They tested the blocks and said, "Harry, if we remove the panzer side block, can you tell if anything is going to fall on you? We don't want to bury you."

"I don't think so. The face side block seems to be taking the weight. The only trouble is I might not be able to squeeze through. I've got broad shoulders."

The digger talked to his mate. "Harry, can you turn on your side and we'll help you through. We will dig a bit deeper under the drum. It will give you a bit more room to manoeuvre."

The manager appeared and looked at the now deeper trench. "Harry, we are going to try and pull you out now. Can you reach out so that we can grasp your hand?" Harry stretched out his arms as far as he could. The manager reached forward and took hold of Harry's hands. "Right, Harry, if you can push with your feet when I pull you and twist your shoulders as you come through into the trench, I think we'll have you out." Harry pushed himself forwards, twisting as best as he could. He was now under the drum and pushing himself forwards as much as he could. Slowly, he felt himself slide into the trench. A sigh of relief as he felt himself being lifted onto the stretcher. "Right, let the doctor check him out and then let's get him to the hospital," the manager said, kneeling down beside the stretcher.

Harry opened his eyes and looked at the tunnel of blocks through which he had just passed. *Looks like a timber yard down here*, he thought. The ambulance was waiting as the stretcher was carried across the pit top. The doctor had given Harry an injection to help with the pain and cramps in his legs. Harry felt himself drifting in and out of consciousness. His mind drifted as one by one his demons passed through his mind. Pat, his cousin, and then Ron and Johnnie entered his mind. He felt a soft hand stroking his face as his wife comforted him on the way to the hospital. Harry fought hard to see his show of chrysanthemums. It had been a good year and everyone had told him how beautiful they were. He blinked at the bright lights as he was wheeled through the hospital corridor. Again the soft hand brushed his face.

***

Susan asked Peter if he wanted to stay the night and then they could go and look at a flat that had come up suddenly. "It's in the town above a shop. The estate agent is meeting me there at 11 o'clock."

Peter said, "Yes, I'd love to come and see it, darling."

A quick breakfast of toast and coffee and they were ready to go. "I bet the neighbours will start talking when they see you leaving my house with me. They will have noticed that your car has been here all night." Susan gave him a broad smile.

"Who cares about neighbours?" answered Peter.

They met up with the estate agent and were led up a flight of stairs to the flat. "It's a bit small," said Peter, walking around the one bedroom.

"It's only temporary," exclaimed Susan.

"What about all your belongings?" queried Peter.

"In storage. I'll just bring what is necessary," replied Susan. "I could start moving in tomorrow, it is vacant?"

The estate agent looked at Susan. "It is partially furnished. I believe all you would need is a new bed. The previous tenant took his own bed with him. The rest goes with the flat, including the washing machine and tumble dryer."

Susan took Peter's arm. "What about it, Peter, will you help me move in?"

Peter asked about parking spaces. "There are two at the rear of the shop," came the reply, "and the flat has immediate possession."

Peter looked at Susan. "OK darling, let's do it."

***

Rosie got up and switched off the telly. "That film wasn't much good. I thought it was a sex film. Not much sex there nor here, Joe. Are you still taking those Viagra?"

Joe let the cat out as Rosie made for the stairs. "Don't be too long, Joe." He lit a cigarette and walked up the garden path. It seemed as if Rosie was in for a night of passion. He felt in his waistcoat pocket and popped in a blue tablet. His mind was on Val, what a fuck she had been. If only Rose was built like her. The cat returned and ran into the house. Joe looked up. With his thoughts of Val and the blue tablet, Joe climbed the stairs. Rosie was already in bed and Joe could see that her nightie was on the floor at the side of the bed. He crawled into bed, hoping Rosie had gone to sleep but her groping hands soon found her target as she pulled Joe towards her. Joe groaned, "Mind my back, Rosie."

***

Dave waited for his mates at the school gates. They chatted away freely as they walked through the estate. Soon they were joined by Kev. He was an uninvited person but the kind that would latch on to anyone. Straight away, he got into conversation with Dave and his mates, boasting about his conquest with the girls. He mentioned that he was getting a motor scooter when he was seventeen so that he could join his two brothers at weekends, zooming all over the place. One of the lads asked what bikes his brothers had. "A Suzuki and a Yamaha," boasted Kev ecstatically. "The Yamaha is the best; it will carry two easily." He then gave a quiet laugh. "We used it during the strike for a special job."

Dave broke away and cut through the estate. His mind was searching for information around the time when a chunk of concrete had dropped on a police convoy from a motorway bridge, almost killing a transit vanload of police reinforcements making their way to the picket lines at Armitage Colliery. The culprits had escaped on motorbikes. Dave waited for Ray to come home and told him what he had heard Kev say. “We need definite proof of that, Dave. You know what a bragger Kev is.”

Chapter 14
Moving on

Dave thought for a while. “How are we going to get proof? They’re not going to admit it even if it was them. I bet the police are still looking for them.”

Ray admitted that if they could prove it was them, then they could grab Kev and use it to get him off the drug pushing. “Keep talking to him, Dave, but don’t show too much interest or he’ll get suspicious.”

***

The team met in the car park. Billy said they had plenty of time and suggested a pint in the club. “I think I’m going to need one,” he said as he turned the key in the ignition.

“A good idea,” echoed Norman. They quenched their thirst and Billy drove through the estate to where a line of cars was parked outside Alf’s house. Abbo seemed to be in charge of organising things.

“Won’t be long, Billy, the hearse is on its way. We’re all set to go.”

The hearse drew up a few minutes later and the floral tributes were loaded. Abbo held his mother’s arm as she was led to the front car of the cortege. As they drove away, the street was lined with friends and relatives who stood solemnly to see Alf leave. “I shall miss my mate,” said Billy. “He looked after me when I got a job at the pit.”

The cars pulled up at the church and made their way into the grounds where they lined the way up to the door. The floral tributes were placed around the entrance. The coffin was placed on a trolley and gently pushed towards the doors. Abbo led his mother behind the coffin into the church and they sat in the front pews. The mourners followed and took their appropriate places. Abbo's sister sat next to her mother and her tears were uncontrollable. Abbo reached over and comforted her and his mother. As the vicar spoke solemnly, a hushed crowd listened to the tributes being paid to Alf. When the service was over in the church, the mourners made their way out to their cars, ready to follow the coffin to the crematorium where another short service was given. Billy touched Alf's coffin as it was moving slowly towards the curtains. "See you, mate," he whispered.

At the clubhouse, Abbo was greeting the mourners as they arrived. Billy gave him a hug. "It was a good send-off, Abbo. You done your dad proud."

***

Peter helped Susan pack her things ready for the move. "Derek didn't want any of this stuff," she said. "So what I don't need at the moment is going into a storage warehouse. We can sort out our requirements when we move into our home, can't we, Peter?"

A few car journeys later, they were organising Susan's new abode. "Not far to the shops from here," said an excited Susan, "and not far to work."

Peter agreed that for a short period it was ideal but added that for their permanent residence, he wanted something better for her. He said he would stay the night with her to see if everything was OK. The following morning, he had an appointment to see Martin at the factory. He drove through the gates and pulled up at reception. Within minutes, he was being shown into Martin's office. "Congratulations, Peter, you've got the job as my assistant. You can start whenever you like, my friend. Welcome aboard."

***

After the doctors had examined Harry, his wife asked if she could get him washed and cleaned up. The nurses said they would get it organised. Harry was still tired even after a long sleep and was somewhat confused. "Post-traumatic stress," the nurses had told her. "He'll be with us for a few days to see how he copes with it. If we can undress him and get him into a chair, we can wheel him into a shower cubicle. We can shower him or you can, if you wish?"

Harry's wife declined. "He's too heavy for me to maul with him. I'm sure he'll enjoy the nurses doing it."

Harry felt half-asleep as he was being undressed. He was half-aware of what was going on when the warm water from the shower hit his body. He thought he was in the showers at the pit but could not understand whose hands were sponging him down. He felt himself being lifted up and his lower half being targeted with the sponge. Finally, he was washed down with cool water and sat down in the chair. As the huge bath towel dried him off, he was aware of two young nurses fussing over him. "Am I in heaven or what?" he asked. Finally, he was dressed in a white hospital gown and returned to the ward.

His wife sat at the side of the bed. "I bet you enjoyed that," she said smiling. "You look more like my husband now."

The doctor came back and said, "You must feel a little better for that, Harry. Now we can check you over thoroughly. No bones broken, heartbeat slightly raised with blood pressure and pulse normal. How do you feel in yourself, Harry?"

He looked at the doctor, a puzzled look on his face. "Why am I here? Have I missed the boxing?"

His wife leaned over and held his hand. "You are in hospital, Harry. You've had a bad experience and they are just checking you over."

Harry seemed to drift off. He closed his eyes and then opened them again. "Where am I, Kath, and what are you doing here down the pit?"

The doctor shone a light in his eyes. "He's drifting in and out of consciousness, his mind won't stay focussed.

Post-traumatic stress can play all kinds of tricks on your mind. We will have to keep him in for a few days and see how it goes. Who are those people he is talking to, Pat and Jean?"

Kath looked perplexed. "I don't know. I've heard him mention other names at various times but I don't know who they are. Sometimes I just think he's talking to himself." The doctor said they would keep him in hospital and asked Kath if she had transport to get home. She told him that the colliery manager had arranged transport. She checked her watch, it was 2:30 in the morning and she was feeling tired. She kissed Harry and said she would see him later.

***

The president arrived at the TV station in Birmingham. He was met in reception and guided to another floor where cameras, lights and all the other trappings of a TV studio stood. A man greeted him who the president recognised as a well-known figure he'd seen many times on the television. He invited the president to sit down in a chair opposite him and started discussing the interview. After the make-up department had done their job, the president was asked to join the man on the small platform in front of the cameras. They sat opposite each other in two comfortable chairs. The lights went up and the cameras began filming. Martin, the man interviewing the president, introduced him to the cameras as the president of the Coal Miners' Union. He asked the president if he was glad the strike was over. "Of course I am. Nobody wants to go on strike but sometimes it is necessary to take drastic action and a show of strength is required when jobs are at risk. If the management won't listen or discuss problems, then what is the alternative? We have a strong case against pit closures that will mean job losses. Families will suffer and villages will be decimated when the government carries out its plans, even to the point of bringing in an outsider, a ruthless American hatchet man to do their dirty work at a cost of one million pounds. Just how low can these people sink?" Various questions were asked regarding the closures and the president was asked how he knew what the government intended. Opening up his briefcase, the president revealed the list of pits nominated for closure. He held it up so that the cameras could zoom in on it. Several signatures were highlighted on the paper. Names of government officials and coal industry bosses who had agreed to the closures and of course, the hatchet man's signature. The president addressed Martin, "Now ask the government to deny the existence of this document." The television programme was recorded and shown on prime time television later that evening. The newspapers were ecstatic and really went to town on the government. The television company was overwhelmed with angry people accusing the government of double-dealing standards and once again sided with the miners. The president was pleased. The opposition had ended up with egg on their faces and the American hatchet man was hounded by his own countrymen, forcing him into early retirement.

***

When Peter announced that he had been offered a job out of the industry, his mates in the office congratulated him and wished him all the luck in the world. "I'm hanging on to see what happens. I'm fifty years old now and I've heard rumours of redundancies being offered," said John.

"Well, I'm only twenty-five and I've got a long way to go yet. I like this job so I'll stick it out and see what happens here," quipped Allan.

Peter said he was looking forward to his new job and was glad his friend, Martin, had contacted him. Also he announced that he had met someone who he was dating seriously and would be getting married in the near future. "Oh, so we've got a wedding coming up as well. You've been secretive about that, Peter lad. Anybody we know?" queried John.

***

Harry woke early after a sound sleep helped by sleeping tablets. He looked around. “Where’s Kath?” he asked a nurse. “And where the hell am I? This isn’t my house.”

The nurse brought Harry a cup of tea. “It’s quite all right, Harry, you’re in hospital and we’ve been looking after you. Kath’s gone home for a rest. She will be back later.”

Harry looked at the nurse. “Well, what am I doing in here? I don’t live here and have I missed the boxing? I wanted to see the Chris Eubank fight.”

The nurse stood looking at Harry. “You don’t remember anything, Harry? You had an accident at work.”

Harry looked at her with a vacant expression on his face. “I don’t remember that. Did Eubank win the fight? I bet Kath forgot to record it for me. Alf liked the boxing as well. He might have recorded it.”

The nurse took the empty cup away, saying that the doctor would be around later to have a look at him. She had made Harry comfortable and told him to relax. Breakfast would be brought around first and the nurses would give him a quick wash. Harry drifted off, walking down the garden in his sleep.

***

Dave chatted away to his mates as they walked from school, keeping an eye open for Kev. It wasn’t long before he appeared behind them. Dave didn’t want to push things but he needed to get Kev talking about the strike. “Been out on the bikes lately?” he asked casually.

“Nah, not yet,” replied Kev. “Got to lay low for a while until things quieten down.” Dave’s mates asked what things he was on about. “The strike,” answered Kev.

Dave looked at him. “What’s that got to do with going out with your brothers on their bikes?”

Kev put his finger to his lips. “Shhh, can’t say but we did a job and the police are making enquiries about anybody with motorbikes. We have stashed them away for a while until things go quiet. Don’t go telling anybody we’ve got bikes.” Dave broke away and made his way through the estate. A little more information but not enough. Meanwhile, he would still keep his eye on Kev and his drug dealing. He made notes of the days and the names of the people Kev was dealing to.

***

Peter answered the phone. It was the estate agent calling to say he had someone interested in his property and would Saturday morning be convenient for a viewing? He had already started packing things in boxes and labelling the contents. He wanted to be ready to vacate. The bulk of his possessions would go into storage with Susan's and it would all be sorted when they found their dream home. He had put in his notice at the pit and was all set to leave on Friday.

At snap time, Allan made the tea and John went to the canteen, returning shortly with a box containing an assortment of fresh cream cakes. Ken, the tractor driver, entered the office with a bottle of whisky and some plastic cups. John looked at Peter. "We're going to drink to your health and future, mate. Ken, pour our mate a drink."

Allan had a parcel in his hand, which he gave to Peter. "Here's to you, mate, just something to remember us by."

Peter opened the package to reveal a framed photo of John, Allan and Ken. "You can always hang it in the shithouse if you get fed up with looking at it," remarked Ken. A chorus of laughter filled the office as the whisky and cream cakes were passed around. Peter thanked them and said he would miss their comradeship. Before leaving at the end of the shift, Peter shook hands with them.

Martin welcomed Peter on Monday morning at the factory. He took him to the shop floor and introduced him to the workforce. He then led him to a section where a machine was being built up. A young apprentice was looking at a drawing. Martin introduced him to Peter. "You have an assistant today, Ian, this is Peter. Show him the ropes."

Peter looked at the drawing. "This is the hydraulic system; I've got to figure out what goes where on this machine. Can you read drawings, Peter?" Together, they traced the pipework from the pump to the control and distribution block.

"It looks like spaghetti junction," Peter said. Martin came around two hours later to see how they were doing. He checked what they had done, pointing out one mistake.

Susan found it hard to cope with all the questions being asked about Derek. The office staff would drop in and sooner or later, the question would be asked. "How's Derek, Susan?" She began scouring the 'situations vacant' columns in the newspapers and looking at the job centre ads. She had done ten years at the Armitage Colliery and now that Peter was no longer there, she was getting restless. "Time for me to move on," she whispered to herself.

Peter had sold his apartment and had moved in with her. They had found, after a while, that the flat was a bit restricted and found themselves going off at weekends to different places to stretch their legs. York was a popular place and there was an occasional visit to Blackpool. Peter sometimes found himself being asked to work on Saturdays and the occasional Sunday when machines had to be prepared for shipping abroad. They talked about various things and Susan said she was looking for another job. Peter said they should start looking at houses. The weeks seemed to be flying by but at least they both agreed they were happier times.

***

Kath sat beside Harry's bed in the hospital. He had been moved to one of the wards where his condition was being monitored. The doctor had been around and said that Harry might be allowed home soon but would have to attend outpatients for a while. "His condition has improved but he is still having problems mentally and relates to things in the past. Psychiatric counselling and therapy may help him but it will take time. He had a traumatic experience and this may haunt him for the rest of his life. The soldiers who have been in the war zone suffer the same thing."

Kath held Harry's hand. "It will be nice to have you home, my dear. It's been lonely without you."

The first thing Harry did was to check his chrysanthemums. They had been neglected and now needed some TLC. He started right away, debudding the side shoots. Kath left him to it, saying she would call him when his tea was ready. Harry felt better in his garden but Kath would often find him gazing with a faraway look in his eyes, talking to imaginary people. "It's Alf," he would say to her. The doctors had arranged for Harry to attend psychotherapy sessions at the hospital once a week.

***

Within six months, Peter had gained a lot of experience at the factory and was now one of the boys. Martin remarked what a good worker he was and that he would now be on the full rate like the other members of the team. Occasionally, Martin would ask Peter to accompany him on an outside job to look at a machine that was having problems. Peter enjoyed being a field engineer and would often volunteer to service problematic machines on his own. The company provided a company van with all the necessary equipment and Peter would go off. He enjoyed the outdoor life, especially during the summer and autumn months. When the weekends came, he and Susan would continue their search for a home. Susan had applied for one or two jobs but nothing suitable had materialised.

***

The president of the C.M.U. had called another meeting to discuss one or two suggestions that had to be resolved before his meeting with British Coal. There had been rumours of redundancies in the industry, which had been welcomed by some but not all. "Gentlemen, if these rumours have any foundation at all then let us make sure that it is the C.M.U. that has control over the issue and that our members will be given a choice. We do not want British Coal to be the axemen. Let us be the ones to decide who goes and who stays. First of all, it will be voluntary redundancies. I want you all to start making enquiries amongst the elderly members who would perhaps welcome a chance to finish work before the current retirement age. Meanwhile, if this redundancy package is mentioned at the British Coal meeting, then be assured that I will be looking into redundancy payments for our members."

Dennis took two paracetamol before he left the meeting. Putting the car into gear, he drove to the Sherwood. Sylvia smiled as he entered reception. "Hello Dennis, nice to see you again. I've booked you into your usual room. I'm in charge as Henry and Gladys are in Blackpool looking for somewhere to retire to. They've decided to put me in charge and take early retirement. Gladys wants to give Henry some quiet time. He's still poorly so they made the decision to quit. I'll bring you up a tray shortly, Dennis, I bet you're ready for some food and drink and a good rest. Those meetings seem to take it out of you." She leaned over the desk, revealing an ample cleavage. "Can you manage your bag or shall I have it brought up for you?"

Dennis said he could manage, taking the key from Sylvia. "See you later," he whispered.

***

Ray talked to Dave about Kev. "You need to open him up a bit more, Dave, but don't get him suspicious. If you can get him on his own, you might learn a bit more. I guess he likes to brag a bit. Try talking about the strike and the things we got up to with the police. Like tell him how we used to let the tyres down on their cars when they tried to stop us harassing the coaches when they pushed their way through the gates and how we used to knock their helmets off and kick them down the road. We had quite a few scuffles with the police at that time but it's all in the past now, Dave. Tell him nothing matters anymore and it's not important now." Dave listened carefully to what his brother was saying. He knew Kev was still dealing at the school and shuddered to think what could happen in the future.

***

Manchester always arranged good exhibitions and Joe noticed a forthcoming event soon to take place. The Traders' Exhibition Guide was a wealth of information and well worth the tenner Joe had splashed out for membership and monthly reviews. He ticked the one off for next week and began phoning around for brochures and complimentary tickets. Janet was his first contact. "Yes Joe, I'm ready to go now. Have you checked on Denise and Veronica?"

Joe said he was doing that now. "There's a good one coming up in Manchester next week, I'll call you when I've arranged it all."

The car had been serviced and valeted. Joe had also remembered to get his shirts back from the laundry. Rosie had planned to visit her sister. Joe declined her offer for him to accompany her. "Oh! She drives me round the twist," he said. "Always on about her bad legs and arthritis. She must think she's the only one with health problems. Besides, I've got physiotherapy twice next week." Wednesday was a good day for the Manchester exhibition so Joe contacted the girls. Veronica asked what sort of exhibition it was. Joe informed her it was a mixture of household and fashionable items to which Veronica replied, "Oh Joe, they'll be some good choices then."

***

Martin joined Peter on the shop floor. He had a pile of drawings under his arm. "Peter, take a look at these," he said, laying them out on the workbench. "This is one of our machines we sold six months ago to one of our best customers in the Middle East. They say the machine developed a problem that their engineers have failed to solve."

Peter scanned the drawings. “Have they given any information on the problem? Have they gone through the fault-finding section in the service manual?”

Martin said he had asked that question. “They can’t find what they call an intermittent fault. Sometimes everything is OK and then the machine just fails. The fault is in the track motors. One or the other fails intermittently. It’s holding things up on that road construction they’re developing. They’re asking for our advice. Help me trace these circuits, Peter, perhaps we can suggest something that they can try; otherwise, I’m going to have to go out there. This machine carries a manufacturer’s guarantee.”

Peter traced the hydraulic system from the pump through every pipe leading to the functioning parts. “It’s like looking at spaghetti junction, only on a grander scale,” said Martin.

After a long period of tracing the circuits, they had both come up with lists of possible causes. Martin rolled up the drawings. “I’ll phone the engineers heading this project. These possibilities may help them solve the problem. If not, I’ll have to start packing my bag.”

Chapter 15
Eastern Crisis

When Peter arrived home that evening, he found Susan looking through several estate agent brochures. “I’ve done a quick trip around the town today and have picked up one or two possibilities for us to look at, Peter.”

He looked at her and put his arms around her. “Of course, darling, but let me please tell you how beautiful you are and how much I love you.”

Susan responded to his kisses. “Have you had a good day at work?” she asked.

“Yes, quite good. This job is very interesting and Martin came to see me with a problem. One of our customers in the Middle East has a problem with one of our machines. We’ve gone through all the hydraulic circuits and have come up with a few possibilities. I hope we can solve the problem or else poor Martin is going to have to go out there and sort it.”

***

Christine answered the doorbell. She had forgotten what day it was and had not thought of the insurance man coming. She opened the door and found Marianne looking at her. “Oh my goodness, what a surprise,” she said. “Come in, Marianne. I’d forgotten what day it was and what a surprise to see you.”

As soon as the door closed, Marianne put her arms around Christine’s waist, pulling her closer. “I’m just filling in today for the usual rep who’s on holiday. It sure is nice to see you, Christine.” Her lips closed over Christine’s and a passionate embrace ensued. Christine felt a sudden urge coming over her as Marianne's hand fondled her. "Gosh Christine, I have missed you," she whispered, planting another kiss.

"Come in, Marianne. Can I pour you a drink or something?" said Christine. "It was quite a surprise seeing you standing there. I've missed you too. It's been quite a while; I thought you had forgotten about me."

Marianne placed her bag on the settee and sat down. "A cold drink will do fine, Christine. No, I never will forget you; I love you too much." Christine placed a glass of cold orange juice on the coffee table and also the insurance payment. Marianne took a sip from the glass and then entered the insurance money into her ledger. "There, that's the business taken care of." Steven was in his pram playing with his toys. "He's grown a lot since the last time I saw him," said Marianne.

Christine had just made a bottle for him. "Yes, it's amazing how quickly they grow," replied Christine, sitting on the settee next to Marianne. "What have you been doing with yourself? Anything interesting?"

Marianne smiled at her. "No, I've decorated my flat and that's about all. Life's a bit boring at the moment. I need some action. How about you, Christine, are you being satisfied?"

Steve had almost emptied the bottle and was dropping off to sleep. "I'm going to put him in his pram." Christine couldn't help smell Marianne's perfume. It was intoxicating and Marianne herself looked inviting. She went into the kitchen and reached for her own, which she quickly dabbed on. As an afterthought, she quickly removed her panties before rejoining Marianne on the settee. "Life's pretty boring at the moment, I'm practically housebound now that Billy's back at work. I've missed having the car to run around in." She looked at Marianne and edged closer.

"We are a pair of poor souls," replied her friend, echoing the 'come on' signs. She reached out for Christine and soon they were exploring the inner sanctums of each other's bodies. Christine lay back on the settee and stretched out, waiting for Marianne to remove her kit. Gently, Marianne lay on top of Christine, her tongue exploring her open cleavage. Christine was soon fondling Marianne's ample bosom and her tongue was stimulating her nipples. "How I've missed you," she murmured. Soon Marianne had one of her toys and gently massaged Christine's body. As she manoeuvred the toy lower down, Christine moaned with ecstasy. She had missed this kind of attention, Billy's *wham bam thank you mam* failed to rouse her sufficiently to climax. But Marianne certainly knew how to perform. She obviously knew what a woman wanted and that was probably what made her what she was, a lesbian. Christine loved Billy for what he was. He was fun, always making her laugh, he was kind, he was sweet, he was handsome but somewhat lacking in their lovemaking. Marianne's tongue explored her body, finding and stimulating the areas that Billy didn't know about. She responded and reciprocated to Marianne who showed Christine what she wanted herself. They both reached their peaks and moaned with satisfaction.

"You must call me," said Marianne, slipping on her clothes. "I'm still in my apartment. You have my number; anytime you need to relax and get satisfied, just call me and we can arrange something. Please, Christine, make an effort. I need you and you need me."

***

Dennis looked up as Sylvia entered the room with the food trolley. "Here you are, my love, get this down you."

He sat down at the table and let Sylvia lay out the food. "You're good for me, Sylvia," he said, taking a sip from the cup of tea. "What would I do without you?"

She moved around him, placing her hand on his shoulders. "And you're good for me, Dennis. I look forward to you coming here." She gently massaged his neck and shoulders. His headache soon disappeared.

"You certainly know what's good for me, Sylvia."

She leaned over and kissed his cheek. “And you know what’s good for me,” she replied. “Now eat your meal and then have a rest. I’ll see you later if you like.”

Dennis touched her lightly on her rear end. “Looking forward to it,” he replied.

***

Dave dawdled through the school gates, looking for Kev. His mates soon caught up with him. “Come on, Dave; let’s fuck off before that prat catches up with us.”

Dave said he wanted to wait for Kev. “I want to know what he and his brothers got up to during the strike. Something serious but he won’t talk about it. Let’s encourage him to talk. Let’s talk about the strike when he comes.” They walked casually along the road. Dave kept looking back. Soon he spied Kev hurrying to catch up with them. Dave began talking about the strike to his mates. “Yes, there was some serious confrontation outside the gates. The police were right bullies; my brother was involved in one or two scuffles, especially when the coaches tried to get through.”

Kev caught up with them and listened in. “My brother was held by two policemen whilst another gave him a hammering,” said Dave’s mate.

“Well, when they blocked the drive off with their police cars, our kid started to let their tyres down,” said another of Dave’s mates.

“That’s nothing to what we did,” butted in Kev.

Dave looked at him suspiciously. “Why, where were you when all the excitement was happening?” Kev hesitated to talk. “I thought so, you weren’t there at all,” answered Dave.

This reply seemed to infuriate Kev into loosening up. “Look,” he said, “did you know that reinforcements from London were being sent? Three transit vans full of cops were on their way to Armitage Colliery, ready to beat the shit out of the strikers. We decided to stop them getting there so we made plans. Me and my brothers found out about this through a friendly cop. We planned to intercept them on the motorway." Dave was all ears.

"I heard about someone dropping a big lump of concrete from one of the flyovers, causing a pile-up and injuring some police. Was that you and your brothers, Kev?" The question was asked by one of Dave's mates.

"Of course, that's what the motorbikes were used for." Dave absorbed this information. "I'm not saying anymore," answered Kev and broke away from the group. Dave related to Ray what he had heard.

In the club that evening, Ray and the B.A.D. boys discussed the situation. "If that information is correct, then we have the means of eliminating a small-time drug pusher. It's better to do it now before he gets overconfident and starts doing it big time."

Ray nodded approvingly. Abbo had summed it up perfectly and the others had agreed. "Dave reckons this Kev is always knocking about the estate most nights. Him and his mates usually get a few cans and hang around the garages."

Andy suggested they lie in wait. "One of us can patrol the area whilst the rest wait in the car until he is spotted. As soon as he breaks away from his mates to go home, we've got him." The boys agreed and arranged to meet Friday night at 7 o'clock in the club car park.

"OK then, that's how we will play it. Our Dave can be the lookout for us; he knows the score here and knows where they hang out. He does it himself sometimes so nobody will be suspicious." Ray beamed across the table. "My round, lads, let's drink to success and another druggie biting the dust."

Andy shook his head in disbelief. "I can't believe how this drug thing has taken off so easily, especially in our town. London and Birmingham yes, but not in our town, and the bastards are even targeting the school kids. It has got to be stopped. I'm all for the B.A.D. boys."

***

Veronica was waiting outside the flat when Joe pulled up. He greeted her with a big smile.

"Are we all OK today, Joe?" she beamed. "Ready for action." Janet and Denise were also ready.

"Northampton, here we come!" screamed Denise as they got into the car. "That's two exhibitions in one week, Joe, how do you manage to keep it up?" she asked.

"It's the blue tablet," laughed Veronica.

"No, I mean finding about these exhibitions. You've got a one-track mind, Veronica." Denise and Janet were in hysterics. Joe listened to the banter filling the car. These girls were in good humour today. It was a quiet drive straight down the M5. The BMW was a lovely car to drive and they arrived at the exhibition in good time. Joe gave out the lapel badges and handed around a few brochures advertising their goods. Veronica was 'Kitchen Designs', Janet was 'Household Textiles' and Denise was secretary to the sales manager, Joe Martin, Worldwide Commodities.

"OK girls, go and get them," said Joe, showing their passes at the entrance. He looked as Veronica walked away, the two bunnies in the sack drawing some hungry looks from the male species. "Oh yes," Joe muttered to himself. "Not tonight, Rosie, I've got something else in mind." Denise accompanied Joe as he sauntered around the exhibition. It wasn't long before he was in conversation with the exhibitors. Denise would saunter along, smiling at the salesmen. It wasn't long before a handsome forty-something salesman latched onto her and was soon guiding her around the stand, whilst Joe kept his partner busy.

Janet sauntered around the various displays, smiling invitingly at the representatives and encouraging any that showed an interest. Veronica wriggled her way around and introduced herself to a number of interested males. She preferred men who showed managerial status. They were the ones with the fat wallets. She was drawn to one of the stands that had attracted a small crowd. Curious, she pushed herself forward to the front only to find it was a religious stand. A priest-like figure was addressing the small gathering and as soon as Veronica had pushed her way through, he seemed to be drawn to her, holding out a booklet. He was a good-looking man in his early forties with a fine figure beneath the light grey suit he was wearing. The collar around his neck glistened white against his papal shirt. He held out the booklet to Veronica who declined the offer. Two other priest-like figures honed in on the small gathering and soon more people joined in. The one holding out the booklet to Veronica moved in closer and soon they were within touching distance of each other. “I’m Brendan Foster, pastor of our religious order, here today to introduce you to alternative belief in the Holy Scriptures.”

Veronica couldn’t believe that she was listening to this good-looking guy trying to convert her. “I don’t believe that your religion is any different to any other I’ve listened to,” she said, handing him a leaflet on stainless steel kitchenware.

“How about if I take yours and you take mine?” said the pastor, holding out his booklet.

She smiled and said, “OK,” and took the booklet.

“And if I may, perhaps I could invite you to have lunch with me at the hotel. The food is very good and we could enjoy good conversation.”

Veronica couldn’t believe what she was hearing. Was this guy trying to convert her or trying to shag her? She could feel his body rubbing against her as he steered her through the gathering crowd. “I break for lunch at 1 o’clock. Will you give me the honour of dining with me, please?”

Veronica was gobsmacked. Did this religious nut realise what she was? The excitement was too much. “Yes, I will,” she said eagerly.

The three girls had all landed their prey. Joe sauntered around the exhibition, then made his way to the bar.

***

Kath was getting a bit concerned. Harry’s behaviour was getting erratic. She would find him in the garden late at night, just looking at his chrysanthemums or watching telly but not listening to it. She heard him talking to someone but he would be alone. There was no one there. Harry was due for another appointment at the hospital. This time, she would go with him. She had questions to ask. The psychotherapist welcomed her into his office. Harry was receiving his therapy in another room. "Well, Mrs Williams, how is your husband coping at home? Is there any improvement?"

Kath shook her head. "No, not a great deal. I find him talking to imaginary people. Names like Joan and Alf seem to crop up. I don't know who they are. Does this mean he's schizophrenic or whatever you call it?"

Mr Jennings shook his head. "No, Mrs Williams, these are people from his past who were killed, people who were close to your husband. These memories keep flooding back and sometimes, any kind of trauma in life can revive these memories and stay with you. Harry has just experienced a severe traumatic accident down the coal mine that has awakened these sleeping memories. Harry came to see me before his accident and we discussed how he could handle them. Do you know that he likes his chrysanthemums and watching football?" Kath said she had noticed that he seemed more relaxed at these times. "That's where he goes to escape from these memories. If he can occupy his mind with something pleasant, the memories return to the back of his mind. They don't go away forever; they're just forgotten temporarily." Kath listened as Mr Jennings explained. "Does Harry still paint pictures?" She said he did sometimes. "Perhaps you could encourage him to do a bit more. Maybe get him to try painting chrysanthemums; they're such a lovely flower."

Kath thought for a moment. "Yes, I think he would enjoy doing that and I might try it myself."

Mr Jennings stood up. "OK then, Mrs Williams, let's try that for a month. Try to keep him busy and if you find him preoccupied and talking to himself, interrupt him and do something like going for a walk. Harry has got a long way to go yet, Mrs Williams, and we must help him all we can. I will be honest with you though, he may not recover completely."

***

Peter answered the phone at home. He was just doing a bit of decorating whilst Susan had gone shopping. It was Martin. "Peter, sorry to bother you on a Saturday morning and your day off, but I have a big problem."

Peter listened as Martin explained what it was. "I shall have to talk it over with Susan first, Martin, I have to consider her. I'll call you back as soon as we've talked it over. She's out shopping at the moment." Peter hung up the phone. An hour later, Susan arrived home, heavily laden. Peter helped unload the car. Together, they put away the shopping and Peter said he would make a drink. "Sit down and rest, Susan, take the load off your feet." When they were sitting comfortably, Peter told Susan about the phone call from Martin. "He needs my help." Susan listened as Peter explained that one of their machines had broken down and their local engineers had been unable to repair it.

"Where did you say it was?" she asked.

Peter looked at her. "It's one of the eastern countries. We would have to fly out there as soon as possible. It's part of a big project and this machine is holding them up. I reckon two to three days to sort out the problem. Would you mind if I left you on your own for a few days, Susan? I owe Martin a lot and I want to help him."

Susan smiled at Peter. "No, of course I wouldn't mind, darling. I'm quite capable of looking after myself for a few days. I've got things to do. No Peter, you go and help Martin; he's been good to you."

Peter called Martin and told him that he would be OK for the trip. Martin was very pleased and would get the ball rolling as regards the flight to Africa. He asked if Peter's passport was up to date. "OK Peter, I'll see you at work on Monday and go over the details."

Martin spread out the drawings on the workbench. "It's this big one with the double-track motors, it seems the machine goes on all right and then suddenly one of the tracks goes into reverse for some reason. After a while, it rights itself and then the other track does the same."

They studied the drawings, each making suggestions. "Where is it we're going?" Peter asked Martin.

"It's on the Somalian border with Kenya. They're doing a road from North to South to keep the two countries separate. It's so that they can erect checkpoints at various places along the border."

***

Janet and Denise were already in the car when a smiling and highly excited Veronica finally turned up. Denise was sitting in the front passenger seat next to Joe. "It looks as if you've had a good day, Veronica," said Janet cheerfully.

Veronica gave a squeal and then burst out laughing. "I've just been fucked by a vicar," she squealed excitedly.

"Holy cow!" came a chorus of voices from the other occupants. "Tell us more."

Veronica managed to compose herself and began to relate the encounter with Pastor Brendan. "He was very handsome and built like a brick shithouse. We eventually made it into the bedroom, after he told me all about his free-loving religion and how God allowed everyone to do what they liked as long as they didn't lose their faith. I went into the bathroom to strip off and when I entered the bedroom, he was already lying naked on the bed. My eyes nearly popped out when I saw his erection. He must have been at the front of the queue when they gave dicks out, he was massive. I asked him what colour condom he fancied. He said he preferred his own and started to put on something from outer space. It was ribbed at the top and had a series of rubber spikes on it, like the back of a dinosaur. Slowly, he put it in and I felt a tingle of excitement as the ribbed dinosaur touched my vagina. It was wonderful, like a gift from heaven, and he knew how to fuck. After what seemed like multiple orgasms, I had to tell him it was time for me to go. I had already told him I had to earn my bonus and he said I had when he presented two crisp fifty-pound notes. I'm as sore as a cat's arse after that but it was fun. Heaven sent, you could say."

The car rocked with laughter. "Did you get his phone number?" asked Denise.

"No but he managed to convert me," laughed Veronica.

Joe dropped the girls off, leaving Denise until last. As he followed her into her flat, she asked him if he had any of those dinosaur condoms. He laughed as he popped in a blue pill.

***

Christine woke up, she had been dreaming and in her dreams she was pushing the pram around the estate on her way to her mother's. Her belly was huge. "Six months, I would say, Christine," remarked a friend she met on the way. She felt her tummy and got out of bed to look in the mirror. There were no signs and her last period had been on time. She laughed at herself. "Stupid dreams," she mused. Steven was now one year old and bouncing about in his cot. She picked him up and played with him on the bed for a while. "Would you like a little brother or sister to play with, Steven?"

***

The president had called another meeting and Dennis began packing his bag. "Another meeting so soon," exclaimed his wife.

Dennis told her that a lot of negotiation was going on behind the scenes with the president and British Coal. "Redundancies," replied Dennis. "These are important issues that have to be discussed and decisions to be made at the top level before our members are consulted. We have to decide what's acceptable to them." He kissed his wife on the cheek and left for Nottingham. It had hardly been two weeks since his last trip up there and he wondered how many more he would be making.

The meeting got under way and the president soon called for their attention. "Gentlemen, as you know, plans have been drawn up to cut down the workforce in the mining industry. You are aware of the closures that are about to take place and plans have been drawn up in an effort to make it easier for this to materialise. Voluntary redundancies for anybody who wants it above the age of fifty-five. At my last meeting with British Coal, it was decided that favourable payouts would be offered depending on the number of years spent in the industry. I am asking you to inform your workforce of this offer and would welcome a list of volunteers from you as soon as possible. The 'Coal News' will be highlighting these decisions in their next publication so all members will be informed of what is going on. Gentlemen, please do your best to let me have your list of volunteers by next month."

Dennis took two paracetamol and left the meeting. He didn't want to stay and talk with the other colliery reps, his headache was intense and he needed quietness. Opening the door of the hotel, he was met by Sylvia and Gladys. The two women welcomed him. "Hi ladies, it's nice to see you," said Dennis, giving them both a peck on the cheek.

"Not for long," said Sylvia. "Gladys and Henry are off again to Blackpool."

Gladys said, "Yes, we're going to view some property we've come across for when we retire and that won't be long in coming if we like what we see. So our Sylvia will be looking after you permanently, Dennis. I hope she will give you a good service."

Dennis nodded. "Of course she will, Gladys." His headache was beginning to ease off as he started to unpack. A slight knock and the door opened.

"Well, this is a surprise, Dennis, so soon. It's been less than two weeks." Sylvia walked over to him and put her arms around his waist. They kissed and soon found themselves entwined on the bed. After passionate exchanges, Sylvia broke free. "Now Dennis, have a good rest. I'll bring some food up to you later."

Dennis closed his eyes and was soon snoring gently. He awoke two hours later to find that the curtains had been drawn and the room was immersed in darkness.

Chapter 16
The B.A.D. Boys Strike Again

The B.A.D. Boys were sitting in the car in a darkened area of the estate, waiting for Dave to arrive. They knew the alleyway that Kev used to get home and when Dave gave the signal, they would leave the car and position themselves at each end, blocking his path. Another half hour passed before Dave appeared. "He's on his way now," he panted. The boys deployed themselves in the alleyway, hiding in the shadows. Dave disappeared, making his way home. Soon Kev's figure appeared. Ray and Andy hid as they watched him pass by. Halfway down the alleyway, Abbo and Sid stepped out as Kev drew near. Realising that something was up, Kev halted in his tracks and did an about turn. Ray and Andy closed in on him. Kev started to panic as the four lads closed in.

"What the fuck's going on here?" Kev asked nervously. "I ain't got no money if that's what you want."

Ray stood behind him and put his arms around his chest. Andy grabbed one arm and Sid grabbed the other. Abbo stood in front as Kev started kicking and screaming. Ray put his hand over his mouth. "We want you to listen," said Abbo.

Kev looked at the masked men and nodded his head. "I'm listening," he tried to say. Ray still held onto the frightened Kev.

"You're dealing drugs to the kids at your school." Kev tried to shake his head to deny it. "We've got proof; we've had eyes on you for ages, we know you're selling to the kids." Abbo pushed his masked face right up to Kev's. "It's got to stop, do you hear? If you don't, the police will be told about your brothers and you dropping concrete onto the police vans on the motorway during the strike. They're still looking for you and we know where the motorbikes are. Don't deny anything; we've got the evidence and witnesses. Do you understand what we're saying? Stop dealing or else you and your brothers will spend a long time in jail."

Ray eased his grip on Kev. "You had better take note of what we're saying, you shithead. Any more drug dealing and you and your brothers go to jail. We will be watching you."

Abbo asked where he was getting his drugs from. Kev said from a guy who worked at the power station. "He comes from Litchfield and we meet in a lay-by on a Monday evening. He pulls in this lay-by and waits for about ten minutes and if we're not there, he fucks off. I only buy a few joints from him, mainly for myself but one or two of the kids at school wanted in so I sold to them. I'm going to stop now, I promise. Please keep quiet about the motorway incident, my brothers will kill me if they find out you know about it."

Abbo pushed his face into Kev's. "We will be watching you."

They released Kev and watched him sprint up the alleyway. As they sat in the car and changed their jackets, Ray asked if they had done enough. "I don't think he'll be dealing anymore; I think we've stopped him in time," said Andy. "But ask Dave to keep his eyes open."

Abbo suggested a pint in the club. "I think we've earned one," he said.

***

Peter kissed Susan and picked up his travel bag. "See you soon, darling; it will only be a few days at the most." Susan wished him a good flight and watched from the window as he pulled away.

Martin had booked the flight and had packed a few small bits and pieces into a holdall. "I've picked up one or two valves and things, Peter, just in case. I hope it's nothing too serious, bigger parts will have to be flown in, if needed." They settled down to a long flight and each had picked up reading material for the journey. "We're being picked up at the airport by a rep from the Eastern Development Company and taken to a hotel. In the morning, transport will take us to the site. I don't know how far it is to the Somalian border but I reckon we'll be seeing a lot of desert," said Martin.

Again, Peter and Martin discussed the problem with the machine. Martin said he couldn't understand why it had suddenly started to play up. "It's been OK and performing well for the last six months. Minor problems arise but usually the site engineers manage to right them, but this one is strange."

Peter suggested they strip the hydraulic feed to the tracks and work backwards to the pump. "If we isolate one track and check the flow and pressure, we should come up with something."

Martin said that this particular fault had never occurred before as far as he knew. "But there's always a first time and it's got us a few days sunshine in the desert," he said.

***

Kath joined Harry in the garden. "Those chrysanthemums look beautiful, Harry, which is your favourite? I like the yellow ones."

Harry walked along the rows of blooms. "I like this one," he said, pointing to the red one. "It's called Gypsy and it's what's known as an incurve because the petals are growing inwards but I also like the other variety with the petals growing outwards. They call them reflex."

Kath suggested that Harry should try and paint one. "And you could show me how to paint. It's something we could do when it rains."

Harry looked at Kath. "Do you mean that, Kath? I've been thinking about it for ages but I didn't think you would be interested. OK love, that's something to think about. I'll get you a canvas."

Harry decided to visit Armitage Colliery. He wanted to know what was happening. Rumours were spreading about voluntary redundancies. His doctor at the hospital didn't recommend that Harry even go down the pit again. "You have a long way to go yet, Harry, before you will be well enough to work. These traumas have a habit of suddenly coming back and I don't think that working in such an environment would help you any." He looked at Harry. "Don't rush anything, Harry, you're not getting any younger."

Harry knocked on the door of the Training Office. Mr Jones was sitting at his desk when Harry opened the door. "Hello Harry, come on in, it's good to see you. Take a seat." Harry sat down and exchanged pleasantries. "What can we do for you, Harry?" asked Mr Jones. When Harry explained about the rumours, Mr Jones nodded his head. "Yes, there's talk about more redundancies, Harry. How old are you?" The training officer started to write things down. "And how's your health, Harry? What are your doctors saying?"

Harry told him what the doctor had said. "I'm fifty-four this year and I don't think I shall be wanting to go back underground."

The training officer looked at Harry. "You will be fifty-five in December, Harry. Now from what I've been told, this redundancy scheme is due to end in December. I am going to see what I can do for you, Harry. Maybe I can get you pushed forward before the scheme ends on health grounds so you stay on the sick whilst I do my best."

Kath was delighted when Harry told her about his visit to the pit. "But you should have taken me with you, Harry. What would have happened if you had been taken ill?"

***

Billy decided to take one of his rest days. Christine had found him a job around the house that he had been putting off—painting inside the cupboards in the kitchen. "Well, it's pissing down with rain so I might as well do it today. The garden will have to wait."

Christine looked out of the window. "Well, I was going to take Steven into Stafford with me but this weather is poxy, it won't be good for him. Can you look after him, Billy, for a couple of hours?"

Billy looked at his son playing on the carpet with his mobile. "Yeah, he'll be OK as long as he doesn't get any paint on him."

Christine kissed Billy. "I appreciate that, darling; it's a nice break for me."

She pulled up in the car park in front of *Matalans*. She looked around the car park but there was no sign of Marianne's car, so she made for the pay phone. "Hello Christine, oh good, I'll come and pick you up. It's so nice to hear from you." A quick visit into the store for some new clothes for Steven and then she stood outside, waiting for Marianne. A tingle of excitement escaped her as she saw Marianne's car approaching. She got in the car and they sped off to Marianne's apartment. They both seemed keen as Marianne put the key in the lock. Two glasses of wine later and they were both standing naked in the bedroom. Christine began by fondling Marianne's breasts but soon they were entwined on the bed. Marianne was hungry for love and was soon enjoying Christine massaging her with the vibrator. "Oh, Christine, you're getting really good," murmured Marianne. She rolled over and was soon pleasing Christine in the same way. Marianne felt under the pillow and pulled out the dildo. Christine helped her put it on and soon the screams of ecstasy echoed in the bedroom, as each of them took it in turns with the dildo. Christine wondered why another woman was better in bed than Billy. *We know what pleases us*, she thought to herself *Men just hump us and please themselves.*

Marianne made the coffee and brought it into the bedroom. "I hope you're not in any hurry, Christine? I haven't had sex like that for a long time. I wish you would leave your husband and come and live with me."

Christine was shocked. "I can't, Marianne. I have a baby and I could never leave my husband and child."

Marianne pulled a face. "It's a pity, Christine, because I have something to tell you. I have been promoted to Area Manager and I have been asked to take over the Liverpool area, which means I'm going to leave here and live in Liverpool."

Christine was flabbergasted. "Does that mean we won't be seeing each other again?" she asked.

Marianne reached out and touched her cheek. "I'm afraid so, Christine. I move out next week. I'm so glad that I've seen you today; it's been lonely."

They drank their coffee in silence. Christine's mind was racing. She had never been in a relationship before that had given her the sexual pleasure that Marianne did. If only Billy could be so pleasing. Marianne lay on the bed and pulled Christine on top of her. "It's the last time, Christine, so let's fuck the roof off this place." With that, they got entwined and pleased each other like it was going out of fashion. As Christine drove home, she could feel the tears welling up. She was going to miss Marianne.

***

Martin and Peter got into the Land Rover that was to take them to the site. There was a lorry full of soldiers in front of them. "Our escort," said the driver. "We have to pick up the engineer along the way and then it's about fifteen to twenty kilometres across the desert. It will be a bit bumpy but when the new road is built, it will be much better." As they passed through the sparsely inhabited town, they pulled up to pick up a smartly dressed man. "This is the boss man," the driver informed them.

Mr Sayeed Abdullah introduced himself and got in the front passenger seat. "I'm so glad to meet you gentlemen. I'm afraid this machine has been causing us many problems. We are most anxious to get it sorted out. We are well behind schedule with this road. I hope you gentlemen can sort out the problem." They travelled along a very bumpy track through the desert. Soon they had left the town behind and could see nothing but sand and rock-strewn tracks. An hour later, they were standing on a flat roughly constructed road. The huge machine stood covered in dust as the hot sun and winds began to bite. "Our site hut is over there," pointed

Sayeed. The lorry load of soldiers had begun erecting tents. Sayeed informed Martin and Peter that the soldiers were there for their protection and would stay with them.

They entered the site hut, which comprised a table with a lot of drawings out on it, two bunk beds pushed against the far wall and a large chest containing all kinds of tools. "Our maintenance men have decided to take a holiday whilst you sort out the problem," said Sayeed. "There are facilities for washing and food preparation. The soldiers are well-equipped for a short stay and will look after you."

Martin looked at Peter. "Let's hope it doesn't take long. I'm missing my comfort zone already."

Mr Sayeed Abdullah led the way over to the machine. Peter and Martin had put on overalls and climbed onto the machine. It took several tries before the machine sparked up. "I'll go and check whether there's anything visible underneath. Martin, listen to what I call out to you."

Mr Abdullah hung around for a while and then decided he had other business to attend to. The soldiers had erected their tents and were preparing food. "I wonder what's for lunch," murmured Peter, climbing back on top of the machine.

"Just try moving it forwards," Martin suggested. Peter pushed the lever that operated the tracks. At first, the machine just juddered. "It's been standing for a while; just give it a chance to pressure up a bit." Peter tried again. The machine moved forwards slowly. Gradually, it began to pick up power.

"Take a look underneath, Martin, and see if there's anything leaking," suggested Peter. After a quick check, Martin reported that everything looked all right.

"Peter, take it forward as far as you can," shouted Martin. Peter eased the pedal forward. The track motors picked up and the machine moved forwards. "Keep it going, Peter." Martin walked alongside the machine observing the tracks. Everything seemed to be in order. Both tracks were doing their job. Peter drove the machine, operating each track individually.

"Seems to be working all right," shouted Peter.

One of the soldiers came over and shouted something to them. Martin told Peter that their lunch was ready. "Switch off, Peter, we will try again later." They washed up and joined the soldiers in the temporary cookhouse.

"Well, that bit of run went all right," said Peter, placing his cooked lunch in front of him. "I wonder what this lot is."

Martin had tasted it already. "Some kind of stew, I think. As long as it isn't cooked camel shit, I don't mind. It tastes all right."

***

Kath leaned over and looked at Harry's painting. "That's good, Harry, mine isn't as good as yours."

Harry smiled at her. "Patience, Kath, a bit more practice is all you need. Don't forget; I've been looking at those flowers for a long time. I can practically see them with my eyes shut. This 'Gypsy' is lovely, such vibrant colours. You'll get the hang of it; don't be afraid to use more paint."

Kath got up to make a cup of tea. "I hope you get made redundant, Harry, then we can go off on painting holidays."

Harry paused for thought. He was hoping it would happen. He feared the thought of returning to work. He still harboured visions of the coal face and the time he had been trapped for ten hours, soaked in his own urine. He had been hoping he could forget the trauma but he couldn't. The memories started flooding into his mind. He rose from the table and walked up the garden. Kath watched as he walked amongst the flowers and it seemed as if he was talking to someone. "Harry, here's a cup of tea," she said, joining him. "The neighbours admire your garden. Perhaps you could encourage them to grow some chrysanthemums. I'm sure they would appreciate your help."

Harry admitted he was proud of his garden. "Very relaxing in the garden, Kath, and you can see something for our efforts."

***

Dennis knocked on the door of the training office and walked in. "Another list of volunteers for the redundancy scheme," he said, placing the sheet of paper in front of Mr Jones. "That will probably be the last of them for now."

Mr Jones scanned the list of names. "I've got one more to add to that, Dennis. Harry Williams has been to see me and he doesn't think he will ever be able to work down the pit again. He's fifty-four and I'm going to try and squeeze him in on health grounds. I'll have a word with the personnel officer today and that will be the last of them, Dennis. The redundancy package has finished now unless British Coal comes up with anything else."

***

Susan busied herself around the flat. Already she was missing Peter's presence. She decided to go into Stafford and look around the shops and maybe the estate agents. She telephoned a friend who readily agreed to accompany her. "Good idea, Susan, pick me up when you're ready. I could do with a day out and some girlie talk."

In one of the estate agent shops, Susan was shown a plan of a new phase of building plots earmarked for early construction, halfway between Stafford and Rugeley. Susan asked for further information and approximate pricing. "It hasn't been priced up yet," said the salesperson. "But leave your address and I'll forward the details as and when they are available."

Her friend asked Susan if things were going well in her relationship and if she was happy. "Yes," she replied. "We are so happy together. Peter is adorable but he's in Africa at the moment. Him and his boss are on an urgent mission to repair some machine but it will only be for a few days. I'm missing him already."

***

Ray joined the boys in the club. "All quiet on the western front?" he asked, taking a big gulp of his beer.

The boys nodded. "Yes," said Abbo, "but we've been talking about that guy Kev was getting his supply from. He's still dealing and he's on our turf."

Ray looked at his three mates. "What are you suggesting?" he asked.

"Well, we thought perhaps we could put the frighteners on him and chase the bastard off." Sid said. "Just put a bit of pressure on him. No violence or anything like that; we don't know how involved he is. It ain't gonna hurt to check him out."

Ray agreed. "Yes, we need to keep active or the B.A.D. Boys will just be a thing of the past. The problem is we can only operate during the dark nights. Kev said this guy worked at the power station and met up in the lay-by. It's still daylight and we'll be seen." Ray said it wasn't an option.

"Let's just pull in the lay-by and see what happens," suggested Andy. "This Friday at 5 o'clock, we just park up and watch. No masks or hats; let's just see if he's dealing to anybody else."

Ray agreed to the plan. "Whose round is it now?" he asked.

***

Joe pulled up outside Veronica's flat. He watched as she bent down to put a note in the milk crate. The two bunnies in the sack put pressure on the tight skirt she was wearing. "I've had a call from Denise. She's out of action this week, Joe, but she's arranged for Val to take her place, so pick up Val on the way."

Janet was waiting when Joe pulled up. "It's Val next, Joe, Denise has arranged for her to take her place today due to severe weather conditions."

Veronica screamed with laughter. "That's one way of putting it."

Val climbed into the front passenger seat. "OK girls, where are we off today?"

"Not far," Joe informed them. "Coventry. Fabrics and Fasteners we are representing today. It's a furniture and hardware exhibition." He chose Veronica to be his secretary today, handing out the sales brochures for the other two girls. "I doubt if you will see the vicar today but you never know," he said quietly to Veronica.

"Who knows," she replied. "Lightening does sometimes strike in the same place twice."

***

Martin and Peter tried the machine again but this time it didn't respond. Martin looked at the drawings. "We need to put flow meters between the track motors and the controls. We can see then where the pressure is failing."

Peter began uncoupling the hydraulic feed to the left-hand side track. Martin did the same to the right-hand side tracks. The flow meters and pressure gauges were fitted into the line. "Right, try it now, Peter. I'll check what's happening." The machine moved forwards and seemed to be running fine. Then suddenly, the right-hand side track failed. "No flow pressure, Peter." Martin uncoupled the hydraulic feed and drained the fluid out.

"Try coupling it back up again," Peter suggested. He pulled the lever and pressed the pedal. The machine moved forwards, both tracks working together. Suddenly, the left-hand side track failed. Again Peter suggested breaking the line and draining the fluid out. Martin did this and then repeated the procedure of recoupling the connections. Peter pulled the lever and pressed the pedal. Once more, both tracks functioned properly for a while until the right-hand side track failed. Martin scratched his head. "I've never had this happen before."

Peter climbed down and looked at the drawings. "I know what it is," he said, smiling at Martin. "We must disconnect supplies to both tracks and trace the hydraulics back to the inline restrictor valves. Let's do that and see if I'm right."

They worked hard stripping away the steel pipeline. Peter removed the inline restrictor valve and examined it closely. Martin brought his valve and gave it to Peter. "OK Peter, my clever mate, tell me what you see."

Peter studied both the inline valves before showing them to Martin. "This machine has been sabotaged, Martin. Can you see those rubber seals? There should be two to each valve. One has been removed from each valve and that is the problem. Do we have any new seals or valves?"

Martin ran over to the hut and brought back his case containing the spares. Anxiously, he sorted through the bits and pieces he had thrown together. They worked into the darkness of the African night to insert new seals and reassemble the hydraulic system. Working by torchlight, Peter jumped onto the machine and powered up. As the hydraulic fluid filled the line, the machine moved forwards, both tracks working together. Peter drove the machine while Martin shone the powerful torch. Peter put the machine through its paces, driving in all directions and testing the tracks. Peter returned to where he had started from. Martin was dancing with joy. "You clever bastard, Peter, the drinks are on me."

They settled down in the hut after a hearty meal from the cookhouse. "We'll give it another good run tomorrow and then we can start packing our bags." Martin was overjoyed. "Was it a guess or what?" Martin asked curiously.

Peter shook his head. "I've had a similar thing happen when I worked down the pit some years ago. I was at a loss what was causing the problem. Just as I was about to give up, I noticed that one of the seals on the right-hand side track feed was damaged and split. I replaced the inline restrictor valve and bingo, problem solved." They decided to retire early. "We can get up early in the morning before it gets too hot and give the machine a good run. I'm feeling confident," said Peter.

It was pitch black when Martin woke up with a start. A gunshot echoed through the night, breaking the silence. He checked his watch. It was 12:30. Were the soldiers gaming about or what? Peter had also woken up. "What was that?" he asked. Martin was looking through the window but it was pitch black. No desert moon tonight. Suddenly, more shots were heard. The two men got dressed quickly. "Can't see anything." More shots rang out as a lorry with its headlights full on drove through the site. Shots were being fired into the tented area where the soldiers were sleeping. Martin and Peter hit the floor. "I think we're being attacked," whispered Martin. The scene was like a war zone. The lorry was full of soldiers who were firing into the tents. It drove up and down as bullets riddled the whole area. "We've got to try and get away from here," Martin suggested.

Suddenly, the door of the hut was kicked in and they were confronted by a group of armed men, all pointing their rifles at them. A man who seemed to be their leader pointed his gun to Peter's head. He spoke in a language Martin and Peter didn't understand. Martin shouted something but was rewarded with a rifle butt to the stomach. The man in charge said something and they were roughly manhandled through the door. The site was now set on fire. The bodies of the soldiers who were supposed to have protected them littered the outside area. Martin and Peter felt their arms being tied behind their backs and then roughly loaded into the back of a lorry. There was a lot of talk going on but neither Peter nor Martin could understand. The lorry moved off into the desert towards the Somalian border. "I reckon we're hostages," whispered Martin.

***

Christine stood on the scales. She had put on two pounds. Her brow furrowed as she hadn't been eating any fatty foods for ages. The following day, her period should have started but nothing showed. She tried to dismiss the idea but as the days passed and there was no show, she began to realise that Billy had knocked her up again after a Saturday night on the piss. "Well, that's put an end to things," she muttered to herself. "It's a good job Marianne's left, no more ladies hanky-panky with dildos." She picked up Steven. "What's it to be, lovely—a girl or a boy?" She put on her favourite CD and began singing along with the music; she felt happy.

Chapter 17
Hostage

Martin whispered, "These must be Somalian rebels, Peter, they don't look like a proper army. There's no proper discipline; they're just a load of bandits." One of the soldiers gave Martin a kick in the stomach and shouted at him. Their ragged clothes might have been uniforms at some time but now they were dirty and tattered. It was possible that the bunch had broken away from the real Somalian Army and set up their own group and were being led by a nut who wanted to rule and rob, a sort of Robin Hood of the desert but not so nice. After two hours of rough travel across the desert, they arrived at what may have been a settlement of sorts many years ago, but was now abandoned and ravaged by the desert winds and sandstorms. However, as the two men were manhandled out of the lorry, they were led into a stone building that had been crudely renovated. Obviously, this was their hide-out. Adjoining buildings had also received the same treatment as women and children emerged to greet the rebels.

***

Kath and Harry made their way along the corridor to Mr Jones' office. Harry knocked and opened the door. "Come in, Harry, bang on time as usual. Hello, Mrs Williams." The door opened again and the union official entered. He greeted everyone and then sat down beside them. "Right Harry, we've been successful in getting your redundancy." Mr Jones opened a folder in front of him. "Dennis and I have worked closely on this and we have been treating you as a special case. A package has been drawn up and I'm going to explain it all to you. You finish employment with British Coal on 31 December of this year. A payout in the form of a lump sum will be made to you, a sum of eighteen thousand pounds." Harry looked surprised. Mr Jones carried on, "You are advised to remain on the sick and your sick pay will be paid each week as it is now. You will also submit a claim for industrial injuries from the D.H.S.S. You may have to fight to claim this but Dennis will be there to support your claim and represent you if required. The D.H.S.S. doesn't like giving money away and you might have to attend a tribunal, but again Dennis will be with you to represent you. On top of that, you are also advised to claim from British Coal for your injuries, which weren't your fault. Do you understand, Harry? There's a lot of claiming to do and your union and I think you have a very good chance of winning a substantial sum of money."

Harry looked at Kath. "We'll be taking a holiday, love, where shall we go?"

Harry had to sign to say he had accepted the redundancy package and thanked Mr Jones and Dennis. He and Kath left with big smiles on their faces. "Christ, Harry, we've never been so rich," said a happy Kath.

***

It was stiflingly hot in the ramshackle ruin. Martin and Peter were forced to sit on a dirty piece of matting. Their hands were still tied behind their backs. After a while, one of the soldiers entered, carrying a bottle of water that he held out to them to drink from. He carried his rifle, pointing it at them. Later, he returned with a plate with pieces of bread on it. He held it up and placed a piece of bread in their mouths. The door was left open when he left and a slight but warm breeze engulfed them. The guard sat outside, watching them, his rifle pointing in their direction. Later, as the hot sun moved towards the west, they heard a vehicle pull up outside. They heard someone shouting orders. The guard came in and pointed his rifle at them, ordering them to get up. They were ushered outside where more rebels were hanging around. The one who seemed to be their leader barked further orders. Peter and Martin were made to kneel down in front of him. He cleared a space around him and produced a large handheld camera and began taking photos of them. He pressed the button on the camera and watched as the photos were produced. He shoved them in their faces to show them. He then had them returned to the building where they were forced to sit on the mat.

"I think we are being held for ransom," Peter managed to say between gritted teeth. The guard looked at him and shouted something.

What seemed to be a couple of hours later, Martin began to groan. "I need the toilet," he said. Peter called out to the guard. Both men had now reached the stage where they needed to relieve themselves. Peter had raised himself into a sitting position and was trying to convey to the guard their need for a toilet. It was difficult but eventually the message got through. Martin was led outside and two more of the rebels escorted him to the back of the building and pointed to the ground. Martin got the message and asked for his hands to be freed. The rebels seemed reluctant at first but then one of them produced a knife and cut one hand free. Martin struggled with his trousers but eventually he managed. The two rebels watched as he emptied his bowels. Peter was brought out next and the procedure was repeated. "What a relief," Martin said. As the night drew in, a paraffin lamp was hung up inside and another drink of water was given. A plate of meat was fed into their mouths by the guard.

During the later hours, there was more activity outside. The sound of motorbikes shattered the still air. "Scramblers by the sound of it," said Martin. "Two of them."

Peter listened. "Probably used as messenger boys or outriders to patrol the dunes where the lorries can't get."

Martin chuckled. "I wonder if we could borrow them for a while."

Susan had filled the washing machine and was just browsing through the mail. The doorbell rang and Susan skipped down the stairs to answer it. Two well-dressed men stood in front of her. They greeted her and introduced themselves as managers from the plant where Peter worked. A cold shiver ran down her spine as she looked into their faces. "What's happened? Has something happened to Peter?"

The elder gentleman asked if they could come in. "Peter's all right at the moment," he assured her.

They sat down in the lounge. Susan was shaking; she feared that something was wrong, she hadn't heard from Peter for two days. Not since he had phoned to say he would be home very soon. "Has there been an accident or something?" she asked.

The elder gentleman said, "I'll come straight to the point. Peter and Martin are being held hostage by a band of Somalian rebels."

The second man spoke quietly, "They are being held for ransom. We have offered to pay their price but our government is blocking us, telling us that we cannot make any deals. They say talks will take place but we cannot pay any ransom money over until other possibilities have been discussed. The Kenyan Government is negotiating with the rebels but not making much progress. They have mobilised their army units who are now patrolling the borders with Somalia. The Somalian Government has denied any kind of involvement with the rebels and is now searching for them. We must tread very carefully as this is a delicate position we are in. You will no doubt hear about it on the news and in the media but as always, things get exaggerated. We will keep you informed of any progress made and please believe what we tell you and not the media."

***

The B.A.D. Boys met at the club at 5:15. "We are just observing him today," announced Ray. "See what he gets up to." They pulled into the lay-by and waited. "It doesn't look as if he's going to show," said Ray, looking at his watch. "It's 6:30 now. Did Kev say the bloke comes here straight from work? Well, he must be doing some overtime or he ain't coming. Oh well, we can always try another Friday night." Barely had the words left his mouth when a blue Vauxhall Corsa pulled into the lay-by, driven by a man in his thirties. He pulled up just at the end of the lay-by and switched his engine off. The B.A.D. Boys sat there, observing his actions. Nothing was happening. After ten minutes, he got out of the car and had a quick look around. He waited a few minutes longer and then moved off.

Abbo said, "I've written his number down so we can perhaps follow him next time and see if he's selling to anybody else in our area."

Ray pulled up in the club car park. "Who's for a pint?"

***

Janet made her way around the exhibition looking for potential customers. She was looking for someone a bit fanciful. "No potbellied bald-headed old farts for me," she whispered to herself. She was drawn to the stand where a small crowd had formed. Pushing her way through, she noticed religious banners and piles of bibles. *Oh my God*, she thought. *Where's Veronica? This is her pitch.*

A suave-looking man with blonde hair caught her eye. He was addressing the crowd and spreading the word about his religion and God's word about freedom of choice. "Anything goes," he was saying, "as long as you do not lose your faith."

Janet moved around, he was certainly a looker. Their eyes met and he honed in on her handing out his religious leaflets. Soon they were engaged in serious conversation. Janet was attracted to him and he knew it. He was saying that he felt he had so much in common with her. Leaving his associates to deal with the crowd, he led her to a quiet spot behind the stand. Janet was remembering what Veronica had said about him being well-built and well-blessed. He certainly was an eye-catcher. After a short while, Janet had arranged to meet him for lunch and further enlightenment on religious understanding. After the meal, he suggested visiting his room where he had some interesting leaflets. Janet made her excuses, informing the pastor that she had to get back into the exhibition and earn her hundred pound bonus by interviewing prospective customers for the company. She handed him one of her leaflets. "Mine will be much more interesting and far more rewarding," he said, feeling for his wallet. He handed her five crisp twenty-pound notes. In no time at all, he had her standing at the side of the bed and peeling off her clothes. He then quickly undressed, revealing his erect member. Janet gasped; it certainly was a two and a half hander. Veronica had been right; he had a huge rib tickler.

She made her way back to the car where Joe and the other two were waiting. "I thought I was going to have to come and look for you," said Joe.

Janet smiled and leaned over and placed a religious leaflet in Veronica's hand and howled with laughter. "I've been converted too, Veronica."

Joe eased the car off the car park. "You know you've been fucked when you meet the pastor," said a smiling Janet.

"Ooh!" whispered Val. "I must meet him."

Joe popped in a blue pill as he drove up to Veronica's flat. He lay on the bed as Veronica disappeared into the bathroom. She emerged shortly, wrapped in a large white bath towel. "How would you like to do it, Joe? Doggy fashion or the slow boat to the Bermuda Triangle?"

Joe said, "An all-round trip would do nicely."

Veronica climbed onto the bed. "How about a Sharon Stone, Joe? I've done the Bermuda Triangle today already." Joe smiled as Veronica mounted him.

***

Peter eased his aching legs as the desert night drew in. Martin tried to adjust his position as well. "Peter," he whispered, "do you think there's any chance of escaping?"

Peter leaned himself a bit closer. The guard outside looked at the prisoners menacingly. He came in and turned the flame down on the lamp and then resumed his position sitting outside the door. Peter whispered very quietly, "If we could untie ourselves, we would stand a chance, but these ties are too tight. I've been trying to loosen them."

Martin eased himself into a sitting position. "So have I, Peter, and I think I might have loosened my right one a bit. What I'd give for a knife."

Peter observed that the guard's head was on his chest as if he was dozing. "They've tied us up with electrical cable, Martin, a knife wouldn't be enough. Keep working on loosening your hand. If you can get a hand free, we might stand a chance."

Morning arrived to find Martin and Peter in a deep sleep, exhausted by their efforts to untie their bonds. The guard had been relieved at some point during the night and replaced by an equally nasty-looking rebel who came in and extinguished the lamp. He pointed his rifle at the two men as he checked their ties. Moments later, the rebel leader came in and barked some orders at them. The guard prodded them with his rifle, indicating that they should go outside. A group of rebels had gathered and seemed to be holding another prisoner. The rebel chief had his camera and was giving orders to his men. The other prisoner was led to a clearing between the buildings and Martin and Peter were held a few yards away. The rebels forced their prisoner to kneel before their leader who began taking photos of the man and then of Martin and Peter.

The leader barked further orders and one of the rebels stepped forward, pointed his rifle at the man's head and fired. Martin and Peter both vomited as the man's head exploded, scattering his brains into the sand. The leader stepped forward to photograph what had once been a human being. Martin and Peter were returned to the building and made to sit on the floor. Martin puked again. "It will be one of us next," whispered Peter. "We've got to try and escape from here." The usual bottle of water was held in front of them followed by some bread. The guard was replaced every couple of hours. It was very hot inside the building and now flies were buzzing around where Martin's stomach had erupted. Peter called to the guard and indicated that he wanted to empty his bowels. The guard pointed his rifle at him as Peter made his way to the back of the building, which served as the toilet area. The guard untied one hand, allowing him to drops his pants. Peter looked around trying to see beyond the building. Two motorbikes were leaning against the adjacent building in a shaded area, keeping the sun off them. Returning to their prison, Peter gave Martin a nod. The guard had retied Peter's hand and made him sit on the floor. "Martin, we've got to get our hands free. There's a way out of here if we can." Martin nodded and began trying to loosen his bonds.

There was a commotion outside and the rebel leader could be heard giving orders. It sounded as if the rebels were getting into the lorry. Shortly, the sound of the lorry leaving reached their ears. "They're off somewhere," said Martin. "That means fewer rebel soldiers left here. Maybe we've got a chance, Peter." During the hot afternoon, the guard held out the bottle of water for them to drink and a plate of meat was offered. He then resumed his position outside the building, occasionally checking on his prisoners.

***

Billy manoeuvred the machine into the back of the rock head. "This is more like it," he said to Norman. Lifting the boom, he began to cut into the rock.

Norman fed the cable behind the machine. "I should think we will break through soon. It will be easier on the level."

Billy said it was only a matter of a few metres and then they would be earning good bonuses. "About fucking time," shouted Jegger. "My car's about knackered and I want to swap it."

Billy laughed. "Get another moped, Jegger, but not a fucking noisy bastard like you had before."

Sitting down on the floor, the men stopped for their snap. "We've driven this road down here and it's taken two years. There's coal down here but there's rumours that this pit is on the list for closure." Billy looked pissed off. "What does the future hold for us if it does close? There's no jobs going for us in this area, there's only the power station and the bog factory. What is there for knackered up miners like us? I've never done anything else. I'm forty years old and on the scrap heap if this place closes."

Norman said that he was fifty and was hoping a new redundancy scheme would be set up. "I'd snatch their fucking hands off if they offered me a payout and then apply for a job on the council, grass-cutting or painting white lines."

"That's about all you're good for," voiced Jegger, ducking to miss the pieces of rock that Norman threw at him. "And all you're good for is letting your girlfriend play with your plonker." The team burst into laughter as they resumed their work.

Chapter 18
Escape

It was getting dark inside the building and the guard had brought in the lamp and hung it up. He checked the prisoners' bonds before resuming his position outside the building. Peter had moved closer to Martin and now they were almost back-to-back. When the guard had retied his hand, Peter had stretched his hand more than usual so it gave him a bit more freedom to manoeuvre. He inched into position so that he could reach Martin's bonds. Slowly, he pulled and twisted at the ties. Martin could feel Peter trying to undo the cable. "It's not very easy as my hands are sweating and I haven't got a very good grip," he whispered to Martin.

"Let me have a go at yours, Peter, while you take a rest." Peter moved so that Martin could try. Peter's ties became looser and after a while, Peter could wriggle his hand free. The guard's head was resting on his chest. It looked as if he was asleep. Peter eased his free hand around to Martin's ties and soon he had eased the knot and he could feel Martin stretching the cable. A sigh of relief escaped Martin as he pulled his hands free. They rested a while, pretending to sleep. The guard had moved slightly into a more comfortable position but was fast asleep. Both men were now free from their bonds. They massaged their wrists to get the blood flowing. Peter whispered to Martin, "The two motorbikes are just around the corner from the toilet area. If we can get past the guard, we can get to them."

Peter picked up a piece of rock from the floor, it was fist-size. Creeping forwards on all fours, he approached the sleeping guard. A swift blow to the head and the guard rolled over, unconscious. Martin looked out of the door; it was very dark apart from a weak moon high in the sky. They pulled the guard into the building and rolled him over on his belly. Peter grabbed the pieces of cable and tied his hands behind him. Martin was doing the same to his feet. They dowsed the lamp and Peter removed a ragged scarf from the guard and wrapped it around his head, gagging him. He picked up the guard's rifle and led the way to where he had seen the motorbikes parked. It was so dark he couldn't tell if they were still there. They crept forwards on all fours, feeling their way around the building. Peter reached out and felt the frame of the first bike. Gradually pulling away the cover, Martin also reached out and found the second bike. With bated breath, they felt for the top to turn on the petrol. They were old bikes with the familiar kick-start. Martin pushed his bike away from the building and straddled it, feeling for the controls. "Don't put on any lights until we are away from here. Are you ready, Martin?" Peter kicked up the machine but it didn't fire.

"Try again," whispered Martin as his machine fired up the first time. Peter held his breath as he tried again. This time, it fired up, to his great relief. Martin led the way past the buildings onto the rough road. The bikes skidded a couple of times as the rough road was littered with debris. Voices could be heard from some of the buildings as the noisy machines were driven slowly at first and then opened up. After a couple of miles, they pulled up to find their direction. A weak sun was emerging, heralding that they were facing east. "We have to keep the sun on our backs and head west," shouted Martin. "I reckon its thirty to fifty miles to the border. I hope there's enough petrol in these tanks." He shook the bike, listening to the petrol sloshing about inside.

Peter did likewise. He pointed to the panniers. "I think there may be some spare cans in there." He undid the straps and looked in. "There's a gallon can in mine." He opened the top and smelt it. "Yes, it's petrol. We should be all right, Martin."

They moved off into the desert, keeping the sun on their backs. As far as they could make out, the rough track was heading in the right direction. They had put the light on now, which helped them avoid the larger pieces of debris littering the road. "What shall we do if we meet anybody?" shouted Peter.

Martin pointed into the sand dunes. "We head up there, Peter, these bikes are made for that." They followed the track, still keeping the sun on their backs. They could see the tyre marks of lorries that seemed to be heading in the same direction. Suddenly, Martin braked and pointed to dust clouds heading towards them. "It looks like we've got company, Peter. Into the dunes quickly before they spot us."

They revved their engines and Martin led the way slipping and sliding up the sandy dunes. "I used to do this sort of thing when I was a teenager," shouted Martin above the noise of the engines. "It was great fun."

Suddenly, shots were fired at them. The two lorries full of rebels had pulled up and were firing at them. "I guess they've found out we escaped," shouted Peter. "Let's get into the dunes as they won't follow us in there with those lorries." They revved the engines and disappeared, still heading west.

After a while, the motorbikes began to falter. "I bet the air filters are getting blocked," yelled Martin. "Let's stop and see." They pulled up at the bottom of a huge sand dune. Martin unscrewed the air filter cap and started to blow out the sand. "I thought so," he muttered. Peter had done the same. They fired up the bikes, which sounded much healthier after the clean out. "Right," said Martin, shading his eyes against the sun. "Let's follow these dunes, keeping parallel to the track. We should have bypassed the rebels now and should be somewhere near the site where we started from." Peter followed Martin, who would occasionally climb to the top of the dunes and peer down the other side.

"It looks all clear down there," shouted Peter.

"Yes, it does. Shall we get back on the track now?" They eased the bikes down the dune and started making their way to where they hoped the site was. All went well for fifteen minutes and then a rifle shot took them by surprise. “They’ve guessed where we’re heading and have turned around to follow us,” yelled Martin. “Let’s get out of here. We can’t be far off the Kenyan border. Maybe they won’t follow us once we’ve crossed over.”

More shots rang out but went wild. “Keep zigzagging,” Peter shouted out. “Don’t give them a clear shot.” The zigzagging had a good effect and kicked up a load of dust, obliterating the view from the lorries. They kept on the track, hoping soon to find somewhere they would recognise. More shots were fired and then soon a whole volley of shots fired but not at them. Martin shouted to Peter, “I think we’ve reached safety. That must be the Kenyan soldiers shooting at the rebels. We’ve done it, Peter.”

Susan picked up the phone. She listened as the managing director gave her the good news. “They managed to escape and are now in the hands of the Kenyan army. We will soon have them home, Susan.” Susan whispered thank you and put the phone down. She sat on the settee and wept.

***

Christine was in a good mood when Billy arrived home. She gave him a kiss, which took him by surprise. “What’s up, Chris, have we won the lottery?”

Christine shook her head. “No Billy, it’s nothing to do with money. Money can’t buy this.” She took his hand and placed it on her stomach.

He looked at her open-mouthed. “What’s this then, you haven’t gone and got yourself knocked up, have you?”

Christine gave him a hard slap across the face. “No, you bastard, you’ve gone and got me knocked up.”

She backed away, not sure whether Billy was pleased or not. He opened his arms and gave her a huge hug. “What a lovely surprise, Christine, I’m a bit shocked but I’m also delighted. I was going to suggest we should have a playmate for Steven but I didn’t know if you were ready or not. Is it definite or what?”

Christine laughed out loud. “Well, I don’t think it’s wind, Billy. You’ve got a dick, not a bicycle pump.”

***

Joe opened the front door. “Is that you, Joe?” Rosie called out.

“No, it’s the postman,” he answered.

“Can’t be, he was here yesterday,” she called back.

“What, are you shagging him while I’m at physio?” Joe asked suspiciously.

Rosie started laughing. “Of course not, Joe. I don’t need to now that you’re on them tablets. By the way, you need another prescription; you’re nearly out of them. I don’t know how you got through them so quickly; you only take one at a time. There were fifty in the bottle and it’s nearly empty, we ain’t been shagging that many times, Joe.”

Joe had to think quickly. “Well, sometimes I take one and find you’ve gone off to sleep before I come to bed,” he said hopefully.

“Well, don’t forget to get some more,” answered Rosie.

“I’ve just been talking to a couple of lads in the club. They say that the redundancy scheme is starting up again and I’m thinking of putting my name down for it.”

Rosie poured Joe a cup of tea. “What will that mean to us, Joe?” she asked.

Joe thought for a moment. “Well, there’ll be a lump sum cash payout for a start. I’m not sure whether I will be able to stay on the sick. If I can, I will still be able to claim sick pay. There’s some who are already doing that.”

Rosie looked at Joe. “And what if they sign you off the sick? You would have to find a job, Joe. A lump sum wouldn’t last until we get our retirement pension, would it?”

Joe took a sip of tea. “I’ll have to make more enquiries,” he said thoughtfully.

***

As the train rumbled along the rails taking them to the backend, Abbo spoke, "Are we still active as the B.A.D. Boys?" he asked, dealing out the cards.

"Of course we are," Andy answered. "There's still drugs out there; we've just got to find the dealer."

Ray looked at his cards. "If they're anything like the fucker who just dealt these cards, it should be easy," he quipped. "Our Dave is onto something at the moment. The trouble is the fuckers who are taking them buy them off their mates or at work. We can't stop them; we can only stop the dealers we find selling on the streets of our town. It's a matter of eyes and ears. We've done well so far but we must be vigilant and act on information received."

The boys agreed with Ray. "We need more informers really," added Abbo.

***

Susan listened as Peter related what had happened and how they had managed to escape. "Who was the man they shot?" Susan asked.

"Well, apparently he was the engineer on the site looking after the machinery. The rebels had kidnapped him previously and threatened to kill his family if he didn't put the machine out of action and so he reversed the restrictor valves in the line so that they didn't work properly. He then said he was going away for a few days and wasn't seen again. The Kenyan government apologised for allowing the rebels to kidnap us and have offered to compensate us for our trauma. Our employers also are going to make up for it and were very pleased that the machine was put right and is now in full working order again. The rebels were killed in a gun battle and the rebel leader captured and is in prison."

"I'm so glad you have returned safely, Peter. I couldn't have been without you. I've been out of my mind worrying about you."

Peter drew her close to him. "Never will I ever leave you, Susan. I've made that clear to my employers and now

Martin and I have been given two weeks paid holiday as a bonus."

Susan reached for the property magazines she had collected. "Let's look through these and find our new home, shall we?"

***

Dennis picked up the phone in his office. "Another meeting," said the president. "British Coal has instigated another redundancy package. Can you make it this Friday, Dennis? I want to get things moving again as our members seem anxious to get things sussed out to see what's on offer."

Dennis went home and started packing again, ready for Friday's departure. He recognised Sylvia's voice when he rang the Sherwood. "Oh Dennis, that will be nice. Gladys and Henry are in Blackpool again so I'll be looking after you all by myself. Ooh Dennis, I can't wait."

***

The first week passed quickly and Susan and Peter made use of the time trawling around estate agents and proposed building sites. They chose a new site looking out across open meadows with the river Trent meandering its way through. Peter stood looking over the planned site; he stamped his feet on the ground, which puzzled Susan. He looked at her and smiled. "I've probably worked below these pastures green," he said, giving her a cuddle. "Let's go and see the plans."

When the second week passed, Peter returned to work. Martin was waiting for him. "Peter, come into the office please, I've got some good news."

Peter listened as Martin informed him that the Kenyan government had decided to pay each of them ten thousand pounds as compensation. Peter clapped his hands. Martin went on to say that their own company had also decided to compensate them and had offered the same amount. Peter couldn't contain himself and he jumped up and gave Martin a big hug.

"You've just made it possible for Susan and me to put a good deposit on our new house. I can't wait to tell her when I go home. I'm absolutely delighted, Martin, I owe all this to you, my friend. Will you be best man when Susan and I get married?"

***

Ray and Dave stood in the cemetery, looking at the grave of their sister. "Can't believe it's been a year," whispered Dave.

Ray put his hands on his brother's shoulder. "We still miss her, don't we, Dave?" They placed the flowers on the stone slab. 'Sadly missed by all' it read. "Mam and Dad come here often too," said Ray, wiping away the tears.

"But we done something about it, Ray, didn't we? That Columbian woman will be having a hard time in jail," said a tearful Dave.

"Yeah but not hard enough," replied Ray. "She's got to answer to me when they let her out. There's a hole waiting for her over in the forest." They walked amongst the gravestones, looking at the names.

"I supposed we're all going to end up here one day," muttered Dave.

"Yeah but in the meantime, little brother, let's go and have a pint."

"Are we still going to remain active?" asked Dave.

Ray looked at Dave. "You bet your life we are," he said.

***

The president brought the meeting to order. "Gentlemen, I have received notification form British Coal that further redundancies are on the cards. They have, however, made certain suggestions regarding pit closures. The redundancies will be offered to men working at the mines that are due to close. Anyone who doesn't want redundancy will be offered employment in areas where the industry is promising. Rehoming and monetary payments will be made for their upheaval. I hope we can still maintain a workforce to enable us to produce coal for this country." The president asked for a vote to indicate whether or not to accept the proposals. "I believe it is a fair offer and I don't believe we can ask for anything more."

Dennis put his hand up. "Mr President, what if the number of volunteers doesn't meet British Coal's requirements? Will other members be invited to apply?"

The president acknowledged Dennis' question. "Of course, these questions will be asked of British Coal. I shall propose that if the numbers aren't met then the quota will be met by other members in the industry."

As the meeting came to a close, Dennis popped in a couple of paracetamol before driving to the Sherwood. It had started raining and didn't look very promising for the weekend. Sylvia greeted him as he entered the hotel. "Do you want something warm?" she asked.

Dennis smiled at her. "Of course, darling, but I'll have a coffee first. If this weather doesn't clear up, I may decide to spend the weekend here."

Sylvia gave a seductive giggle. "Oh Dennis, please do."

He made his way to his room and began to look through his notes. He was fifty years old himself. How about him taking redundancy? He shook his head. "No, I'm not ready yet," he whispered.

Sylvia entered the room with a tray, two cups of coffee and cakes. "Are you joining me?" he asked.

Sylvia placed the tray on the table and sat on the bed beside him. "How about a nice welcome kiss?" She loomed in towards him and offered herself.

Dennis took a sip of coffee. "How come you haven't remarried, Sylv? You're a good-looking woman and you know how to look after a man."

Sylvia shook her head. "I was married once, Dennis. We had two kids, a boy and a girl, and I thought we had everything but he changed. He started womanising and then beating me. He would disappear on a Friday and come home on Sunday night as if nothing had happened. I knew he had a bit on the side. I tried to keep my kids from knowing about it but eventually they found out. My son, who had turned thirteen, followed his father one night and saw him and his woman get on a bus together, arm in arm, kissing and cuddling. My son was so upset when he came home and I could see he had been crying. That's when I decided I had enough. We moved out and came to live with Gladys and Henry. Eventually, we got a place of our own and lived together until both my son and daughter made a life for themselves. They are both now happily married and I've got three grandchildren who I adore. I see them all regularly so what more do I need, Dennis? I have friends both male and female and I lack for nothing."

Dennis gave her a hug. "I hope we will always be friends," he whispered. "But that's all I can offer you, Sylvia. I have a sick wife who I have to look after."

Sylvia snuggled up to him on the bed. "That's all I want too, Dennis, just to be good friends."

***

Christine watched as Steven bounced up and down in his bouncer that Billy had put up in the doorway. She leaned against the kitchen work surface, feeling her stomach. "Definitely pregnant," she murmured but her thoughts soon began to meander through her mind. She missed Marianne and began to feel horny. "I still miss you, Marianne," she whispered. "You gave me what I wanted. I'm going to find your address and write to you." Putting Steven into his chair and giving him toys to play with, she began searching for the piece of paper Marianne had given her.

"Dearest Marianne, how I have missed you," she began.

It was almost two weeks before the letter arrived. Christine smelled the perfume and right away, her heart began to beat faster.

"My dearest Christine, I too have missed you but I do have to come and visit Stafford for a meeting on 25 October. Maybe I can come and see you?"

Christine read the letter. "Oh yes, Marianne, please do," she said out loud. She stroked her belly. "I shall be two and a half months by then but so what? Billy will still be humping me so why not Marianne?"

***

Susan and Peter signed the papers in the estate agents' office. "Good, that's secured your plot and now we can give the builders the go-ahead." The young man shook their hands as he escorted them to the door. "It won't be long before you move into your new house," he added.

They held hands and wandered around the town. "I've worked it out, Peter. A year from now, we will have moved in and I shall be thirty-five and you thirty-six. I want us to start our family, Peter, the clock's ticking, let's do it."

***

Rosie put the teacup on the table in front of Joe. "Did you get them?" she asked.

Joe reached into his pocket. "Yes I did, here they are." He placed the packet on the table.

"These aren't the same as you had before, Joe," exclaimed Rosie, checking the label. "Are they any good?"

Joe took them off her. "The proof of the pudding is in the eating," he said.

Rosie smiled. "Well, I shall want some pudding tonight, Joe, so rest up for the day."

Joe closed his eyes. *If only Rosie's arse was like Veronica's*, he thought, *two bunnies in a sack and not an elephant in a nylon stocking.*

Chapter 19
Flooded

Billy eased the machine forward and began drilling into the rock. Norman checked that the cable didn't get caught up in the tracks. "This fucking water's getting worse," shouted Jegger.

The deputy looked. "It's coming up through the floor. Keep an eye on it; we shall have to get the pump brought in."

Billy swung the boom across. "We need some wellingtons; my feet are soaked."

Bruce made a note in his book. "I'll get a note off to the gaffer for the morning."

Mr Burns, the underground manager for area five, sat in his office. He wasn't feeling very well and his stomach felt on fire. He picked up the phone and rang the colliery manager's number. "I'm feeling a bit rough, boss. I'm going to have to go home. Can you arrange for someone to take over for me?"

He managed to make it to his car and drove home. Mrs Burns immediately sent for the doctor. She had noticed how her husband's complaint had been getting worse. "It's not indigestion," she said. "Let the doctor check you out."

Within two hours, the doctor had examined her husband. "I'm afraid he's going to be admitted to hospital, Mrs Burns, your husband is seriously ill."

The ambulance arrived and drove them to the hospital. She waited whilst her husband was examined. The doctor diagnosed Mr Burns as having peritonitis and needed immediate treatment. She waited patiently in the waiting area with her son and daughter who had joined her.

The hours ticked by and it was almost midnight when a nurse and a doctor approached them. His sad expression said it all. "Mrs Burns, I'm very sorry but your husband passed away ten minutes ago. His condition was very serious and despite all our efforts, we were unable to save him. We are extremely sorry."

The notice was put up on his office door, informing the workforce that Mr Burns had passed away during the night. Funeral arrangements would be made. The men of area five crowded around, muttering their disbelief. "He was a good gaffer," some said. "Yes, a gentleman."

***

Billy looked at the water level in the head. "It's still rising," he said, climbing up onto the machine. "It's twice as bad as yesterday." As he looked closely, he could see bubbles of water coming through the floor. "Let's get the fuck out of here quick," he shouted to his mates. They clambered back along the road. "Fuck it," shouted Billy. "I've forgotten my safety lamp." He turned around and hurried back the fifty yards they had travelled.

"Fuck the lamp, Billy, there's plenty in the lamp house," shouted Norman.

Billy trod carefully until he reached the spot where he had hung his lamp. The water was lapping around his ankles. He reached for his lamp and then he froze. Alf stood in front of him, barring his way. Billy broke into a cold sweat as he looked at the apparition. Alf was telling him to go back. Billy tried to speak but no words came out of his mouth. The water was still rising as Billy backed off. He looked again but Alf had gone. Billy raced back to where his mates were waiting. He only said two words, "Let's go," and started climbing up the hill.

"He's in a bit of a hurry," said Norman, trying to catch up with Billy. They met Bruce coming down the hill. Billy told him that the water had broken in and was flooding the head.

"It's rising rapidly, Bruce, don't go in there."

Bruce said he had to see for himself so that he could give a good report to the manager. "Be quick then, Bruce, we'll wait here for you."

The rest of the team caught up. "Fuck me, Billy, you was legging it. Are you on a promise or something?" quipped Jegger, sitting on the floor. "I'm knackered."

Billy said nothing as he watched Bruce walk down the hill. "I'll go and see if he's all right," said Norman. They watched and waited until they could see the lights of the two men returning. "OK, let's go," said a pale-faced Billy.

"It's coming in fast," Bruce remarked. "I think it might just close this place down." They walked steadily up the hill. "It's taken two years to head this road out. What a fucking thing to happen," he added.

The train pulled in to pick them up. Jegger pulled out the cards. Billy hadn't spoken and he just gazed out of the carriage. He shook his head when Jegger asked if he was playing. Bruce said that they should accompany him to the bosses' office and give their report to back up his. The boss listened. "It sounds bad. I shall have to arrange for someone to go down and monitor the water level."

Billy spoke for the first time, "We've isolated all the electric supply, boss, just as a precaution."

The boss thanked them and told them to take the rest of the day off. "We'll see what the morning brings, lads."

Billy quickly dashed through the showers. He didn't bother going into the canteen for the usual cup of tea that always tasted like piss anyway. He got into his car and drove to the club. He downed the first pint in seconds and ordered another. "Got a thirst on today, Billy?" remarked Hazel the barmaid.

"Yeah, you can say that," said Billy as he asked for another pint. He closed his eyes and tried to recall what had unnerved him. Had he imagined it or had Alf appeared before him to warn him of the danger? He finished his beer and drove to the cemetery. He walked amongst the gravestones until he stood in front of Alf's. Billy could feel the emotions building up inside as he gazed at the flowers that the family kept replanting. "Thanks Alf," he said loudly.

***

Christine had put Steven in his buggy and covered him with his blanket. He was sucking his dummy and dozing off. She quickly tidied up and ran upstairs to the bedroom. She quickly brushed her hair and put on her make-up, dousing herself in her favourite perfume. She ran downstairs to answer the doorbell. Marianne stood there with a huge smile on her face. "God, Marianne, you look gorgeous, come on in."

Once inside, they greeted each other intensely, Marianne's tongue finding all the right spots that Billy didn't even know about. They sat down on the settee. Christine looked at the clock. Just on half past eleven; Billy would be sweating his cobblers off down the pit. Marianne took control and soon they were pawing over each other, bras and knickers thrown on the floor. "Oh Marianne, I've missed you so much," she whispered as Marianne's tongue teased her innermost sanctuary.

"You've put on a bit of weight, Christine, what happened to that lovely flat belly of yours?"

Christine giggled. "I've got a baby in there now, Marianne, Billy's knocked me up."

Marianne looked surprised. "Oh Christine, I can't introduce you to my new toy now, it would be too much." She felt in her bag and showed Christine the huge penis.

Christine gave a laugh. "Well, Billy's still humping me so I think it's safe, Marianne."

Marianne lay back. "You can fuck me with it, Christine. It's very good and most stimulating."

Christine took hold of the toy and pleasured Marianne. "Oh, I must try it, Marianne." They changed over and Christine was soon experiencing the monster penis. "Ooh, I must get one of these, Marianne."

"It takes three batteries, Christine, and they last a long time." Well-satisfied, they got dressed and Christine put the kettle on. Marianne played with Steven. He had just woken up. A look of horror crossed Christine's face as she heard the front door being opened. Billy walked in and smiled. "An early day today."

Christine looked at him, surprised. "A wet note?" she asked. "This is Marianne. She used to be our insurance agent but now she's a manageress and has just popped in to say hello."

Billy shook hands. "Shall I take him off you?" he said, reaching out for Steven. "Yes, I thought so, he needs changing."

Christine walked with Marianne to her car. "Phew, that was close," she said.

"Yes, it was," agreed Marianne. "But still we got away with it and it was most enjoyable, Christine. I don't know if our paths will cross again but it was good while it lasted." Marianne drove off, leaving Christine waving to her.

"What brings you home so early, Billy, has something happened to you?"

Billy had finished changing Steven. "Yes love, the rock head is flooded. Water has broken in and flooded the place. We had to get out quick."

Christine put the kettle on. "So what's going to happen?"

Billy shook his head. "Don't know yet. Somebody's going to have to find out where it's come from. We didn't expect it." He thought for a minute. "They'll probably put a pump in there and pump the water out."

***

Kath leaned over and looked at the cheque Harry was holding. "Look at this, Kath, we've never had so much money. We'd better go down the town and bank it."

Kath squeezed Harry's arm. "It's like a dream come true, Harry. Let's do it now before I wake up and find out I'm dreaming."

They put on their coats and walked down the road to the bus stop. “There’s a travel agent in the town, Harry, can we pop in and get a brochure?” Kath browsed through the brochures whilst Harry looked on.

“What about the garden?” he asked.

***

Denise sat in the front passenger seat. “Pick up Val next, Joe. Veronica is off this week due to the usual breakdown in services.” Joe followed the road around to where Val lived. He couldn’t help notice how stunning she looked in her tight skirt and ample cleavage protruding over her top.

I must have her again, he thought wistfully as she climbed in next to Janet.

“Where are we off to this time?” she asked.

Janet informed her that it was a Tupperware and Stainless Steel Kitchenware show in Sheffield. Joe added, “We are in the cutlery business today, girls. Don’t forget your free samples.”

Denise looked at Joe. “I hope you mean knives and forks, Joe, I ain’t giving nothing else away free.” The girls howled with laughter.

“If they want the other, it’s gonna cost them,” screamed Janet.

They entered the exhibition hall with the girls carrying samples of cutlery in fancy boxes. “How do you manage to get all this stuff?” asked Val.

“I know a man who knows someone in the trade. It’s who you know, Val, in this game.”

They dispersed and worked their way around the huge hall. Denise made several approaches to reps, showing off her samples. All were encouraging but not to her liking. She honed in on the group of people surrounding one of the stands. She observed the religious notices being distributed amongst the gatherers. Val was showing a lot of interest as the blonde-haired pastor held her attention. Denise slipped away, leaving Val to do her bit. Her attention was held by a young man on one of the Tupperware stands. He was staring at her. Slowly, she immersed herself in the few people around the stand. His companion, who was an older man, drew the attention of the small gathering. The younger man followed Denise as she moved around. "Is there anything I can interest you in?" he asked.

Denise displayed her samples. "I was about to ask you that," she said, giving him a warm smile.

The rep smiled back at her. "Ooh, what a question," he mused, looking at her samples. "I would have to look at these more closely; perhaps over lunch in a quiet location, like the hotel."

She thanked him for the invite. "I might just be able to spare you a few minutes of my valuable time being as you are such a handsome fellow and you have asked me so nicely. Anything else will cost you."

He beamed at her. "Of course," he whispered. "1:30 at the entrance."

Val reached out as the pastor held out a leaflet. His eyes opened wide as her breasts looked up at him. "If you need further information, it can be arranged," he whispered.

Val nodded. "Yes, I would like to know more."

The pastor moved around and took her arm. "Perhaps a private lunch at the hotel and then maybe I can indoctrinate you in my room."

Val pushed herself against him purposely and could feel a bulge moving closer to her. "But I do have a job to do, my time is priceless. I have these samples to show to would-be customers."

He looked at her and smiled. "You show me yours and I'll show you mine." After lunch, he led her to the lift leading to the third floor. He opened the door to his room. Already his hand was on her arse but at least the five twenty pound notes were in her handbag.

Denise glanced around the hotel restaurant. She couldn't help noticing Val and the pastor making for the lift. Her own man was rabbiting on about how he had worked his way up in his company and was now an assistant manager with good prospects. He said the company allowed good money for spending on prospective customers at these exhibitions and he hadn't spent anything yet.

"So I'm the first prospect of the day?" she asked coyly. "But I don't have much time; I have to earn my bonus or I don't eat."

The rep touched her arm. "First, let's eat and then we'll talk about your bonus and how you can earn it quickly."

***

"No. Area five is at risk of a complete shutdown," said the colliery manager, looking at the maps in front of him. "There's a big underground lake north of Litchfield, which was way off to our right. We've gone past that and are well below its level. We thought we were safe but the geologicals have come up with a possible answer. If, at any time, a slight tremor occurred in that area, it could have caused a breach in the lake's bed. Such a tremor did occur last year and now it is thought that there's a leak, allowing water to find its way to where we are. They are testing to find out if the water level has dropped in the lake by testing bore holes around it. Maybe it's just a trickle but we can't take the risk of continuing into the area before we are given the go-ahead. Meanwhile, we are putting in a Lee Howell pump and pumping the water out into a pound hole at the top of the hill. It will be monitored daily by the deputy and I will follow the reports. We are planning to come back far up the hill and start heading off at an angle and down at the shallower gradient just in case we can't go back to the road we've already put in. There's a lot of coal down there and it's a pity to lose it. We've spent two years putting two roads in. Let's see what we can do."

Billy and his team made their way across the pit top. "We shall have to break the belt structure first and then start cutting in. We need a drill and some bits as well as powder."

Norman said the deputy would be on the job and would organise the supplies. "We will need the surveyors to put a line in first and show us where we've got to start," said Billy. "It's going to be a pick and shovel job to get started and another two years if we've got to go in this way. The sooner we cut in and get some machinery in, the better."

"I hope we don't have to put up with that crap drill rig we had before. A Doscoe is better," muttered Jegger.

***

Susan and Peter stood on the threshold of their new house. The rep handed them the keys. "Congratulations on your new home. Have a wander around and ask me if there's anything you're not sure of."

They explored the house, admiring the views from each window. Susan checked the kitchen, trying out all the appliances. They were pleased with everything and told the rep so. "Good, I'll leave you to enjoy and make your plans. Thank you for choosing our company. You will find a courtesy bottle of wine in the kitchen with the compliments of our company."

Peter followed Susan up the stairs. "Shall we have the front bedroom for ourselves?" she asked.

Peter nodded. "Yes, why not. We can see who's coming down the street."

Susan wandered into the second bedroom. "You know who's going to be in here, don't you?"

Peter put his arms around her. "Yes I do, the kids."

Chapter 20
Rosie in Bloom

Joe had gone up to the surgery to keep his appointment. He leaned heavily on his stick as he was called to see Dr Elaine. "How are you, Joe?" Is the physio helping you?" Joe muttered that some of the exercises hurt his back but the heat lamp eased it a bit. "Well, severe arthritis isn't much fun, Joe, but at least you can move around with the aid of a stick. Some people can't even do that. How are you getting on with Rosie and the tablets?"

Joe looked away, embarrassed. "Well, she doesn't moan so much these days and she's told me to get another prescription."

The doctor looked at Joe. "And what about you, Joe, are you coping any better? Did that booklet help?"

Joe said Rosie had taken charge of that and was studying it. "She's a bit heavy to have her on top so we avoid that one," said Joe.

"Well, I'm sure you will find a way around it, Joe. Try to keep Rosie happy and in the meantime, I'll give you a sick note for six months. Keep up with the physio."

Joe called in the club for a pint, he felt as if he deserved one. He spoke to a couple at the bar before taking a seat at the table where his mates were. "You need to ask her to put you on permanent sick, Joe, and then go to the pit and put in for redundancy." Joe listened to his mates. They were experts in getting things done. They knew all the angles.

Rosie was hanging some washing on the line when Fred, her next-door neighbour, looked over the fence. He had been on his own since Ethel passed away two years ago. "Gotta problem with my washing machine, Rosie; is Joe in?"

Rosie shook her head. "No Fred, he's at the doctor's and then he'll pop into the club. What's up with the washer; has it conked out or just misbehaving?" Fred said it was misbehaving. "I'll pop around and have a look at it for you."

Fred opened the back door and let her in. "It does play up now and again," said Fred.

"Oh, it probably just needs a woman's touch," exclaimed Rosie, bending down and looking through the glass door. Fred noticed the curvature of her body in front of him. He had always liked women who were well-built.

"It's not the only thing that needs that," he whispered.

Rosie pressed all the buttons but nothing worked. "Have you turned the water on, Fred?" She squeezed past him and then bent down to reach under the sink. "No, you haven't, Fred."

He leaned over her to look and his hands slid around her waist. "Oh! Rosie, I must have forgotten." Rosie tried to stand up but Fred had still got his weight on her.

"Fred, what are you trying to do?" she whispered. She managed to stand up but Fred was still holding on to her. He manoeuvred her towards the kitchen table and bent her over it. "Oh Fred, you're getting me all hot and bothered. Do you know what you're doing?" Fred lifted her skirt and began to pull down her knickers. Rosie felt him enter her from the rear. "Ooh Fred, that's nice." Rosie was enjoying what Fred was doing, realising that Joe was lacking in that department.

"Thanks for putting my washing machine right, Rosie," said Fred, opening the door for her.

Rosie gave him a big smile. "Don't mention it, Fred. Anytime, just call me."

***

Dave told Ray that some of the lads who hung around at night were still smoking joints so someone was supplying them. "Is Kev still doing it?" Ray asked. Dave said he hadn't seen Kev for a long time.

“I think he may have found a girlfriend somewhere. He doesn’t deal at the school now. In fact, I hardly see him.”

Ray asked Dave to try and find out where the kids were getting the joints from. “It’s time we went on patrol around the area. I bet some bastard has crept into our town. We gotta keep vigilant. I’ll get the lads together for a drive around on Friday night. Meanwhile, keep your eyes and ears open, Dave.”

Abbo agreed it was time for another recce of the area. “There’s always something going on over the Chase at night. Shall we start with that bastard from the power station?”

***

The train pulled out of the pit bottom and dropped off the leaders and supply lads. “We will want them rings in sharpish,” shouted Billy to Abbo. “We’ve broken into the new road and need them urgent.”

Abbo shouted back, “You’ll get them today, Billy. We’re the ‘A’ team, aren’t we?”

Billy or someone shouted back, “Yes, ‘A’ for assholes.”

The deputy informed them that the water was still rising in the head and had not levelled out yet. The new pump was keeping it down but it was still rising steadily.

***

Susan opened the door for the carpet fitter who had arrived on time. “Carpets top to bottom, Mrs?” asked the fitter.

“Yes please, I don’t like these wooden floors, they’re too noisy.”

The fitter climbed the stairs. “They’re all the rage these days. The young ’uns love them.”

Susan and Peter had spent most of the week in carpet stores carefully selecting what they both liked. Susan had been very particular about the second bedroom carpet, it had a special purpose. The result of her pregnancy test had shown positive but she wanted to confirm it with a doctor before telling Peter. She stroked her stomach and smiled. During the following week, they sorted the furniture, discarding some of the old stuff and renewing various pieces. One thing was for certain—money was no object. They had procured a good mortgage and had kept a good sum in the bank. They handed the keys in for the flat and made their way home. Peter opened the front door and then turned around and picked Susan up. "I want to carry you over the threshold into our new house."

Susan giggled. "Yes, this is our home."

Peter put Susan down in the lounge. "Now Susan, will you marry me? I've waited for this moment."

Susan put her arms around him. "Yes darling, as soon as possible. I've been waiting too." During the evening, they talked about the wedding. Susan desperately wanted to tell Peter about her suspected pregnancy but refrained. The wedding would take place soon and she would tell him on the wedding night.

***

The B.A.D. Boys met in the car park at 5 o'clock. "We'll try the power station first. We can park close by and look for him," Ray suggested. "Our Dave reckons the kids on the estate are getting joints from somebody but he doesn't know who." Abbo said it could be anybody. "Drugs are available all over the place, especially in these discos and pubs. They just meet up in the bogs and buy; it's as simple as that." Ray thought for a while. "We gotta find a contact who uses the stuff, someone who wants to get off it. Put your feelers out, lads, there's gotta be someone out there."

Jegger thought for a moment and said, "There's always a lot of activity over the Chase at night. I bet that's a hot spot for druggies."

Abbo said it had always been so. "There's more shagging goes on over there and I've even done a bit myself."

Ray laughed. "Yeah, that applies to some of us as well but we're not interested in the shagging, it's the drug pushers we want but it ain't gonna hurt to check it out from time to time."

They parked up near the power station. It was almost 5:30 and still light enough to see the number plates of cars as they pulled out of the island. After a while, they observed a blue car approaching the island. "Check that number plate," said Abbo, winding down the window.

"Yes, that's him," whispered Andy. Ray put the car into gear and pulled away, following the blue car. It started to get dark and the driver put on his lights. He indicated and turned off, making for the Litchfield road. Ray followed at a distance. He hadn't yet switched on his lights. The suspect headed for Litchfield but soon he was pulling into a lay-by where two people were waiting. Ray pulled in but stayed back to observe.

"That's our man all right, let's put the wind up him. Mask up, boys."

They waited until the driver did his business with the two people. They soon grabbed the small package and hotfooted it farther along the lay-by to where their car was parked. The B.A.D. Boys eased their car forwards, closer to the blue Vauxhall. They slipped into the darkness and descended on the unsuspecting man sitting in the car. A look of horror appeared on his face as the boys got into the car. "What the fuck's going on?" he yelled.

Ray sat behind him and reached over. "You're pushing drugs, mate, in our area and we don't like it. We're going to take you out."

The man started screaming as the boys searched for his stash. "I only do a bit," he screamed, struggling to get out of Ray's grip. Abbo had found the packet under the seat.

"What's all this then?" he asked.

"If you want money, I'll give you all I've got," said the panicking driver.

Abbo tipped a packet of white powder all over the man. "Here, you have some," he said, tipping a second packet into the driver's mouth.

"Now fuck off from here and don't ever come back," said Ray. "Or next time, it will be the needles and you know what that stuff does to you."

Jegger leaned over. "We will be watching out for you; keep out of this area or its curtains for you."

Abbo had emptied all the packets over the interior of the car. "Right, let's fuck off," said Ray, releasing his hold on the very frightened man.

Ray pulled over at the first public phone box. "Just going to report a man selling drugs," he laughed.

***

Rosie looked through the kitchen window at Fred who was busy in his garden. He was 60 years old but still had a good body on him. He had powerful shoulders and good muscular arms, not like Joe who had let himself go and had developed a belly on him. She watched as Fred turned over the soil. He had stripped off to his vest, revealing his upper torso. Joe shouted that he was going out now. "Going to the pit to see if I can get redundancy."

Rosie watched as he closed the front gate. "Yes, dear, and then up to the club for a pint," she whispered.

"Morning Fred!" she called out as she wiped the clothesline.

Fred straightened up. "Morning Rosie." They looked at each other and smiled.

"Is everything all right?" she asked.

"Yeah, sort of," he answered. "Got a problem with the curtains upstairs. I took them down, washed and ironed them but I forgot to notice which way they go back up." Rosie said she would show him a bit later. "Thanks, Rosie, I hate being a nuisance but I do miss having a woman around."

Rosie agreed. "We do have our uses, Fred."

It was an hour later when she noticed Fred putting his tools in the shed. She looked in the mirror and sprinkled toilet water on her breasts and body. Combing her hair, she made her way around to Fred's. He had just stripped his vest off and splashed his upper torso, wiping away the water. He was putting on a clean vest when Rosie knocked on the door. "Is it all right now, Fred, if we sort your curtains out?"

He opened the door wider. "Yes, come in, Rosie." He closed the door behind her, "I've got the steps upstairs ready." He took a sniff at her as she moved past him. "By God, Rosie, you smell like a million dollars." The steps were already by the window. Fred held up the curtains, "I wasn't sure which the front was and which was the back."

Rosie held them up and then started to climb the steps. She felt Fred's hands hold onto her. "Don't let me fall, Fred," said Rosie with a slight laugh, "or I might fall on top of you." Rosie's dress rode up her body as she stretched. Fred moved his hands to her inner thighs. He felt Rosie's legs part slightly as his hands ventured a bit further. Rosie looked down at Fred. "If you want to fuck me, Fred, wait until I've finished up here."

Fred smiled at her. "You know I do, Rosie."

***

The B.A.D. Boys headed off over the chase, looking to where the cars were parking. It was 8 o'clock at night and already the forest paths were a hive of activity. Cars were pulling into small, secluded areas. "So much for having cars these days," said Ray. "We had to manage up against the fence or behind the garages."

Abbo laughed. "It's hard to tell who's doing what up here. What do we do—go out on foot looking into each car?"

Andy said he didn't fancy that idea. "There's a lot of 'dogging' goes on along here."

Sid looked perplexed. "What the fucking hell is dogging?"

The boys erupted into laughter. "Well, it ain't walking the dog," laughed Abbo.

Ray looked at Sid who was the youngest of the group. "You don't know, Sid?"

Sid shook his head. "No, I've never heard of it."

Ray sat back. "Well, Sid, it's where men and women come here to get fucked. Not with their husbands or boyfriends, on their own. They just come here and park. The men look around for a single female, and if she gives the nod, the man or men get in the car and fuck her silly or in some cases, they just want to watch while somebody else does it. Didn't you read in the paper about a well-known footballer who was caught doing it?"

"So it's free?" asked Sid.

Ray looked at his mate. "Yes, it's free, Sid. If you want to try it, just go and have a look around and we'll wait for you. Just look for a single female and ask her if she needs company."

Sid looked at his mates. "Are you having me on or what?"

A chorus of various voices said, "No Sid, you just do what Ray told you."

Sid got out of the car. "Take off your mask and turn your jacket inside out," suggested Abbo.

They watched as Sid walked along the path, looking for parked cars with only a female in it. He passed one or two that were occupied by women and men. Finally, he came across one that looked as if it was occupied by a lone female. He slowed down. The woman had long blonde hair that she was brushing. He could only see by the light of the moon. As he got closer, he heard the window being opened. "Looking for some fun?" she called out. Sid felt a shiver down his spine as he approached the passenger side and opened the door. The interior light came on, illuminating the interior. The woman looked at him and smiled. Sid took a good look at the woman who he guessed was in her late fifties. Her face was wrinkled like a prune and her ill-fitting dentures were almost falling out of her mouth. Sid almost pissed himself as he slammed the door shut and ran like the clappers back to their car. "You bastards," he yelled, "you stitched me up good and proper there."

The boys fired questions at him. "Did you find anything, Sid?"

Sid sat back in the seat. "Yeah, I did. A blonde woman who must have been over sixty. This is 'grab a grannie shagging' place, ain't it?"

The boys howled with laughter. "Did you look around, Sid? There must have been others available," asked Abbo.

Sid said, "No, that was enough to put me off dogging for life."

***

Peter and Susan arranged to have their wedding locally, making it easy for friends and relatives to attend. They made all the necessary arrangements and planned it for a month ahead. Their honeymoon location was kept secret but they had booked in at the Metropolis in Blackpool and had timed it nicely for the illuminations. The time up until then, they spent shopping for a wedding ring and more household items. Everything was going according to plan for them. Peter put his arm around Susan as they sat on the settee. "You know, Susan, with what we put down on our house and the mortgage we've taken on, we have quite a good bank account to our names. That reward from the firm and what the Kenyan government gave us has made us quite comfortable moneywise. We can well afford to start a family now."

Susan bit her lip; should she or shouldn't she spill the beans? That was what was going through her head at that moment. "Yes, we could, darling, but let us wait a little bit longer, it will happen when it happens." She gave a little giggle and squeezed his hand.

***

Rosie climbed down the steps and stood back looking at the curtains. "They look good, Fred, now what else had you got in mind?"

She felt Fred put his arms around her waist. "I want you, Rosie. I want to reward you for what you've done."

Rosie could feel Fred rising to the occasion and moved towards the bed. She began to feel horny and welcomed his advances. “You don’t mind a bit of fat on a woman, Fred?”

Fred started peeling off her clothes. “Oh no, Rosie, I like to feel something under me.”

They lay on the bed and Fred began to explore Rosie’s big breasts. He didn’t rush like Joe did to get it over with quickly. He took his time and Rosie was enjoying every minute of it. “Ooh Fred, that’s nice,” she whispered as his fingers probed the promised land. She massaged him gently before he penetrated her inner sanctum.

“By God, Rosie, there’s nothing on earth like it,” he whispered.

***

Bruce stood looking at the yardage of the new head. “I reckon the new machine will be here by next week, Billy. I think it’s a Doscoe.”

Billy grunted, “I hope so too, I don’t like this pick and shovel work; it’s too much like the olden days.”

Bruce laughed. “Yeah, the good old days, eh! I just hope that water doesn’t break in anywhere else or area five will be closed and that could mean this pit will close.”

Billy talked to his mates. “I hope this pit doesn’t close. I don’t know what other jobs are going in this area that would be suitable for us and I don’t want to move to another part of the county. I’ve done that once and I didn’t like it.”

Norman agreed that it was too much of an upheaval at their age. “Another ten years would see us taking redundancy packages probably,” he said. “The younger ones would probably fit in with the new small businesses setting up in the area. They could probably adapt to the new technology but we older ones don’t know anything else except the mining industry.”

The younger miners had been job-hunting locally and several small businesses had set a lot of them on. More businesses were being encouraged to open up in Rugeley and slowly but surely, the pit began losing its younger men.

***

Peter stood at the altar and his best man, Martin, stood at his side as the organist started to play. “A few minutes left as a free man,” whispered Martin. “Do you want to change your mind?”

Peter smiled at him. “No way, Martin, she’s the love of my life.” He turned to see Susan being led down the aisle by her uncle who had flown in from Spain to give her away. Peter’s heart was racing as she drew closer.

“She looks beautiful,” whispered Martin.

It was a breath-taking moment as the vicar conducted the ceremony. The reception was held in a village hall not far away. Peter and Susan greeted their guests as they arrived. Soon they were seated and more photographs were being taken. Peter gave his speech and soon everyone was enjoying themselves. Cards were read out by Martin and he gave his speech. As the evening wore on, Susan began to feel tired; her feet were sore from much dancing. Peter looked at his watch, it was 7:30 and almost time for them to depart for the railway station. Martin had offered to drive them to Birmingham where they would catch their train to Blackpool. They announced that it was time for them to leave and wished everyone to stay and enjoy the evening. Amidst a hail of confetti and a loud send-off, Martin pulled away with the bride and groom in the back. Peter thanked Martin and said how pleased he was with his friendship.

The train sped thought the evening twilight hours and in no time at all, they had arrived in Blackpool. The taxi driver gave them a tour of the lights free of charge as a wedding present. Peter and Susan thanked him and soon they had flaked out on the bed, exhausted. They awoke next morning to bright sunlight shining through the window. Susan leaned over and kissed Peter. “And now, my husband, it’s time for your wedding present.”

Peter smiled through half-closed eyes. “You’re my wedding present,” he said, responding to her kiss. “What more can I ask for?”

Susan gave a huge smile. "Our baby is on the way." Peter looked puzzled and then suddenly realised what Susan had said.

***

Fred leaned over the fence and beckoned to Rosie, who was hanging out the washing. "Our Mary is coming to live with me. She's divorcing her husband for various reasons and wants to know if she can move in with me. She will bring her daughter with her."

Rosie looked at Fred. "Well, it'll be company for you, Fred. Is that what you want?"

Fred looked a bit confused. "Well, I don't know really. I don't mind a bit of company but her daughter is almost sixteen and you know what teenagers are like—loud music and generally untidy."

Rosie smiled back at him. "Well, Fred, it's your home; you make the rules and stick to them." She pulled a face. "I shall have to put up with having Joe around me all day. He thinks they will be making him redundant soon." She then smiled at Fred. "Let's wait and see, shall we? Besides, it's nice having a woman around the house. We have our uses, don't we?"

Fred gave a big smile. "You can say that again, Rosie, I certainly miss my missus." Fred looked up at the sky. "Rain on the way, Rosie, don't leave your washing out too long. I'm just making a cup of tea; do you want one?"

Rosie looked up at the sky. "This lot will be dry in an hour. I think the rain will hold off for an hour, Fred. Yes, I could do with a cuppa. Shall I come around?"

***

Joe lay on the bed whilst the nurse manoeuvred the heat lamp over his back. "My God, that's good," he murmured. When she had finished, he dressed himself and left the surgery. A steady walk down the road brought him to the Miners' Club. "Why not?" he said to himself as he pushed open the door. A couple of familiar faces greeted him as he approached the bar. “Hi Joe, come and join us,” shouted Bill. “How did you get on at the pit?”

Joe sat down and took the top off his beer. “All right, I think. Nothing definite but Mr Jones has put me on the list.”

“Wash day today, Joe?” voiced Bob.

His other mate raised his glass. “Best out of the way on such days.”

“Well, I’ve just been to the surgery for some physio. Our Rosie knows I’ll be calling in for a pint. Not much else to do these days.”

Chapter 21
Winding Down

Ray steered the car around the estate. "It seems quiet enough around here so let's try over the chase again."

"I'm not doing that dogging thing again," said Sid. "So don't suggest it."

The boys erupted with laughter. "You just didn't look around enough," suggested Abbo. "There's some smart cookies visit this place. Enough to attract a well-known footballer."

Ray drove around; pulling up occasionally to observe what action was taking place in the parked cars. "Just shagging," he said and pulled back onto the main road. "Well, we've cleared a few pushers from our town so I think we can ease off for a while but still remain vigilant and listen out. I'm sure they'll be back and we will be waiting for them."

***

Dennis pulled into the car park of the Sherwood. It was another union meeting that had brought him to Nottingham but he didn't mind. It had many advantages. "Hello Dennis, it's been a while since I last had the pleasure of your company. It is one night or two?" Sylvia looked her usual self, very attractive and desirable.

"Just one night, Sylvia, as my wife is rather poorly and I must get back tomorrow."

She handed him the key to the room. "I'll bring up a tray soon, Dennis."

The meeting had gone on longer than expected and as Dennis drew the curtains, he could see the late afternoon sun disappearing in the west. Sylvia knocked on the door and walked in, carrying a tray of food and drinks. She put the tray down and then turned to Dennis. She kissed him and then sat down on the bed. "I've got something to tell you, Dennis," she said. They drank their coffee as Sylvia looked sadly at Dennis. "I've found someone who's very interested in me and wants to start a serious relationship."

Dennis looked at her. "If that's what you want, Sylvia, then I'm happy for you. Don't let our friendship get in the way of your happiness. Just make sure he's everything you want. Make sure, before you commit yourself. I sincerely hope this one works out for you, Sylvia. If I didn't have my responsibilities back home, I would be the one for you. I really mean that, Sylvia."

She put her arms around him. "Oh Dennis, if only." She looked at him. "We haven't slept together yet but I know he wants to. I'll keep him in suspense a little longer. In the meantime, Dennis, let's celebrate a good friendship; tonight I'm yours."

***

Billy climbed up on the Doscoe and started it up. Pushing the levers forward, he put his foot down on the pedals. The machine moved forward. He raised the boom and the head bit into the rock head. "Right lads, let's earn some money," he shouted. "If we can get this road in, there's a few more years ahead of us."

Jegger kept his eye on the cable. "Is that what the gaffer told you, Billy? What about the water?"

Norman shouted, "It's levelled out. We should bypass it when we get further in."

Jim watched as the giant paddles fed the rock into the conveyor. "I'm glad that's sorted. I was getting a bit worried. Another ten years will do me."

***

Peter put his arms around Susan's waist as they looked out onto their garden. "That's a nice place for our baby to play in. I shall have to put up swings and things and make it look pretty."

Susan melted into his arms. "You're not disappointed, are you, Peter, with me getting pregnant so soon? I stopped the birth control tablets ages ago but I didn't think it would be so early to get pregnant after taking them for so long."

Peter looked at her. "You have made me the happiest man in the world, darling, what else can I wish for? Now I have everything I ever wanted."

The months passed by and soon, spring was knocking at their door. Susan was getting restless, as it wouldn't be long now before the baby's arrival. They had decorated the baby's bedroom in wallpaper depicting various animals. The scan had shown that Susan was carrying a little boy. Peter was over the moon but promised the next one would be a girl. The delivery went well and soon Susan was nursing their new baby. When they finally left the hospital, Martin was waiting for them at their house with a bottle of champagne. He poured the wine and raised his glass. "Here's to a happy future for my best friend, Peter, and his beautiful wife, Susan and to baby Craig, of course."

The End